ONE

Tate
———————

"*C*an I go play with my puzzle? Pleaaaaase!" my nine-year-old daughter asked, batting her eyelashes.

"Sure, Paisley. And after we all finish breakfast, we'll go out on the boat."

"You're the best daddy in the world."

That made me smile, even though I definitely didn't feel like Dad of the Year today.

Half my family was gathered in the living room of my Chicago home. My grandma Beatrice was sitting on the couch next to me. My brothers Declan and Tyler were scattered around the kitchen island, finishing off their breakfast.

I could tell by their expressions that they couldn't wait to give me shit. I wondered who was going to start first.

To my astonishment, it was Gran.

As soon as my daughter was out of the room, she sighed, shaking her head. "I can't believe you scared off yet another nanny."

"I didn't scare anyone off," I replied smoothly. "She wasn't right for the job."

"Yeah. Can't have anything to do with you being all

1

demanding, right?" Declan asked with a smirk. As the oldest of six brothers, he didn't miss a single opportunity to lecture us— or, as he liked to call it, *advise* us.

But I didn't give him too much shit about it. At thirty-four, I was the third oldest, and even I'd done my fair share of lecturing as a kid. Mom always said we were her trusted generals when we were young. To this day, I wasn't entirely sure if it was a compliment. She had a skewed sense of humor.

"No. It has everything to do with the fact that she was putting Paisley in front of the TV while she wasted time on social media, and I flat-out told her that was unacceptable."

"Tate, I told you I'm always happy to look after her," Gran said.

I cleared my throat, looking straight at her. I knew she meant well, but Paisley was a handful. I needed to be subtle about this. "Gran, you don't have the energy to keep up with a nine-year-old every day."

"Young man, are you calling me old?" She glanced at Declan. "Did he just call me old?"

Declan grimaced. "Sort of, but he didn't mean to." Glaring at me, he cocked a brow. "You didn't, right?"

I shook my head. *So much for being subtle.* "Sorry, Gran."

I had to find another nanny, and I had to do it fast. As a divorced single dad, I made it a point to be home for dinner every evening. I wanted to give my daughter some stability while her mom jet setted around the country. Nora and I married young, when I was fresh out of college. We divorced four years later, when Paisley was three and Nora decided she couldn't be a model *and* a wife and mother. I tried to reason with her and even went to couple's therapy. I gave it my best, right up until I found out she was sleeping with a photographer.

"I spoke to the agency, and they're already looking for candidates." I needed someone to look after Paisley full time

PROMISE ME FOREVER

LAYLA HAGEN

now during summer vacation. When she was in school, it was different. But in the summer, she was home nonstop, except for the occasional camp outing or sleepover at a friend's house.

As the CEO of Maxwell Wineries, one of the biggest companies in the industry, I spent the day in the office. I needed someone I could trust to spend that time with Paisley.

No matter how successful I was in business, I couldn't stop this sinking feeling that I wasn't a good father. I couldn't give her the happy family life I'd had growing up, or even keep a nanny around for too long. But I was going to be very careful with the one I chose this time.

"What kind of candidates did you tell them to look for?" Gran asked.

"I told the agency it's important for them to send someone who is experienced, likes children, and isn't taking this job because they couldn't find anything else to do. I need someone who wants to do this for a living, not as a temporary job until they find something better. Paisley needs stability in her life, and it's my responsibility to give her that."

"Tate, she has all of us. That's more than enough," Gran said. "It's not your fault her mother left."

I stood up, pacing my enormous living room and looking out the window. I'd bought the house in the Lincoln Park neighborhood right after the divorce, wanting to give Paisley as much space as possible while still staying in the city and not moving to a suburb. It was far too big for the two of us.

"I don't want to get into that today," I said. The divorce wasn't my fault, but that didn't mean I liked the outcome. Nora wasn't a big part of Paisley's life. She'd been happy that I wanted full custody. She called her every few weeks and visited on Paisley's birthday. Once a year, they went on a vacation together for a week. Last time Nora took her to a spa hotel. Paisley wasn't impressed.

This train of thought wasn't going to do me any good. I

needed to focus on finding the best nanny for Paisley. My parents would be back from their vacation at the end of next month, but they couldn't watch her nonstop either.

"Well, I'd offer to help you decide on a candidate, but that's not my area of expertise," Tyler said with a lazy smile. "I can, however, help you get that stick out of your ass. You're looking tense, brother. I don't think you'll impress any candidates like that."

"It's the other way round. They have to impress me."

Declan cocked a brow. "Yeah, no. I'm with Tyler on this one. No one's gonna want to work for you if you scare them away."

I groaned, pacing the living room some more. "Back off, both of you. I don't need your advice."

It's not like I could tell them all to fuck off in front of Gran. My brothers could be a handful sometimes.

"I disagree. I think it's exactly what you need. I wonder who Travis, Sam, and Luke would side with. Maybe we should call them and find out," Tyler continued conversationally.

This time, I chuckled.

We did this a lot, randomly giving opinions on each other's lives. Things could get out of hand when we were all together. It had always been this way.

Declan and I were Mom's "generals" only because Luke, the second oldest, had made it his mission to cause mayhem. The funniest fact was that he almost always convinced us to get into trouble—to this day, he still counted talking Sam and Travis into pranking Gran that they had chickenpox by painting red dots on themselves as one of his top ten achievements.

It was probably why Declan became a lawyer. He spent so much time getting us out of hot water that it was an obvious career choice. Sam and Travis, the youngest ones, were like a weird mashup between Declan and Luke. Depending on what the situation required, they were the troublemakers or the saviors. It had been fascinating to watch.

"I dare you to call them this early on Saturday," I said. "They're gonna bust your ba—"

I cleared my throat, stopping before I said "balls."

Gran shook her head. "I'll pretend I haven't heard anything. But I think Tate's got enough on his plate with the three of us offering our opinions. And I don't think you can get ahold of Sam or Travis."

That was true. Sam was on the other side of the world working for Doctors Without Borders. Clearly he'd followed his savior instinct. Travis was in the process of selling his hugely successful startup—and he was working nonstop.

Tyler only had so much time on his hands because he was the goalie for the Chicago Blades—the hottest hockey team since they won the Stanley Cup. He had summers off, but otherwise he was always busy.

Gran sighed. "Well, if you ever change your mind and decide I could handle it, I'm up for the job. I love my great-granddaughter and would adore spending more time with her."

I knew she did, but Gran was eighty-two, and no matter what she said, she couldn't keep up with Paisley for more than a weekend.

Checking my watch, I said, "I promised Paisley I would take her out on the boat today. Anyone want to come with us?"

"No, no. I don't like boats. They make me queasy," Gran said. "I came to have breakfast with you all."

Saturday was the unofficial get-together day of the Maxwells, but I suspected the news about the nanny also had something to do with these three dropping by unannounced for breakfast.

Declan clapped a hand on my shoulder. "As much as I like spending time with my niece, I've got a lunch date today, and I have to leave. I don't want to be late. Gran, want me to drop you off at home?"

"That would be lovely. Thank you, dear."

"I'm coming with you, Tate. I don't have anything better to do today," Tyler said to me. "Maybe I'll get lucky and end up with a date too."

I stared at him, narrowing my eyes. "You're not going to use an outing with my daughter and me to pick up women."

Tyler smirked. "I can't use *you*, that's true. But women have a thing for hot uncles. For hot single dads too, I hear—not that it's working for you."

"Very funny. Don't make me take back the invitation," I warned.

"Paisley asked me earlier, and I said yes, so don't even try it. You don't want to disappoint your daughter, now do you?"

"Tyler. Behave," Gran jumped in.

"Never," he responded, walking over to Gran kissing her cheek. The man had no shame.

Gran laughed, shaking her head. "You six are responsible for every strand of white hair I have. And that goes for your parents too. I'd always hoped you'd all have boys just as rambunctious as you were to see what you put us through. There's still time. And then I'll sit back and chuckle as you try to outmaneuver their shenanigans."

Neither of my brothers was seeing anyone seriously, so I doubted Gran's wish would come true anytime soon.

After she and Declan left, I headed up the spiral staircase to my daughter's room while Tyler waited for us downstairs. She was lying on the bed, reading her favorite story, *Snow White*.

"Paisley?" I said. "Want to go out on the boat?"

She jumped to her feet. "Yes, Daddy." Running up to me, she laced her small arms around my legs and looked up at me. "And can we also walk along the shore and collect stones, please?" She was batting her eyelashes, making me laugh. Paisley looked a lot like the Maxwell side of the family. We all had dark brown hair, though she didn't inherit my blue eyes. Paisley had my mom's green ones, just like my younger brother Sam. My dad and other brothers had the dominant brown shade.

"Sure, Pea. Come on. Let's go."

When I got back, I'd have to look at a stack of applications to figure out the next steps, but it was only Saturday, and I had until Monday to tell the agency which candidates I wanted to interview. I was going to spend tomorrow looking at résumés before preparing for the week ahead. It was going to be busy. Summer was one of the peak times in the wine business, and I didn't mind one bit putting in extra hours. Maxwell Wineries was my pride and joy. I got the wine bug from Dad. The two of us spent hours on the family vineyard when I was a kid.

As Paisley and I went down the spiral staircase, her laughter echoed throughout the house.

It was good that my family came and went whenever they pleased, and the door was always open to them. Between Gran, my parents, and my siblings, we never lacked company, but even so, it didn't entirely feel like a home.

Many years ago, I'd wanted a huge family, but I'd made my peace with the fact that it wasn't in the cards for me. For now, I had one goal: find the best nanny for Paisley.

TWO

Lexi

_____

"*L*exi, you don't have to do this," Dad said.

"Dad, we're not having this conversation again. Besides, my interview is in half an hour. No way will I back down now. How is Mom feeling?"

"She's taking it easy."

"I'll call you both after the interview. I have to get ready. I'll talk to you later, okay?"

"Good luck, hon. And thank you."

"Love you, Dad. Bye."

As soon as the call disconnected, I started getting dressed. My interview was at eight o'clock sharp. I checked the weather, to make sure it wouldn't rain. I enjoyed Chicago in the summer. Most people didn't like the hot and humid climate, but I loved it. It felt like one long vacation, which was pretty appropriate in my case. As an elementary school teacher, I had summers off, and usually I occupied that time with long, lazy days in the sun on Lake Michigan. But this summer, things were a little bit different. I decided to take a temp job.

My mom was in and out of the hospital after undergoing two heart surgeries this past year, and the medical bills were piling up. My parents were both retired, and there was no way they could afford everything. Even though they didn't ask, I offered to help. I put out my résumé, looking for any temporary job that would fit my qualifications.

I'd been looking for some sort of summer camp, to be honest, but the agency sent me something entirely different. I'd laughed as I went through the job description. It said "childminder," which was a fancy way of describing a nanny.

I looked in the mirror, nodding appreciatively at my bright yellow dress. It had a boatneck and wasn't too short. It looked professional yet fashionable enough, and I felt totally comfortable in it. I braided my long brown hair, detangling the strands as I went. My hair was naturally wavy, especially in the summer when the air was so humid. I'd only applied a little bit of makeup around my eyes to make the blue in my irises stand out, and I was ready to go in no time.

I lived in a super-tiny apartment in a forty-story building near Edgewater. Besides the relatively low rent, what sold me on this area was that I had the beach and the lake literally in front of the building. I wasn't overlooking the lake, because those apartments were one-third more expensive than mine, but all I had to do was to take the elevator twenty floors, and I'd be outside right along it.

I loved walking, even in summer, but today I Ubered. My potential employer lived in Lincoln Park, which was about a fifteen-minute drive away. I could bike the distance, but I risked arriving a sweaty mess, and I wanted to make a good impression. Even mid-June was hot and humid in Chicago.

I left a bit early, not wanting anything unexpected to make me late for my interview. In the Uber, I drummed my fingers on my thighs while looking out the window. I was so curious to meet the little girl and her father. The job description didn't give me much to go on, except that it was a single parent household and that she was nine years old. It was a great age. I loved being an elementary school teacher. At that age, an educator could have so much influence in shaping those little minds and feeding their curiosity about the world. I loved seeing everything through their eyes.

Kids had an innocence I adored. At thirty-one, I'd always hoped to have two kids by now, but things didn't work out, unfortunately. I'd had two long-term relationships that didn't end well, but it didn't matter. I had my friends and my parents, although they lived in Boston. I loved my tiny studio and my job. And I got so much love from all those kids I taught. Well, during the school year, at least. In summer, I was on my own.

Although, this summer was going to be different. I was hoping this job would pan out because it paid well—more than what I'd get at a summer camp. Besides, focusing on one child for once would be a nice change from my usual pace. But if things didn't work out for whatever reason, I was determined to find something else.

My jaw dropped when the car stopped in front of the house—though mansion would be a more appropriate word. It was huge, with two stories, a white stone facade, a wraparound porch with columns, and a majestic staircase up to the entrance.

Wow. I rarely ventured on this side of town, though I knew they had lovely homes. But this wasn't pretty. This was like a small palace.

I wondered if it had a backyard. But even if it didn't, I was sure I wouldn't run out of options to entertain little Paisley in this huge house. I was a master at coming up with ways to keep kids busy, even when space was limited to a classroom.

"Thank you," I said to the driver before getting out of the car. I was still five minutes early, so I paced in front of the gate, glancing through the bars. A small stone patio led up to the steps of the front porch. There were gorgeous flowers and plants on either side of the pathway going around the house. I assumed there was a backyard too.

I was becoming a bit nervous. Plus, I hadn't been on a job interview in about seven years, ever since I started at my current school, The Stone Academy.

Two minutes later, the front door of the house opened, and my jaw clenched. The most handsome man I'd ever seen was looking straight at me. He had dark brown hair, cropped short, and blue eyes so mesmerizing that even from a distance I felt the sex appeal rolling off him in waves.

"Ms. Lexi Langley?" he asked.

"Yes."

"I'm Tate Maxwell. Come on in. You don't have to wait outside."

"Okay." *Good God, Lexi, get a grip. You're not going to get this job by giving one-word responses.*

Tate climbed down the porch steps, coming closer. He was seriously movie-star handsome. His eyes were somewhere between tourmaline and turquoise. The white shirt he wore was rolled up at the sleeves, revealing very sexy forearms. Through the fabric of his shirt, I could see his biceps were just as muscular.

My mind immediately went to other places. Would his abs be as defined? Probably.

Swallowing hard, I forced my gaze to stay on his face.

Way to be inappropriate, Lexi. He could be your future employer. No sexy thoughts about him, even though his body is delicious, and that face... yummm.

He had a short beard, and the dark stubble made his eyes pop even more. I was tall at five foot eight, but he was even taller, at least six foot three.

I cleared my throat as he opened the front gate, holding out my hand. "Lexi Langley. Nice to meet you."

"Likewise. Come on in." He opened the door, and I

stepped inside. He walked right next to me up on the steps of the front porch. I could feel his presence at my side, solid and hot as sin. He had an energy surrounding him that felt downright magnetic.

"You have a very nice home," I said, trying to focus on a neutral subject.

"Thank you." Opening the front door, he ushered me inside, and it was all I could do not to sigh. The interior of the house was as amazing as the exterior, decorated in old-fashioned, classic furniture complete with chandeliers.

"Let's go inside the living room. We'll be comfortable there."

"Yes, of course," I said.

"Do you want anything to drink?" he asked. "Coffee? Water? Anything else?"

"No, I'm good."

"Okay. Please, have a seat." He pointed to one of the white leather couches.

I immediately sat down. He sat on an armchair opposite me. His presence had seemed larger than life and all-consuming even outside, but right here, enclosed in this room, the energy coming off him felt downright intense.

"Ms. Langley, I have looked over your résumé, and you have excellent qualifications. I was hoping to find someone for my daughter who has formal education in childhood development."

"Well, yes, I've been an elementary school teacher for seven years."

"And now you're looking to change jobs?"

I frowned, not really understanding. "What do you mean?"

"Why are you applying for this job?"

"I have time during my summer vacation, and honestly, I need some extra money. This seems like a good job."

His expression darkened as his frown deepened. He got up

from the armchair, pacing in front of me, crossing his arms over his chest. "That's going to be a problem. I want someone who can be with my daughter long-term, over the next few years."

"Oh! I didn't see that on the job description."

"I'm sure I told the agency to put it there."

"Maybe I just missed it. I'm so sorry. But may I ask, why do you need someone for her full time? She goes to school, right?"

"Yes. Paisley is in the fourth grade."

"I thought she might be. That's the grade I teach." Tate still looked confused, so I explained what I was getting at. "So, then, you presumably only need someone to pick her up from school and bring her home and stay with her for a couple hours until you come home from work? Is anyone else with her in the afternoons?"

"It's just me." His tone was clipped.

"Okay." I was curious to know more, but I didn't want to push. Was he divorced? A widower? Well, clearly he was a single dad. But it was none of my business to know the rest.

I noticed a hint of vulnerability in his gaze. It contrasted so starkly with his tough exterior that I didn't even know what to make of it. It was gone the next second, though.

"Look, I'll be honest. I'd love to have this job because I love kids. The second I got out of the Uber and saw the house, I had all kinds of activities in my mind to keep Paisley busy. It's an amazing space to raise children. Not to mention that you have the lake nearby."

He looked pleased that I had already planned things for his daughter, which I was glad for, so I continued. "I'm not sure how long it might take you to find a permanent nanny. I honestly can't imagine there are too many people with a formal education in child development looking to do this as their full-time job for a prolonged period of time. But I could do it until you find someone who can."

His frown deepened even more. Damn, this man knew how to brood. My heart was beating faster. How could he look even hotter when he was frowning?

"I'll think about it. My daughter gets attached to the people she spends time with. I'm not sure if that's a good idea."

My stomach bottomed out. How did I miss that this wasn't a summer job? Regardless, I didn't want to press, because his daughter's well-being came first. If she didn't like changing nannies, it would make more sense to hire someone who wanted to stay longer from the start.

"Okay. Well, do you have any more questions for me?" I asked.

"No, it was all on your résumé. Do you have any questions for us? I mean, for me?"

That was encouraging. Maybe he was still seriously considering me after all. "Yes. How many hours a day would I be here, and what would you like me to do with your daughter?"

"I'm at work about eight or nine hours a day, so I would need you here in the morning. I always prepare breakfast for Paisley and me, and we eat together. Otherwise, you can do whatever you feel is best for her. I'm not one to think that every moment has to be a teachable one for kids. I think they should be allowed to play."

My face exploded in a grin. "Oh my God, I think you're a species that's about to disappear. I have not heard those words from a parent in forever. Thank you for thinking that. I'm on the same page. Playing is how they discover the world. It's their way of learning. And not many people believe me, but what they learn from having fun sticks with them more than book learning does sometimes. It's the way they absorb it, and it's natural."

For the first time today, the corners of his mouth tilted up in a small smile. He had two dimples. My heart rate intensified. *Seriously? Why is he so hot?* I never thought dimples would work on this man, but they so did. I had a hunch anything would look sexy on him.

"I like you, Ms. Langley."

"Well, I love to teach kids. It's why I became an elementary school teacher. Do you often go out of town for business? I mean, would it require me to sleep here or anything?"

"I do go out of town sometimes. But when that happens, my parents or my grandmother usually spends the night with Paisley."

"You have extended family close by?" I asked, a bit envious. My parents were in another state. I felt a bit lonely this summer. My best friends, Jenny and Ella, weren't in the city. They were both working at a language camp in Louisiana. "That's great."

"Yes, it is."

He didn't expound, so I had to ask, "How come they aren't spending the summer with Paisley?" Then I cringed. "I'm sorry if I'm overstepping my boundaries."

"You're not. They did offer, but Paisley is energetic—like all children, I imagine—and no matter how much my parents and grandmother think they can keep up with her, they actually can't."

"That makes sense," I said with a grin. Typically, kids will take advantage of family members, whereas with a nanny, they tend to behave more. "May I meet her?"

He hesitated. "It's best if she doesn't meet all the candidates." Of course he was right, and I should have thought of that. "And considering that you don't want to do this long-term, it probably won't work out, so it doesn't make sense."

"Oh, okay." I deflated a bit but tried not to show it. I pushed a hand through my hair, crossing and uncrossing my legs. Despite the icy chill inside from the AC, my skin was a bit clammy from the heat outside. I raised my eyes to his and, to my astonishment, caught him looking at my legs. Goose bumps broke out on my skin—because he was *looking*? Okay, maybe it was for the best if I didn't get this job. If I needed to fan myself when he checked me out, I couldn't imagine how I'd feel if I were around him for too long. Perhaps it was best not to find out.

"I'd still like to know a bit more about the job. When would I have to be here?"

"From nine in the morning until six in the evening. I come home then and eat dinner with Paisley."

"Would you like me to cook too? My skills aren't fancy, but I can make simple meals."

"No, that's fine. I always make our dinner."

I had no idea why, but the thought of that made me swoon. I could imagine this guy in the kitchen, sleeves rolled up.

"Okay, then, I think that's everything, right?" I asked.

"What *would* you do with my daughter?" he said abruptly.

"Well, first I'd get to know her a bit and see what she likes to do in her free time and find out if she enjoys books, or going out in nature, or staying indoors. Every child is different. I haven't had the chance to focus on just one until now. But I'd love to." My words faded as the patter of feet reverberated from the spiral staircase to our left. I instinctively looked in that direction, noticing a lively nine-year-old girl descending them in a rush.

"Daddy, can I go in the backyard?" she exclaimed, her dark brown hair floating around her. She was wearing pink cotton pajamas with nothing on her feet. She skidded to a stop when she saw me, eyes wide. "I'm sorry, Daddy, I didn't know you were with someone."

"Hey, Paisley," he said.

Oh my God. I felt it in his voice that he was smiling.

When I turned to look at him, my heart went into overdrive. He was completely transformed. His face lit up completely. His eyes weren't intense now. They were happy.

Yeah, broody Tate was hot, but smiling, happy Tate was drop-dead gorgeous.

Paisley ran up to the TV console, and though it took me a second to realize it, he was playfully trying to block her way.

"What do you think you're doing?" He grabbed her around the middle, tickling her little tummy.

Good God, this is too much for my hormones.

"Getting chocolate, Daddy." Her innocent green eyes looked pleadingly at her father. The whole scene was adorable.

He looked at the console over his shoulder. "You're stealing chocolate every morning?"

"I am not stealing it. I'm eating it. You never told me I'm not allowed to eat chocolate in the morning when you aren't looking."

"No, I wasn't that specific. My bad."

He burst out laughing. I couldn't help but smile big. Paisley was one lucky little girl.

Tate looked at me directly, and my stomach somersaulted. "Lexi, this is Paisley. Paisley, this is Lexi. I'm interviewing her to be your new nanny."

He released his daughter, and as Paisley straightened up, she looked at me curiously. "You're pretty," she said.

"Why, thank you," I replied.

She looked at my braided hair longingly. "Can you teach me how to do that?"

"Sure. I could braid it right now if you want to. Do you have a mirror here?"

"Yes." She pointed to the wall opposite the TV console. There was a mirror in the corner I hadn't noticed. I looked at Tate questioningly, and he nodded.

Taking Paisley's hand, I brought her to the floor-length mirror. "Okay, let's do it sideways. This way, so you can see what I'm doing." Her hair was silky and already brushed perfectly, so it was easy to braid it.

"Dad, can you record it on your phone? That way I'll know how to do it later."

"Sure," he said, coming up right next to us. This was the closest we'd been since he walked me inside the house. I couldn't help but draw in a sharp breath. My fingers trembled a little, and I lost my focus for a few seconds. His body radiated heat and masculinity. Just being inches away from him was messing with my senses.

"There, you're done," I said a few minutes later.

Paisley looked at her braid in the mirror, smiling broadly.

"I love it. Daddy, when are we having breakfast?"

"After Ms. Langley leaves. Why don't you go to your room and change, and I'll call you when it's ready, okay?"

Paisley nodded, heading toward the staircase right away.

"She's very well behaved," I said once she was out of earshot and while we were still standing next to the mirror. He was a foot farther away than he'd been when he was recording but still too close for my peace of mind. I couldn't understand how his nearness could impact me so much. But I suspected Tate Maxwell was the kind of man that made an impact on a room no matter how many people were in it. He had a dominating presence that took up all the space available.

"She's a great kid," he said, looking up at me from his phone with a slight smile.

"Okay, well, I'm going to go, then. Give me a call if you think I'd be a good fit." As we started to walk to the door, I asked, "How long do you think you're going to need to make a decision?"

"I have more interviews today and tomorrow, and I'll probably make up my mind afterward. I need someone as soon as possible. I'm working from home until then."

"Okay. I'll order an Uber." I took out my phone and was lucky there was a car nearby. "It's going to be here in two minutes."

As we stepped outside, Tate offered, "I'll walk you to the gate."

"Thank you."

We walked side by side on the porch steps. When Tate reached the gate, he opened it with one hand. Our arms brushed in the process, making me shiver. I straightened up instantly, looking up at him.

"Thank you for your time. I'll be waiting for your call." My voice was a bit uneven, and I was hoping he didn't notice. *How is this happening?*

"I'll be in touch, Ms. Langley." His eyes darkened.

I averted my gaze. *Oh wow. Is my imagination playing tricks on me, or was he checking me out again?*

His presence didn't feel magnetic right now but almost dangerous. Like if I stayed too close to him for too long, I might lose myself. And I couldn't let that happen, could I?

I had a golden rule. I didn't go out with parents. It seemed unprofessional, and I didn't want the kids to think I had favorites. Paisley wasn't at my school, but I was still sticking to my rule.

But that didn't mean I couldn't indulge in a little daydreaming.

Oh, Tate Maxwell. Why do you have to be so hot that my imagination is already wandering to forbidden territory?

Forbidden but soooo delicious.

THREE

Tate
___

*T*wo days later, I was with my brothers at the Maxwell Wineries headquarters in one of the office buildings on LaSalle Street.

My passion for wines began at a young age. We grew up on a vineyard on the west side of the state. It was small, and my dad only produced wine for personal consumption, but I'd had the bug since I was a kid. I always knew I wanted to get into the wine business, even though I grew up on the floors of Maxwell Bookstores, the chain of bookstores my grandparents founded. My grandma, uncle, and parents ran it after Grandpa passed away. Ten years ago, they sold it in one of the highest transactions in that industry. My parents set up trust funds for each of us. I hadn't touched mine—I put it directly in Paisley's name.

Maxwell Wineries was taking off. In fact, I moved the company into this building only two years later.

It started when I rented far more space than I needed for my employees, and then gradually, each of my brothers moved their business here. Declan, Travis, and Luke also had their office in the building. Tyler often stopped by, especially during the off-season. Sam joined us whenever he was in the country.

After work, we sometimes went to the top floor where there was a bar with a view of the Chicago skyline. That was currently where we were. It was one of the perks of working in the same building.

"Man, maybe we should help you pick," Declan said. They'd asked about my interviews and what I decided. I couldn't tell them the truth.

I groaned, tipping back a beer. I had interviewed four candidates over the past two days, and so far, I only wanted Lexi Langley. She was the one who bonded with my daughter and who seemed to actually like children. The others had held several different jobs besides childcare. One had been laid off from her computer science research job. The other worked as a bank teller until recently, and the last one was an aspiring fashion designer. But Lexi was different. And I liked her far too much, which was a fucking problem. If she was going to be my daughter's nanny, as temporary as it was, I couldn't lust after her.

She was so damn beautiful that remembering her in that yellow dress was driving me crazy. It had looked sexy as fuck on her.

"Dude, he's lost in thought," Tyler said. "That never happens to him. Someone must have revved his engine."

"True," Luke pitched in with more smartass comments. "You have an iron determination and focus, isn't that what you say is the key to your success? So who is she?"

"Why are you mobbing the guy? He's having a hard time picking the next sitter, knowing he'll probably fire her before the summer ends," Travis said.

"Or the month," Luke added.

Our inability to keep our opinions to ourselves was chronic.

"I don't fire people because I'm an asshole. Those I fire do things on the clock they aren't supposed to. Most leave because they get tired of the job. It's tough on Paisley because she gets attached, and now the only candidate I like is Lexi, an elementary school teacher who told me upfront that she can only work until the end of the summer."

"But she's your best candidate, right?" Luke asked. I nodded.

"Wait a second," Travis added. "He's too silent. My money is on the fact that he likes Miss Lexi a little too much. Don't you?"

Busted.

Tyler burst out laughing. "Dude, don't do that. Don't go there. Hooking up with your daughter's nanny is a bad idea."

"She's not my daughter's nanny yet, and I haven't hooked up with her," I said.

Luke patted my shoulder. "Yet, right?"

Declan raised a hand, motioning to the bartender. "Give us a round of tequila shots. Beer isn't going to cut it tonight." He looked at me with what I called his lawyer face, and I knew he was going to warn me off. "Tate, don't go there. The last thing you need is a harassment lawsuit. And—"

"Declan, save your breath. Give me some credit, will you? I've never even looked at one of my daughter's nannies, and I'm not going to start now."

That wasn't exactly true. I'd looked a lot at Lexi, and I'd fantasized a whole lot more.

"Okay. Why don't we talk about something else?" Tyler said. "Anyone spoken to Reese recently?"

Reese was our cousin from Dad's side. She and her sister, Kimberly, had practically grown up in our home, and we were all very close. Reese was going through a rough time since discovering her scumbag ex-fiancé was cheating on her. To make matters worse, they were going to go into business together.

"I speak to her daily," Declan said, "but she's not telling me much. Mostly, she's worrying about Gran's building."

When selling the chain of bookstores, Gran insisted on keeping the building where they'd opened the first one. It was symbolic because it reminded her of Grandpa. It meant a lot to her. Reese and the scumbag were going to turn it into a spa. Now everything was a mess. Declan was helping with the legal ramifications.

I turned to Luke. He was closest to Reese and Kimberly. "She's coping. But it doesn't help that the scumbag isn't making it easy on her. He still wants to open the spa."

"He's going to be trouble," Declan said.

I gritted my teeth. "Then he's not just an asshole but also an idiot. He doesn't know who he's messing with."

He was going to be very sorry for hurting Reese. I was very protective of her—all my brothers were. Business was business, but family was the most important thing for us. I wouldn't allow my family to get hurt.

———

I SPENT time with my brothers until later in the evening. Paisley was at Gran's house tonight. Once at home, instead of heading upstairs, I went down into my home office.

I could ask my Gran to look after Paisley for a while longer while I told the agency to send me more applicants, but I didn't want to do that. It wasn't fair to them. Besides, I'd searched for nannies often enough to know I wouldn't come across someone like Lexi Langley again too soon. The way she'd instantly bonded with my daughter shifted something inside me, something I didn't want to analyze. She'd been real; it wasn't just a job to her. And the way she'd clicked with Paisley proved there *was* such a thing as chemistry.

Paisley had asked to meet with the other women I was

interviewing too, and I gave in. After all, they would be spending time together. It was fair for Paisley to weigh in. As it happened, she liked Lexi best too.

I sat in my leather armchair and picked up the phone. There was no point postponing this. I was going to employ Lexi Langley, and I was going to keep my distance. I wouldn't ruin this for my daughter.

I dialed her number before I could change my mind yet again.

She answered after a few rings.

"Hi, it's Mr. Maxwell, right?" she asked loudly, but I could still barely hear her over the music in her background.

"Yes. Is this a good time to talk?"

"Sure. Let me move a bit farther away from the music."

"Where are you?" I asked.

"I'm at the lake. There's music, and I came down to enjoy it." A few seconds later, the music was fainter. "Okay. I'm listening."

"I promised I'd be in touch. I finished the interviews, and I'm happy to say that Paisley and I would like you to start as soon as possible."

"Oh, wow. Really? That's amazing. I thought the time issue was a deal breaker." Her voice was a bit edgy, making me think she suspected there was another reason. She'd caught me looking at her a couple times. I had to be more careful.

No, damn it, Maxwell. What you have to do is not check her out at all.

"You're very qualified, and you and my daughter had chemistry. It's not ideal that you can't continue the job after school starts, but we'll deal with it."

"I've been thinking about it too," she said. "You can keep looking, and if you find someone before the summer ends, I'll look for another job."

I frowned and almost asked why she needed a summer job

24

at all. She'd briefly let it slip that she needed the extra money, and now I wanted to know why. I'd find an opportunity to ask once she started.

"I'm going to pause the search for now, and I'll resume it at the end of summer, so don't worry about that. Your job is secure. I think we're going to get along great," I told her. "I mean, you're not going to see much of me, of course, but I'm sure you and Paisley will get along well."

"Okay, then. I'll start Monday morning? Still nine o'clock?

"Yes. Good memory," I told her.

"Great. Did Paisley tell you what she wants to do? I'm not sure what to wear. Maybe I'll wear jeans and a T-shirt. And I can bring a change of clothes." I could tell she was mostly talking to herself now. "Something that's not too revealing."

"And why is that?"

"Oh, shoot. I didn't mean to say that out loud," she blurted, making me laugh.

"But now you've made me curious. Tell me, Ms. Langley."

She cleared her throat. "I meant something professional and not too revealing."

"Ms. Langley, your yellow dress wasn't at all revealing. I imagine you'd look stunning in anything you wore."

She was the one who burst out laughing that time. Damn, I liked the sound a bit too much.

"I apologize. That was out of line," I said, determined to keep this professional.

"I didn't think you noticed my outfit."

It was on the tip of my tongue to say I spent half that interview memorizing every detail of her gorgeous body—but I didn't.

"And I'm sorry. I was out of line blurting my thoughts," she whispered. "I'll… see you on Monday?"

"Yes. Don't let me keep you from your evening. Have fun, Ms. Langley."

"You too."

I leaned back in my seat, shaking my head. I'd told myself I couldn't even look at her, but now with one phone call I was already imagining what *fun* we could have together.

This summer was off to a dangerous start.

FOUR

Lexi

$\mathcal{T}$he next morning, I arrived at the Maxwell house on time. I was on pins and needles. I kept tugging at my shirt and looking down at my jeans. His words reverberated in my mind. *"You'd look stunning in anything you wore."* A little sigh escaped my lips. If I hadn't been thinking out loud on our call, he probably never would have said that, but still, he'd said it, and now I couldn't forget it.

I rang the bell, and while I waited, I snapped a selfie of myself and sent it to my parents. I was beyond happy that the job searched panned out this quickly. I'd spoken to the agency about getting weekly paychecks instead of monthly so they could start paying the bills as soon as possible.

Lexi: First day on the job. Wish me luck.

Mom: You'll do wonderful, dear. Have a great day.

I bit my lower lip when the front door opened, bracing myself for my hot-as-hell boss to show up, but it was Paisley. She was barefoot again as she ran toward the gate with the key. "Hi, Lexi. Dad said I could open the gate for you."

"Hey, Paisley. Thank you, it's good to be here."

"I'm so happy you're here. I like you most."

So, he did ask his daughter's opinion after all. Nine was old enough to tell if you completely disliked a person, and I always thought first instincts should not be dismissed. Well, unless that first instinct was to check out a ridiculously hot single dad. Those impulses had to be ignored at all costs. What had gotten into me? It was true, I hadn't been on a date in almost a year, but still. He was the parent of a child in my care, and I had my *golden rule*.

Paisley took my hand and lead me inside the house.

"It's so nice outside today," I said. "Did you already decide what you want to do?"

"I want to go on the bike."

"Okay. You have one, then?"

"Yes. It's pink."

"I like pink," I said. Unfortunately, I was far too old to get away with owning a pink bicycle. "Do you also have one for me? If not, I can bring mine tomorrow and keep it here."

Paisley frowned. "I think there are more bikes in the garage. We can check."

"Sure." I braced myself as she led me through the house. I'd been in the living room, but now she took me to the right side of the house into an enormous kitchen with white country-style cabinets and a marble countertop.

In front of the stove, Tate was making waffles. Holy shit! Once again, he was wearing a shirt with his sleeves rolled up.

"Morning, Lexi," he said, and my stomach somersaulted.

He hadn't called me by my first name before, but it made sense now that I was working for him. I didn't know if I should call him Tate or Mr. Maxwell, so I went with the safer option. "Good morning, Mr. Maxwell."

"Call me Tate, please," he said.

He held out the chair closest to him, and I drew in a breath, sitting down.

"I made a lot of waffles," he said. "Did you already have breakfast?"

"Yes, I did, but I'll never say no to waffles."

Paisley laughed, clapping her hands. "Daddy makes them for me twice a week."

Tate shrugged, smiling. "I've tried to make a rule of waffles only once a week, but I fail at enforcing it."

"That's understandable," I said. "Don't be too hard on yourself. I work with kids daily, and even I'm not immune to their charm. They are tiny and lovely and know how to use that as a weapon."

I put maple syrup on my waffle and ate it quickly. Tate stood, drinking coffee and only eating half a waffle. Apparently he wasn't much of a breakfast guy. I suspected he did this to spend time with his daughter, and that impressed me, as well as the fact that he didn't have his phone nearby, so his attention was wholly focused on her.

"Lexi and I are going out bike riding today. She asked if we have one for her."

He looked up, and my heart skipped a beat when he trained those piercing blue eyes on me. God, he was handsome. I could admire his looks, though, right? As long as I kept in mind that he was off-limits, I couldn't see why not.

"We do have one that should fit you nicely. We have two adult bikes. One is mine, and one belonged to a previous nanny."

"Great. I'm sure one of them will fit me."

"I'm also going to leave a credit card for you. Use it to pay for anything you and Paisley need. If you pay out of pocket for anything, give me the receipts, and I'll reimburse you."

"Will do," I said.

"Okay, you're both set?" Tate asked as he set his empty cup in the dishwasher. "I'm going to the office."

"Paisley, I'm going to walk your dad out and ask him a few things, okay? I'll be right back," I said.

She nodded, digging into her breakfast.

Tate looked surprised but didn't say anything. As we both walked out of the kitchen, I could feel the air between us change. It became more charged.

"Tate, do you want me to update you during the day with Paisley's schedule? I can send you pictures."

"I'd like that. I miss her so much during the day."

Wow. My heart burst at the thoughtful look on his face. And right then I realized it wasn't just his impossibly good looks that were messing with me. The fact that he was such a dedicated father touched me deeply.

"Okay. Then I'm going to take her out today and keep you posted," I said, more for myself than for him. "I'll take a change of clothes for her. I also brought one for myself, and—"

I stopped abruptly, remembering our conversation from last evening. I'd gotten both of us in trouble by talking about my clothes, and I didn't intend to do it again. Judging by the playful glint in his eyes, he was thinking about it too. I was rambling again.

He was standing only a foot away from me, and I could smell his aftershave.

"Do you have any questions for me?" I asked.

He looked at me intently for a few seconds, making me squirm. Then he shook his head, clearing his throat. "No, that would be all."

Remember your golden rule, Lexi. Besides, my parents were counting on me. I couldn't mess up this job. But it was our first morning together. I was sure I wouldn't be as impacted by him as time went by.

I needed time. That was all. I was sure of it.

———

PAISLEY and I had a lot of fun. She was a great kid. We biked along the Lakefront Trail at a considerable speed. She had a lot of stamina, and we only took a break when we reached Oak Street Beach. I'd brought a blanket with us, so we made a picnic of sorts overlooking the water. I took the peanut butter and jelly sandwiches I made out of the backpack and handed one to Paisley.

"How often do you bike ride?" I asked her.

"Oh, in the summers, a lot. My dad sometimes takes me, or the nanny does."

"You've had a lot of them?"

She nodded. "Yes. About two a year, I think. When I'm at school, I only have someone in the afternoon, but summers are different."

I wondered what happened to her mother, but I didn't want to ask. She'd tell me when she was ready, or maybe Tate would. It was important for me to know what to expect so I could handle any situation.

"My uncles also like to take me out," she said after a few mouthfuls of her sandwich.

"How many do you have?" I asked her.

"Five," she said proudly.

"Five. Wow." I couldn't imagine six Maxwell brothers. I was sure all of them were hot, and that was too much for the world to handle.

"I also have two aunties. Dad's cousins. They all live in Chicago. Sometimes they pick me up at school. I think my teachers like it when my uncles stop by."

Yeah, that confirms my theory.

In between bites, I got a lot of intel. She loved Selena Gomez, her favorite color was pink, she could watch *Snow White* every day and wasn't much of a reader. She did like coloring books and crafts, though.

After we finished the sandwiches, I took out the sunscreen.

We'd smeared ourselves at the house, but it was time to reapply; the sun was burning, and we were sweating a lot. A few minutes later, we went on with our bike ride, only taking another break to eat hot dogs from a food truck for an afternoon snack. Once we got home later that afternoon, we worked on a puzzle of the Chicago skyline while drinking lemonade. As six o'clock approached, I was on pins and needles again, bracing myself for Tate's arrival.

He came home at six on the dot. The second the front door opened, Paisley jumped into his arms. He gave her a tight hug, smiling over her shoulder. When he looked up, his gaze met mine, and I was delighted at the look of happiness in his irises. He put his daughter down and walked toward me, and I swear to God, with every step he took, my body temperature seemed to rise in anticipation of his nearness. This was going to be much harder than I thought.

"How was the day?" he asked. "Thanks for the pics, by the way."

"You're welcome. It was great. The pics were from the Lakefront Trail. We were there for a while and then we came home and spent some time inside the house working on a puzzle."

"It was so fun, Daddy," Paisley piped up. "Lexi can ride really fast, not like the last nanny. And she made a really good lemon drink too."

Tate was obviously pleased with this bit of news. "So the bike fit okay, then?"

I nodded. "Yes, it was fine."

"I'll have to try the lemon drink. Is there any left?"

"Of course!" My voice was a bit high-pitched. Why his interest in my lemonade made me nervous was beyond me.

He poured himself a glass in the kitchen and downed it in big gulps.

"This is great. Do you want to stay for dinner? I'm making

chicken kabobs. They'll go great with lemonade." He winked at me, and it definitely didn't help with my nerves.

"Chicken kabobs? Wow. I'm impressed."

"Please stay, Lexi," Paisley begged. "Dad is a really good cook."

I was hungry, but I didn't want to interfere, even at Paisley's insistence. Besides, I wasn't sure it was very smart to spend more time with him than necessary. He was my employer, and I didn't want to get into a messy situation.

"I'm hungry, but I think it's best to go," I said. *Damn it, why did I admit I was hungry?* I really couldn't get my wits together around this man.

He cocked a brow. "Why aren't you staying if you're hungry?"

I swallowed hard, whispering, "I don't want to interfere during your time with your daughter."

"I'll walk you out," he offered, looking at me intently. I suspected that he actually wanted to be alone with me for whatever he wanted to say next.

"Okay."

"Paisley, I'll be right back," he said. We stepped out into the corridor and walked toward the front door.

"Lexi, if you want to stay, you wouldn't be interfering. Are you sure that's the only reason you want to leave?"

Oh Lord, the way he says my name sounds so decadent.

I looked straight at him and wondering if I should take the bull by the horns and openly discuss everything.

"Or is it because I was inappropriate on our phone call?"

Okay… so I'm guessing he's the take-charge guy all the way.

I liked that.

"Well, I was inappropriate by running my mouth in the first place," I murmured. "Tate, listen, I've been a teacher for seven years, and I have a golden rule. I don't get personally involved with parents."

Finally, I found it in myself to look straight at him. Amusement danced in his eyes.

"Define 'personally involved.'"

The tips of my ears felt hot. "You know what I mean."

He looked at me for a few moments, and the temperature of my body seemed to rise with every passing second.

"It can get confusing for kids, and—"

"Lexi, I know. Paisley is my priority. I'd never do anything to confuse her. She's everything to me."

He can't say that and expect me not to swoon.

"I can tell."

"You and I can keep it professional."

There was a slight edge in his voice that told me he didn't quite believe that.

"But that doesn't mean you can't stay for dinner," he added.

Hmm... here was the thing: if I stayed, I was sure to swoon some more, and that made me more susceptible to him. I couldn't say that out loud, though. That would get us in trouble.

"I'll take you up on the invitation another time, but tonight I'm off. It was a great day. Enjoy your evening."

———

FOR THE REST of the week, I skirted around Tate. I did have breakfast with them every day because he always prepared it right when I arrived, but I left before dinner.

On Wednesday, he worked from home in the morning, and I swear to God, I could feel his presence no matter where I was in the house.

Paisley and I were going to a museum, and she was taking her time choosing an outfit. I waited for her downstairs in the kitchen, leaning against the island and browsing an online foodie shop on my iPhone.

"What are you doing?" Tate asked, startling me. I hadn't heard him come up.

"Waiting for Paisley. And using the time to search for a present for my parents. My mom was given the all clear from the doctors to add some goodies to her diet."

"Was she sick?"

"Yes, she's had two heart surgeries. The bills are adding up."

"That's why you took the job?"

I nodded. "I offered to help, but a teacher's salary barely covers my bills. Anyway, I'm going to look for a present for them later."

He narrowed his eyes. I tried so hard to keep eye contact, but he was wearing a white shirt, and the top button was open. I was dying to take a peek.

Eyes up, Lexi. Eyes up.

"Do they like wine?" he asked suddenly.

"Is the sun yellow? Yes, they do."

"I can send them a special collection from Maxwell Wineries."

My jaw dropped. "Wait… Tate Maxwell? Oh my God! You own Maxwell Wineries?"

He chuckled. "My last name didn't give it away?"

"Honestly, I didn't put two and two together. Until now. *Wow.* You're related to *those* Maxwells."

I'd loved their bookstores and spent a lot of time there as a teenager. The Maxwell family was something of a legend in Chicago. It never occurred to me that he was one of them. Aside from the huge house, he seemed very down-to-earth, and so was Paisley.

"Umm… okay," I recovered. "And yes, they'd love a collection. How much does that cost?"

He cocked a brow. "Nothing. Tell me their address."

"Wow, thank you. That's so generous. They love Maxwell Wines. So do I. They're my favorites," I exclaimed, feeling a bit off-kilter. I was not used to generosity. There he went, making me swoon again. He was going to spoil my parents!

He flashed me a stunning smile. He even had a twinkle in his eyes that set me on edge. My breath caught.

"Good to know, Lexi. Good to know."

It was on the tip of my tongue to ask why, but perhaps I was better off not knowing.

Oh, Lexi. You're playing with fire.

FIVE

Lexi

$\mathcal{O}$n Friday afternoon one week later, I could sense victory. Saturday and Sunday were going to be completely Tate-free. Last weekend had helped me clear my head, but being near Tate every morning this week muddled it all up again. If being near him didn't help, then distance should do the trick. I was hoping, at least.

Paisley and I went biking again, but we also stayed on North Avenue Beach, enjoying the sun and swimming in the lake. It was far too hot outside. The water was cold, but neither of us cared; we wanted to cool off, and this was what we needed. I kept a close eye on her, but she was a proficient swimmer. Even so, I was next to her the whole time we were in the water. She liked swimming even more than I did, and I only convinced her to get out of the lake when black clouds rolled in. They'd announced this morning that there would be a storm in the evening, but I honestly didn't buy it because it was so sunny until now.

"I'm tired and sooooo hungry," she said once we were back in dry clothes.

"So am I. We can Uber home if you want. I'll order a big car so the bikes also fit."

Paisley shook her head. "I can do it. And then Daddy promised veggie curry for dinner. I can't wait."

The mention of Tate made my stomach somersault. The bright side was that I had half an hour on the bike to brace myself for seeing him and then probably another hour or so in the house. That was plenty of time to get my act together.

"Okay."

Uber was still my backup plan, though, in case it started raining. The clouds were dark gray, and the air seemed heavy, the way it usually did before a summer storm.

We were lucky—we only felt a few raindrops on the way, but the thunderstorm rolled in as soon as we got inside the house.

To my dismay, Tate was already home, even though it was only five o'clock. He came toward us, walking slowly. He was wearing a black T-shirt that clung a bit to his torso like his skin was still humid. Clearly he'd just showered. He was also wearing jeans. I'd never seen him dressed so casually, and I could barely keep myself from checking out his abs.

There went my plan to brace myself.

"Daddy, I am hungryyyyyyyyyyyyy," Paisley exclaimed, running right past him and into the kitchen.

"I already made sandwiches until dinner is ready," he called after her.

Instead of following Paisley, he advanced toward me, blue eyes trained on me. "And you, Lexi? Want to stay until the thunderstorm is over? The rain is pretty damn strong. Even with an umbrella, you'll get soaked walking to the car."

That was a great excuse.

I bit my lip, wondering if this was smart. He must have picked up on my hesitation, because he cocked a brow. "I'm not letting you walk out in this storm, Lexi. It's not safe."

"You're not *letting* me?"

My God, the alpha vibes rolling off him weakened my knees.

"No."

"Well, then. Okay."

I didn't have the willpower to say no, and I could only describe the look in his eyes as triumphant.

Oh, Lexi, what did you do?

The thunderstorm only intensified during dinner. Tate made a veggie curry with basmati rice, and it was utterly delicious.

"Your cooking is amazing," I said.

He winked. "I've had lots of practice."

Paisley beamed. "Daddy is the best cook. Once we had a cooking competition in school and he won it. All the other moms were so mad."

I pressed my lips together, biting back a chuckle.

"Notice the emphasis on moms," he said out of the corner of his mouth. "Says a lot about gender expectations, right?"

I nodded, taking another mouthful of rice. I liked that he didn't care about any of that. I could imagine him showing up at school at a cooking competition. He was a man of many talents, that was for sure.

After dinner, Paisley said she wanted to sit on the couch and watch TV, but she fell asleep two minutes later.

"We went swimming in addition to biking today," I whispered. "It's not a surprise that she's asleep."

"I'll take her upstairs really quick," he said. Looking straight at me, he added, "Wait for me here."

My heart thundered in my chest. I knew being alone with him wasn't a good idea, but I couldn't bring myself to say no.

"I have an excellent wine," he continued.

And he was bribing me with drinks!

"I'll stay, but only on one condition."

"And what's that?" he asked.

"I want something that's not on the market yet."

"I'm sure I'll find something to your liking, Ms. Langley." His eyes widened.

Was it an involuntary flirty line? Yes. Yes, it was. And his daughter was asleep a few feet away from us. I wasn't sure staying was such a good idea. But we were both adults, and we'd drawn a line in the sand.

"Okay. I'll wait here," I said.

"Good."

I tried not to melt too much when he picked up Paisley in his arms. She immediately put her head slightly lower than his shoulder, and he brought his hand to the back of her head, sustaining it with so much ease that it was obvious this happened often.

How could this mountain of a man be so gentle?

I paced the kitchen, unsure what to do with myself while I was waiting for him. I still had some rice to finish, so I sat back in my chair and continued eating.

He came back a few minutes later. I glanced up as I heard his footsteps and really looked at him for the first time tonight.

The man was too handsome. His attraction score skyrocketed in casual clothing. Not like he needed it. The black T-shirt molded perfectly to his sculpted abs and revealed more of his arms than the shirt. The sleeves cut into his biceps. Yum. I trained my gaze on him, but he cocked a brow, making me blush.

"You want seconds?" he asked, pointing at the pan with the curry.

"No, thanks. I'm good. I finished eating this portion. It was huge, but I ate it all anyway. It was so good that I didn't want to miss one bite."

"I'm glad you liked it." He'd finished his plate, but he sat in the chair next to me. We'd been sitting in the same spots before too, but without Paisley here as a buffer, the tension between us was palpable. His presence was overwhelming and all-consuming.

"Are you happy after the second week?" he asked.

"It was fun, and it's easy to be with Paisley. She's so curious about everything."

"What about me, Lexi? How easy am I?" He pinned me with his blue eyes, and I was instantly on edge, squirming.

"I'm still not sure about that." Licking my lips, I averted my gaze. "Back to Paisley. I wanted to ask you if some topics are off-limits and if there's any stuff you don't want me to talk to her about."

He frowned. "Like what?"

I cleared my throat. "Like boys."

He jerked his head back, eyes wide. "She asked about boys?"

Oh, I can see an overprotective father in the making. "No, she didn't. But, you know, in case she asks."

"Do girls even think about that at her age?"

"Sometimes. You'd be surprised all the things girls think about, and they usually don't want to ask their parents, so they ask me."

His expression darkened. "Well, it's not like she can ask her mother."

My heart sank. "Did she pass away?"

He shook his head. "No, nothing like that. We divorced when Paisley was three years old. She moved away to Seattle, but she's rarely there. She's a model, so she travels a lot. It's one of the reasons she gave me full custody of Paisley."

"Oh, okay. She didn't mention her mother at all, so I was wondering if it's an off-limits topic as well."

"It's not. Nora is not very involved in Paisley's life. She calls every few weeks and visits once a year. Paisley also spends one week with her each year, but that's it."

My heart bled for Paisley, and for him, because he was clearly hurt and still suffering, even though the divorce happened years ago. "I'm sorry."

"I have my family here, and we're all very close, but not having a mother is difficult for my daughter."

"It is," I agreed. "If it's okay, I'd like to tell Paisley that she can ask me anything she feels she can't ask you, and if I find that something's very delicate, I'll ask you before saying anything."

He looked at me intently, nodding. "That sounds great. Thank you. I'm very happy you took the job, Lexi. I've never had… Well, Paisley and I have never had anyone like you. You seem to understand what kids need."

"Well, I love them. That's why I became a teacher. I don't know why, but I always understand where they're coming from and what they think, especially when they're Paisley's age. I'm not very good with toddlers, but I'm great with elementary school kids."

His expression changed. His eyes softened, and that was my kryptonite. Not his smoldering look or his intense gaze, but that right there was slicing through me, and I had no idea why. I couldn't understand how Paisley's mom had left the two of them.

"Was the divorce amicable?" I asked without thinking. "I'm sorry. If I'm way out of line, you don't have to answer."

He leaned in closer, looking straight at me. "You and I passed 'out of line' on that first phone call, Lexi."

I laughed, running a hand through my hair, liking this lighthearted side of him. But then he frowned.

"And no, it wasn't exactly amicable. She'd been a model before Paisley was born, and when Paisley turned two, she decided to pursue it again. I was supportive, because I understood passion for a career. Then she decided she didn't like being a wife and that she wanted to dedicate herself to her career. I thought she'd want to stay more involved in Paisley's life, but she isn't. I think Paisley is slowly coming to terms with that."

"And you?"

"I came to terms with the fact that she wanted to be out of our life for good when I insisted on couples therapy and she told me it was no use because she had an affair with a photographer."

I gasped. "That's awful."

He waved his hand, shaking his head. "It is what it is. Not everyone can have a happy marriage like my parents. Before marrying, I thought divorce rates were exaggerated. Now I know they're not."

He didn't say anything more, and I didn't press, not wanting to bring up old wounds. I wanted to distract him, and then I remembered I had a very good reason.

"You promised me wine, remember? I don't see a bottle around here."

He pulled back, smiling so confidently that my knees weakened. Masculinity rolled off him.

"I have a wine cellar. I can give you a tour, and you can choose which one you want."

I straightened up. "Oh my God. You have a wine cellar here?"

He chuckled. "Yes, I do. What kind of winemaker would I be otherwise?"

"I don't know. I figured maybe you had it at the production site or something."

"I have one there too, but this is my own personal cellar. Come on. I'll show it to you."

He rose from his chair and then pulled mine back.

As I got up, my arm brushed his chest, and I heard him suck in a breath.

Oh my. Feeling those hard muscles against my arm did things to me.

What is wrong with me? He was Paisley's dad. True, she didn't go to my school, so there was no risk of students thinking I had favorites or colleagues gossiping, but I still didn't think this was a good idea. Especially after what he'd shared with me.

Focus on the fact that he's Paisley's dad, Lexi.

It didn't matter that he was also the hottest man I'd ever seen. But if I was honest, the fact that he was such a dedicated father was also part of his irresistible sex appeal.

I looked up at him and was surprised that his pupils had dilated a bit. I swallowed hard, fidgeting in my spot.

Clearly I wasn't the only one shaken by this incredible chemistry between us.

SIX

Tate

I was losing my mind. This was the only explanation I could find. I couldn't take my eyes off her. I barely kept my hands to myself.

"How are your parents?" I asked as I led her to the back of the house.

"Better. Super happy with the gift box. Thanks again. That was beyond kind."

She was fucking amazing. Not many people would take a second job to help out their family. For me, family was what mattered most in this life, so knowing that about her made her all that much more appealing to me. She stirred something inside me, and no woman had ever managed to stir anything in me since the divorce. It was like I'd shut myself off from everything. It had been as much a conscious decision as an instinct. I'd put up a wall between myself and everyone else. But I was drawn to Lexi.

"You're a great person."

"Thank you," she said softly. "I'm so happy I got the job."

I turned, watching her. "I'm glad you said that. You and

45

Paisley are a good fit. She likes you." I tipped my head to her. "I like you, Lexi. More than I should."

She pushed a strand of hair behind her ear. I barely kept from reaching out and doing it for her.

Fuck. Me.

"Come on, let's go. We're going to have to spend some time downstairs before we pick your wine."

"How many bottles do you have?" she asked.

"About a thousand."

Her eyes bulged. "Can I move in here? I can live in the cellar, honestly."

I let out loud, unrestrained guffaws. She was grinning.

"I made you burst out laughing. You only do that when Paisley's around."

"Or you."

She licked her lower lip. I couldn't look away from her mouth.

"The wine cellar?" she murmured, bringing me back to reality.

I straightened up, gesturing for her to walk in front of me as I opened the door to the cellar. "After you, Ms. Langley."

What was it about this woman that made me laugh so often? The things she said were always so unexpected that I couldn't help myself. She was right. I needed to laugh more. And when I was with her, I felt happy.

The lighting was dim in the staircase, but then it abruptly turned dark. I tried a nearby switch, but the light didn't turn back on.

"Something's wrong with the electric circuit down here."

"Should we go back upstairs and grab a flashlight?" Lexi asked.

I took out my smartphone from my pocket, turning on the little flashlight button. "It's okay. We have enough light with this."

46

"That's true. I left my phone upstairs, but this will work. I'm going to focus on the fact that there is wine; otherwise, I'd feel a bit like we were in a horror movie."

"Are you afraid of the dark, Lexi?"

She shivered. Fuck, I was close enough to feel the goose bumps on her arm.

"Not tonight," she whispered as we stopped in front of the shelves. "Wow. This is amazing. You know how most people would love to see a real-life version of the bookcases in *Beauty and the Beast*?"

"I have no idea what you're talking about."

She turned her head sideways at me. I tipped my head and was so close that my lips almost brushed hers. "You have a young daughter."

"I know, but my brain always blocks out whatever she wants us to watch."

"Understandable. Well, anyway, there's a scene in which there's a huge library, and people are always like, 'Oh, I want this to happen in real life.'" She pointed at the wine bottles. "But this is what I've always wanted to see."

I chuckled. "You're always welcome here, Lexi. Tell me, what kind of wine do you like? Describe it as best as you can."

"I love white wine. I want it to be fruity but not sweet. Light, with a hint of smokiness."

"I have what you need. Come on. Let's pick it out together from the shelf." Instinct overpowered rational thought again. I put a hand on her waist. She moved, knocking my phone out of my hand, disengaging the light when it fell so it was completely dark.

"Oh, shit. I'm sorry," she said.

"No problem. I'll get it." Bending down, I brushed my hand around the floor and picked it up. Pressing the bottom of the screen, I managed to turn the light on again.

"Can you find the bottle?" Lexi asked.

I had to laugh at the apprehension in her voice. She was legitimately worried about not getting wine. I liked this woman more and more.

"It was the fifth bottle from the floor." Taking it out, I held it to her, jokingly asking, "Want to keep it to make sure I don't drop it or anything?"

"Oh, no. I trust you with wine more than I trust myself. Although… you *did* drop the phone, so give it here. I'll keep it safe."

She clasped the bottle, laughing.

I put a hand on her arm, resting my fingers on her bare skin. She squirmed against me. I heard her suck in a breath. She was so sensitive to me that it drove me insane.

"So, you like wine? Tell me more. What else do you like?"

"Your delicious cooking," she said.

"I meant in general, not about me, but since we're on that slippery slope, please do say what else you like about me."

We reached the staircase and stopped.

"Tate," she whispered. Her breath landed on my neck, and it was all I could do not to pin her against the wall. I wouldn't stop just at kissing her. I knew that. If my lips ever touched hers, it wouldn't end with a kiss. It would end with me sinking inside her and making her mine. And I couldn't risk that.

"I'm not sure why I'm always on a slippery slope around you," she murmured.

I laughed, skimming my hand up from her waist to her shoulder and then her neck, feathering my thumb on her jaw. "I like you, Lexi, far too much, and I don't know what to do about it."

The next moment, I heard Paisley calling my name from upstairs. The spell broke and I groaned, taking a step back.

"Is that Paisley?" she asked.

"Yes."

"Does she have nightmares?" She was back in her professional mode. Good, because someone had to keep us in check, and it wasn't going to be me.

When we reached the stairs, I realized it wasn't just the cellar light that was out. The whole place seemed to be in the dark.

"It's a blackout," she said.

"Probably from the storm. Now I know what woke Paisley. She has a night-light, and it probably went off. I'm going to go upstairs and talk to her, okay?" I wondered why the backup generator hadn't kicked in.

"Okay, sure. Should I go home?" she whispered in the dark.

"The storm's still strong, Lexi."

"I see. So, you're still not letting me out?"

"Exactly."

"I'm your prisoner?" Her tone was playful.

I stepped closer. "Wait for me here."

"Okay. I left my phone on the kitchen counter. I'll feel my way there, grab it, and pour us wine."

"Thanks."

I headed upstairs, knocking on Paisley's open door to announce myself before entering.

"Daddy, is that you?" she asked, her breath frantic as I sat down at the edge of her mattress.

"Yes, baby." I caressed her hand, and she instantly calmed down, scooting closer to me.

"What happened to the light?" she asked.

"The electricity is out, but I'm going to fix it, okay? I'm going to turn on the generator."

"I can't sleep in the dark," she said.

"That's okay. We'll turn on the light on your phone, and then when the electricity is back, your night-light will automatically turn on, okay?"

Some people—including Paisley's teachers—raised their eyebrows that I'd bought her a phone when she was only nine years old, but I liked knowing that I could get in touch with her anytime.

She nodded, leaning against me. She didn't do this often anymore. When she was little, she used to want me to rock her to sleep, but then she said she'd outgrown it. I turned on the phone's flashlight, placing it on the nightstand so the light reflected on the ceiling. About two minutes later, I realized she'd fallen back asleep.

I kissed her head, but I didn't leave her room right away, waiting just in case she woke up so she wouldn't be scared. I messaged my brothers in the meantime, asking if one of them could check on Gran. Tyler answered me that her generator had started automatically, but he was already on his way to her house to check on her anyway.

When I was confident that Paisley wouldn't wake up again, I tiptoed out of her room before closing the door and heading downstairs.

"Lexi?" I asked.

"I'm on the couch," she said. I could see the light from her phone. "It's not the house. A huge chunk of the city is out of electricity. They're working on repairing it, but it might take a while," she said.

"Yeah, I figured that might be the case."

"Is Paisley okay?"

"Yeah, she's fine. She fell asleep."

"You're a great dad," she whispered.

"I'm glad you think so."

"So listen, I didn't uncork the bottle. We can drink it another time. With the storm and everything, maybe it's better that I get home."

"Is your building okay? Do you have electricity there?" I asked, standing in the doorway.

"No, but that's fine. We have emergency generators, so those probably kicked in."

"What floor is your apartment on?"

"Twenty," she said on a groan, coming to the same conclusion I did.

"Think it's smart to go there? What if the generator hasn't started yet and you have to climb twenty flights of stairs?"

"Yeah, you're right," she said. "I should wait some more."

"I have another proposition," I said.

"Oh?"

"Spend the night here. We have enough bedrooms. Power outages can be a hassle even with generators."

"Hmmm… I sense some alpha vibes going on. Can't say no to that, can I?"

"What?"

"Never mind. I was talking to myself. Umm…" Damn, she was cute all worked up like this. "Is Paisley going to be okay with that tomorrow morning?"

"You're going to sleep in the guest room, Lexi, not my bedroom." I groaned at the thought. "I'll explain to her tomorrow morning that you couldn't go home while the electricity was off. Come on, let's have that wine before we go to bed."

"I never say no to wine," she said in a chirpy tone.

"I'll go turn on the generator manually since it didn't kick on. You can pour the wine."

"Okay."

———

TEN MINUTES LATER, the generator was up and running. I found Lexi at the kitchen island. She'd taken out two glasses and uncorked the bottle.

I poured us each half a glass and took the bottle with us back to the couch. Sitting down, we clinked glasses.

"I want your honest opinion on the wine," I said.

"Okay." She swirled it once, sniffing the glass before taking a sip, then another one. "Mmm."

The sound went straight through me, and I couldn't hold back a groan. She inhaled sharply, licking her lower lip. Our gazes crossed, and something snapped inside me. The next second, I leaned in closer, cupping the side of her head, tilting it, brushing my mouth over hers. She tasted delicious, I was right, but not because of the wine. It was just her—sweet and so damn perfect. I kissed her hungrily, exploring her mouth, coaxing her tongue with mine until I felt her shudder. The reverberations went through my body. I couldn't stop kissing her, wanting to claim more sounds of pleasure. But Lexi pulled back, groaning.

"Tate...," she murmured.

"I can't think straight," I warned her.

"Mmm," she whispered. "I can't either. But I think it's safe to say we're on a dangerous path, mister. No more wine for us."

"It's not the wine. It's just you, Lexi."

She sighed, and I barely resisted the urge to kiss her again.

"I should go home," she said.

"No," I said determinedly. "You're not going to climb twenty flights of stairs in the dark. I'm not gonna let that happen."

"Oh, sweet heavens. You're already going alpha on me."

"Lexi! It's not safe."

"And you think I'd be safe *here*, Mr. Maxwell, after you kissed me like that?"

I made a sound at the back of my throat instead of answering. Jesus, I was turning into a Neanderthal.

"I think that proved my point. Let me check with a neighbor if the power is back on." A few seconds later, she shook her head. "It's not."

"I'll show you to the guest bedroom, and we'll call it a night, okay? And we can talk about this tomorrow."

She swallowed hard. "Okay. Okay, that sounds smart. Let's do that. Where is the guest bedroom?"

"On the third floor."

"And where is your bedroom?"

"On the second one."

"Oh, good. We have a floor between us. That should be enough."

"Don't be so sure, Lexi. Come on, let's go upstairs before I do something crazy."

Her breath caught. "I was about to ask what, but maybe it's better if I don't," she whispered.

"Yeah, it is. Trust me."

I ushered her to go first on the steps, staying behind her. When we reached the second floor, I said, "Wait here." I headed to my bedroom, grabbed a clean white T-shirt that I usually have under my shirt, and walked back to her.

"What did you bring?" she asked as we moved up to the third floor.

"A shirt for you so you have something to sleep in," I said.

"So gallant," she murmured. "Tate, should we talk about this right now?"

I shook my head. "I need to clear my head first, Lexi. I'm too wrapped up in you."

She groaned. "Oh God. You sure know how to say all the right things."

The bedroom was at the top of the stairs, and she stepped inside.

"Good night, Lexi."

I headed back downstairs, needing a glass of wine to cool off.

A few minutes later, I realized there was no cooling off as long as she was under my roof.

And she was going to be here the whole summer.

SEVEN

Lexi

The next morning, I woke with a start, pushing myself up in bed. I looked around groggily, and then my heart jolted.

Oh my God.

Then I remembered I wasn't at my place.

Looking at the nightstand, I grabbed my phone to check the time. It was eight o'clock. I sprang from the bed, heading directly to the en suite bathroom. I was smiling as I got in the shower. Starting the warm spray, I soaped up quickly, and I also rinsed my mouth. When I stepped out of the shower, I was surprised to find toothpaste and a toothbrush in the medicine cabinet above the sink. I brushed my teeth until I had a minty flavor in my mouth.

My mind raced as I remembered our kiss last night. I wasn't sure what to do. Should I pretend it didn't happen? That kiss was still making me swoon. But that didn't mean I didn't feel guilty for breaking my own rule. I had it in place for a reason. I took pride in my job as a teacher, and boundaries were important to me. And I felt like, even though Paisley wasn't at my school, Tate was my boss, and I needed to remember that.

Oh, who was I kidding? Not only had we kissed, but I'd flirted with him. Part of me wanted to talk to him and ask him to look for another nanny, but I felt even guiltier at the thought of leaving Paisley and Tate in the lurch. I could imagine her eyes filled with disappointment, and my stomach turned into a tight knot.

I mulled this over some more as I dressed in yesterday's clothes, but I didn't reach any conclusions. I was far too sleepy for that.

When I left the room, I heard Paisley's and Tate's voices coming from the kitchen. They were early birds, both of them, even on the weekend. I didn't want to disturb their time together, but I couldn't leave without saying goodbye, so I poked my head in the kitchen.

My heart gave a mighty sigh. Tate was cooking again, but there was something different about him this morning. For one, he wasn't wearing a dress shirt. He was wearing a T-shirt like the one he'd given me for last night—and he looked glorious. The contours of his muscles were visible, and I couldn't help remembering last night.

Heat coursed through me, and I shook my head as if that could do anything to dispel the memory.

"Knock, knock," I said in a cheery voice, tapping against the doorframe.

To my surprise, there was someone else inside the kitchen too. A woman. She had dark brown hair styled in loose curls and deep green eyes, like Paisley's. She was wearing a beach dress with a pattern of yellow daisies and a pendant with an infinity knot hanging on a black thread. I loved her style.

"Good morning," she said. "I'm Reese, Paisley's aunt and Tate's favorite cousin."

"Hi! Nice to meet you."

I shook her hand briefly before glancing at Tate behind her. The second we made eye contact, the heat in my body magnified. Sweet Lord, I'd thought I could forget our kiss? Well, I was completely wrong. I was on edge just because we were in the same room.

The sound of a phone vibrating filled the air. Reese groaned.

"Sorry. I'll step in the other room to answer this."

Tate looked after her with a troubled expression as she left the kitchen.

"When did you two get up?" I asked.

"An hour ago," said Paisley.

"She always wakes up early." Tate's tone indicated that he'd like to sleep in on the weekends, but here he was making breakfast for his daughter. It was adorable.

"I'm making waffles," he said. I couldn't help but laugh again.

He shrugged. "Saturday's waffle day, but sometimes Paisley convinces me to also make them during the week. We have more time on weekends, so that's why I prefer to do elaborate breakfasts either Saturday or Sunday."

I realized what seemed different about him today. He was more relaxed because he didn't have to go to work.

"Look, I don't want to disturb you two. Thanks for letting me sleep here. I texted someone from my building, and the elevator is working, so..."

"You're not disturbing us, Lexi," Tate said. "We'd love to have you, but I understand if you'd prefer to leave."

He looked straight at me. His gaze was hard and intense with a silent question.

I licked my lower lip, drawing in a sharp breath when I realized he'd dropped his glance to my mouth. I did want waffles, and to spend time with Tate and Paisley, even though I knew it wasn't smart to linger outside my work hours. But I couldn't help myself.

"Pleaaaaaaaaaaaaaaaaaaaaaase," Paisley said.

Shucks. I couldn't say no to her when she looked at me like that.

"The waffles win again," I said, dashing into the kitchen.

Tate looked at me triumphantly.

"Yay!" Paisley screeched. This girl was winning my heart.

There were no plates on the kitchen island, so I headed straight to the cabinet next to the stove, where I knew they were stored. Paisley dashed off to her bedroom, saying she wanted to get her coloring book.

"How did you sleep?" Tate asked me.

I hesitated while reaching for the plates and glanced at him out of the corner of my eye. His gaze was trained on me.

"I slept well, thank you."

"At least one of us did, then."

I turned to him. My breath caught. "You didn't?"

"Hell no. All I could think about was you lying one floor above me, wearing my shirt."

I grinned, whispering back, "How do you know I didn't sleep naked?"

Oh my God. My flirtiness was getting worse! Something about him made me impulsive, especially after the kiss.

A growl reverberated in his throat.

"I didn't. I was joking."

He straightened up, and so did I. We both glanced at the living room, but there was no sign of Paisley.

I was blushing. Tate looked from one cheek to the other, satisfaction clear on his features.

Well, well. He likes to make me blush, huh?

He was playing with fire, because I could be full of mischief when I wanted to.

And right now, I really, *really* wanted to. But I reined myself in. I had to at least try.

"Don't burn the waffles, mister," I warned, pointing to the stove with a half smile.

He focused his attention on the pan while I took out the plates. When I turned around, I brushed against him. It was a tiny touch, my arm against his torso, but heat curled through me, tugging at my nerve endings.

Holy shit. What's happening? Chemistry like this didn't exist in real life. I'd never felt it with anyone.

Paisley returned with her coloring book and sat in the chair at the kitchen island. I set the plates, and Tate immediately came with waffles, putting three on each plate. I brought the honey, maple syrup, Nutella, and fruit from the fridge, having learned quickly where everything was because I prepared snacks every day for Paisley.

As I cut an apple in two, intending to dice it, I felt Tate come up next to me. He stood a few inches away, but my body was already on hyperalert, feeling his nearness.

"Paisley, what do you want on your waffles?" I asked.

"Nutella and banana," she said cheerfully, and I was about to cut the banana on the waffle when she added, "No, not like that. Daddy, can you show her? He always makes the funniest shapes with waffles on the weekend."

"Paisley, I only do that when it's two of us," he said.

Paisley frowned. "But we like Lexi."

I sighed, hugging the little mouse, and my heart felt like it was about to burst when she hugged me right back. "I'm glad to hear that."

Tearing herself from my arms, she looked at Tate. "We like her, don't we, Daddy?"

He looked at me, a corner of his mouth lifting. "Yes. We like her very much."

I licked my lower lip, pointing to the waffle, hoping to

distract him from my blush. "Okay. Show me what you can do."

Amusement danced in his eyes.

"What's your favorite place in Chicago?" he asked.

"The Millennium Ferris Wheel. And believe it or not, I've never been on it. You want to draw that?"

"Nah. My skills aren't that good."

He took the plate in front of him, along with the banana, the bowl of grapes, Nutella, and whipped cream. Seriously, this man was every woman's dream.

Well… my dream at least.

He moved his hands quickly, and I couldn't exactly tell what he was doing, but when he shoved the plate back to Paisley, I realized he'd made a smiley face. It was quite good. He'd smeared the Nutella on the waffle and used the grapes as eyes and slices of banana as a mouth. He'd made a halo of hair around them with whipped cream. I couldn't help but laugh, looking up at him.

He pointed at me. "Don't laugh."

"It's an appreciative laugh," I said. I was melting because this serious, take-charge guy could be a total goof around his daughter.

And he's an excellent kisser, a voice said at the back of my head. I had a hunch that the more I tried to forget that, the more clearly I'd remember it.

"Do I get to have a special waffle?" I asked, batting my eyelashes.

"Yeah, Daddy. Make one for Lexi," Paisley said, clapping her hands, looking between us.

Tate sobered up, and my heart leaped in my throat, wondering if I'd overstepped in some way. Paisley also went a bit still, glancing at me from the corner of her eye. "That's Daddy's serious face," she said in a whisper.

"I know," I whispered back.

"But he doesn't mean it."

The next second, Tate's expression morphed, and a huge grin spread on his face. "All right. I'll do a waffle for you, but you do mine," he said.

"But you're not allowed to make one that looks the same as mine," Paisley said.

I raised a brow. "Oh, okay. We have rules. Anything else I should know?"

Tate looked at me as if he was laughing at the private joke but didn't say anything aloud.

I glanced at the waffle, thinking what I could do. Looking at the chopped banana, I got an idea. I arranged grapes on one side of the waffle, left the middle empty, then put three banana slices on one edge before I proudly presented it to him. He was still working on mine, but he stopped, glancing at his plate and frowning.

"What's that supposed to be?"

"That's the lake, beach, and the grapes are skyscrapers," I said cheerfully.

Paisley pushed herself up on her chair and looked closer at my waffle. Then she glanced up at her dad. For a few seconds, no one said anything. Then both of them burst out laughing with so much joy that I couldn't help but join in, even though I knew they were laughing at me. The ease between the two of them and their closeness was melting my heart.

"All right," he said. "I guess you'll get better with practice."

"Okay. Let's see how you do," I said in a challenging voice.

A few minutes later, he pushed my plate to me, and I had to admit it was much better. He'd made yet another smiley face, but this one I recognized. This was the emoji that made sexy eyes. To Paisley, it probably meant nothing, but I felt my cheeks heat up.

"You're cheating, Dad. That's another smiley face," Paisley said.

"Exactly. It doesn't count," I added.

He kept his eyes trained on me, but I didn't look away.

"Dad, when is Aunt Reese finishing her call?" Paisley asked.

"I don't know."

"Is everyone in your family an early riser on Saturday?" I inquired.

Tate shrugged. "Not really, but Reese needed some company."

"Did something happen?"

"Her ex-fiancé is giving her headaches," he replied in a harsh tone.

And his door is always open to his family, huh? This was completely unexpected.

"That's it, I turned my phone to airplane mode," Reese announced, entering the kitchen.

Sitting next to Paisley, she helped herself to a mouthful of her niece's waffle.

"Tate, you make the best waffles." She sighed with appreciation. "When is everyone else arriving?"

"Probably not until lunch," Tate said.

Paisley turned to look straight at me, pushing herself up onto her feet, and standing on the chair. She pointed one forefinger at me.

"Lexi! We're having a barbecue. Pleaaaaaase stay. I want everyone to meet you."

She was adorable.

Before I had a chance to reply, Tate intervened.

"Paisley, Lexi is free on weekends. She's only here this morning because there was a power outage and it wasn't safe for her to go back home. Now, sit back down in your chair before you fall."

A knot formed in my stomach. He was right, of course. I was the nanny, not part of the family. I had to keep that front and center in mind. I'd only been here two weeks, and we'd kissed. And now I was swooning because he'd made me a waffle. I was on a *very* slippery slope.

"But our cookouts are fun," Reese put in. "Do you have plans for today?"

"I'm meeting a friend in the afternoon. But now, I was going to go home and get something to read, a blanket, and maybe picnic out at the beach in front of my building. I don't have anything planned for lunch."

"Then stay. Besides, you might need intel about your employer," she said with a wink.

"What?" I asked, genuinely curious.

"He ran off a lot of nannies because he's so demanding."

Tate groaned. "Reese!"

"He should be," I replied. "They're caring for his daughter, after all."

"Pleaaaaase," Paisley repeated as she slowly sat back down in her chair.

I pressed my lips together before bursting into laughter. I really couldn't say no to her, huh? Not when she stared with those pleading eyes. I couldn't disappoint her.

"Okay. If it's not an inconvenience to anyone, I'll stay," I said.

"It's not. Lexi, let's step outside the kitchen for a minute," Tate said.

My heart was hammering in my chest. I nodded, carefully getting up from my seat and walking ahead of him. I felt his gaze on me every step of the way.

We rounded the corner to the TV area so we were out of sight.

"Sorry about Paisley. She's not too clear on boundaries. Neither is Reese, apparently."

I shook my head, fiddling with my thumbs. "Should I go? I don't want to overstay my welcome."

He stepped right in front of me, eyes hard and unrelenting. "You're not overstaying. But I meant what I said. The weekend is your free time. I don't expect you to stay. But I'd love it if you did."

"Really? Well, I can't say no to Paisley anyway. I can't resist her."

"But you can resist me?" he asked in a flirty tone.

"I think I'm doing a better job of that, yes," I replied in an equally flirty tone.

"I see."

"Daaaaaad, are you scaring Lexi off?" Paisley called from the kitchen.

I chuckled as Tate said loudly, "No, I'm not."

"So she's staying?"

He looked at me intently. I squirmed in my spot, nodding.

"Yes, she is," he announced loudly before adding in a whisper, "And you and I will find a quiet moment alone to talk about last night."

EIGHT

Lexi

———

"So, what exactly is the family gathering about today? Something special going on?" I asked.

"It's a cookout," Paisley replied.

"Everyone brings something, and we throw it all on the grill," Tate explained.

It sounded so normal. They were one of the most influential families in Chicago, but they spent their weekends having a cookout.

"Gran is coming too," Reese said.

"Your parents too?" I asked, looking at Tate.

"No, they're traveling. But trust me, there's going to be plenty of people to confuse you."

"I'll do the introductions," Reese offered. "Three of his brothers are coming. Travis and Sam will be the ones missing. And my sister is in Paris, so she won't be here either. But like Tate says, there's gonna be plenty of people. Between all of us, you should get a good picture of Tate here so you don't have any surprises down the road."

She wiggled her eyebrows at Tate, who shook his head. "Keep it up and I'm revoking your breakfast invitation."

Reese pouted. "You can't do that. You love me too much. And besides, I'm in a bad place: heart crushed, shitty ex-fiancé, and all that."

Reese spoke with ease, like it was all a big joke, but there was no mistaking the emotion in her eyes.

Tate pointed at her. "Stop it. That's where Paisley is learning all her emotional blackmail techniques."

"I'm an excellent teacher," Reese replied with a grin.

Tate shook his head, snorting. "Not everyone's like Reese, I promise."

I grinned. "Hey, I like Reese. She's fun."

The rest of his family arrived a short while later, and everyone gathered in the kitchen. His brothers Declan and Tyler came first, then Luke. His grandmother, Beatrice, arrived last.

All the guys were tall, towering over me by at least a head. They had slender yet strong builds, with muscular but lean bodies.

Tyler was the tallest, and his frame was bulkier than the rest of his brothers. He revealed that he was a hockey player, which made sense. Declan resembled Tyler a lot. I suspected he was a professional athlete of some sort, but he was a lawyer, to my surprise. I could imagine those blue eyes and impressive stature coming in handy in the courtroom.

He also seemed to be the direct opposite of Tyler, who had smiles for everyone. Declan was more serious. Luke seemed more sedate as well, but I wasn't sure if it was because he'd just met me or if that was his personality. Physically, he resembled Tate with his dark hair, but he had green eyes like Paisley and Reese.

Tate introduced me to all of them.

Tyler grinned. "He's already making you work on weekends? Please don't quit because my brother is insensitive." He turned to his brother, saying, "Tate, that is not the way to make people stick around."

"That's okay. I volunteered to stay, and anyway, since I slept here, it wasn't an inconvenience." The second I said the words out loud, the room went silent.

"You slept here?" Declan asked before I could cover my faux pas. He was looking straight at Tate and not at me.

"Yes. With the blackout last night, the elevator in my building wasn't working, and I live on the twentieth floor," I said quickly. Perhaps a bit too fast. Even Tyler looked at me suspiciously with a knowing smile. Declan cocked a brow at Tate.

"What did I miss?" Luke asked, walking into the kitchen. He'd gone to his car to bring a box of fresh veggies.

"Nothing much," Tyler said. "We're giving Tate here advice on how *not* to run Lexi off after only a few weeks."

"Oh. How should we prepare her best?" Luke said in a teasing tone. "That's right. When he looks like this," he said with an exaggerated frown, "it's best to stay out of his way. You never know when he's going to lash out."

Ha! I'd pegged him all wrong. He was more like Tyler than Declan. The razzing between these brothers was hilarious.

"Yeah. I think as a rule of thumb, it's best to stay out of his way entirely," Tyler said.

I liked their dynamic. Tate was taking it all in stride.

"Does anyone have any input that's proactive?" I asked.

"Oh, she's a brave one," Luke said. "I like you, Lexi."

"Thank you. And yes, I like to think of myself as being brave."

"Well, my brother does like good conversation. And wine, of course," Tyler offered.

"Duly noted," I said, glancing at Tate, who was looking at me with amusement in his eyes. I searched his features for any sign that I was overstepping boundaries. Instead of playing with Paisley outside, I was here with him and his brothers. But he seemed to be enjoying this.

"I think I'm a better source," he said. "Anything you want to know, just ask me."

I glanced at Luke, schooling my features to look serious. "Do you think he means it, or will he bite my head off if I ask him things?"

Luke turned to Tyler and Declan. "What do you guys think? Should she go for it, or should she hedge her bets?"

Tyler crossed his arms over his chest. "Always hedge your bets."

"Okay, everyone, let's move outside," Luke said, "before Gran hands us our asses for not starting the grill."

There was a bit of commotion in the kitchen as everyone walked outside. I stayed behind, helping Tate put everything he'd taken out on the counter on a tray. There were a gazillion sauces: ketchup, barbecue, mustard, and whatnot.

"I like your brothers," I said after a while.

"I meant what I said, Lexi. You can ask me anything you want. But a word of warning. You might not be ready for the answer."

I sucked in a breath, a million questions playing on my lips. But I didn't get a chance to ask anything, because Declan said loudly, "Move your ass out here, Tate."

I didn't have a lot of nanny duties because Grandma Beatrice was glued to Paisley. I spoke to Reese, who confided in me that she was excited to work at Beatrice's bookstore starting Monday.

"I didn't know she still had a bookstore," I exclaimed.

"It's because she couldn't keep the original name. This one is called The Happy Place. Gran insisted on keeping it because it was the first store they had, and they lived above it for many years. She owns the whole building. She doesn't actually run it, of course. She's got a manager. Anyway, I've helped out there since I was in high school. I've always loved the place. It was one of the reasons why I wanted to turn the upper levels into a spa with my shitty ex, Malcolm. It's sitting empty, and will continue to stay that way, unless my ex gets his way."

"Why don't you open it on your own?"

"I might, at some point. Right now, though, I'm honestly not in the right frame of mind to start a business. I need something to ground me now."

She seemed so disheartened that I wanted to hug her. I'd had my fair share of heartbreak over the years.

"Do you want to talk about what happened?" I asked her, then added, "Sometimes talking with someone unfamiliar with the situation can be helpful."

She nodded, then blurted out, "He slept with my best friend."

I gasped, covering my mouth with my hand.

Reese sighed. "Man, I've said that out loud a million times and I still want to drink a shot of tequila whenever I repeat it."

"Oh, Reese. I'm so sorry. That sucks. If you need a partner to spray-paint his car or something, I'm your girl. If that's not your style, forget I said anything."

Reese started laughing, inching closer to me. "I've already had that offer from my sister and several of my cousins. Don't tell Declan or he'll behead us."

"My lips are sealed."

"You're a lot of fun, Lexi. I'm glad Tate hired you. Now, let's see what goodies we're having for lunch."

———

ONCE THE BROTHERS started the grill, the food just kept coming. After I filled my plate, Beatrice waved at me and patted the spot next to her on the rattan sofa. I looked around for Paisley, but she was with Tate. The sight made something twist in my chest. I went straight to Beatrice, sitting down.

"Do you need anything?" I asked. "Something to drink?"

She was already holding a plate of food.

"No, no, I'm fine. Tyler handed me this, and it's more than I'll ever eat," she said. "I'm glad you stayed today. I told Tate I wanted to meet you."

"You did?"

"Yes. I speak to Paisley every evening, and she's talked my ear off about you. That's a good sign. I think she likes you more than anyone who's ever watched her."

"Really?" My heart swelled. I was already starting to care about Paisley too, and I was happy that she liked me.

"It's a pity you can only stay until the summer ends."

My smile faded a bit. "Yes, Tate and I talked about that, but I'll help him find someone else."

"I told him I can watch Paisley, but he insists this old bag of bones can't keep up."

I glanced from Tate to Beatrice, searching for the right words. I needed to put it delicately, but I was with Tate on this one. "Well, Paisley is very active. We bike a few miles every day."

Gran shuddered. "Good Lord. What is it with kids these days? They have more energy than I ever remember."

I couldn't help but laugh.

"You know what? I don't think it's just Paisley who's happier since you came around." She leaned in with a conspiratorial whisper. "Tate is too."

"Oh?" I asked, hoping I sounded innocent and that my face wasn't red, though it felt suspiciously warm.

"Yes, he's cheerier. I can't explain it. Maybe he's at ease that he finally found someone who knows how to interact with Paisley so well. Ever since Nora left, he's closed himself off," she added.

"A divorce does leave scars," I murmured. "I've seen the results on the kids I teach, and it does have its impact."

"It's not that. He blames himself for the marriage ending."

"Oh no! Why?" I shook my head, realizing what I'd asked. "Sorry. I didn't mean to intrude."

"Not at all, my girl. They were never a match. When I first met her, I remember thinking that she wasn't a bad person, but she and Tate... I couldn't see it working. Imagine my surprise when they got married. She was seduced by the family name, I think."

"Some things aren't obvious from the start."

"That's true. But with some things, you *know*. You don't need to see them. You don't need someone to tell you it's there. You *feel* it." Narrowing her eyes, she added, "Tell me a bit about you."

"About me?" I asked blankly.

"Tate said you're helping your parents pay off some medical bills."

"Yes. They had a hard time, so I'm hoping what I contribute will help a bit."

"Do you have other siblings?" she asked.

"No, it's just me. I'm an only child." When I was younger, I always wanted a sister, and Mom and Dad wanted more children, but things didn't turn out the way they'd hoped. And I'd planned to have at least three kids, but, at thirty-one, I wasn't sure I had enough time for three. But I'd be happy even with one little bundle of joy.

Beatrice was looking at me intently. "I think it's wonderful that you're helping your parents."

"Thank you," I said.

"My parents were also sickly in their old age, but I have two sisters, and we helped them together."

"Did your husband also have siblings?"

"Yes, three. And everyone had many kids. I always

dreamed about having at least four kids, but I only had two. Tate's dad and his brother."

"Where is his brother?"

"He moved to London after we sold the bookstore business. My two boys gave me a lot of grandchildren, though. Loved looking after them when they grew up."

"Six is quite a bunch."

"Eight, including my granddaughters, Kimberly and Reese. They were at our house so often that they were practically all siblings. And now Tate thinks I can't look after Paisley."

I pressed my lips together, sensing that was for the best.

"Tate wanted a lot of children too, but things didn't work out. I can't believe he thinks I can't watch my great-grand-daughter. I'm still fit enough to run a bookstore, am I not?"

"Are you there every day?" I asked in surprise.

"Well, not a lot. I go there a couple times a week, and the manager I hired handles the daily tasks." With a wistful smile, she added, "It was the first building my late husband bought, and we opened the bookstore when my sons were young. I feel closer to him when I'm there."

Oh, Beatrice. She was such a lovely, warm person.

"My grandkids also spent a lot of time there growing up. I liked having them in the bookstore. Everyone knew Declan was going to be a lawyer even before he knew it. He was the most outspoken, always getting the rest out of trouble or at least trying to. Once, the school caught all of them smoking under the bleachers." She chuckled at the memory. "Declan tried to convince them it was a science experiment."

I burst out laughing. "He didn't."

"No one believed him. The most I could get out of them was that they did it on a dare, but they wouldn't tell me who dared them. My hunch is it was probably Luke. He always liked his dares, and the fun in it was riling up everyone to join him. Tyler was also into dares, but his were more along the lines of physical activity. He walked around bossing them into workout sessions after reading that it prolonged your lifespan. Sam was his most arduous listener. Then he went on and became a doctor."

"And Travis?" He was the brother I knew the least about.

"Oh, my Travis took after his grandfather in a lot of ways. Always fearless. A bit terrifying for everyone else. Had a mind of his own. Whenever he didn't like someone, he'd put frogs or insects in the pockets of their coats. Scared them off for good."

"Very efficient."

"But don't let me keep you with my tales. Fill your plate again. They just made the grilled corn, and it's fabulous for everyone who still has their *real* teeth. Take advantage of it," she said.

Laughing, I stood up. "It was nice talking to you, Beatrice."

She winked at me. "You're good for Paisley." After a brief pause, she added, "And for Tate."

I felt my cheeks heat up to my ears. I walked away quickly, heading to the grill.

Tyler was operating it this time. I held out my plate and asked, "May I have an ear of corn?"

"Yes, ma'am," he said, putting one on my plate. He looked up at me with a twinkle in his eyes. "I'm putting it out there that you can always ask me stuff about my brother. I promise 100 percent honesty."

"Does he know you're going around offering information about him?"

"I bet he does." He smirked. "In my defense, I don't do it often, just for the people I like. And I like you, Lexi."

I grinned, liking the ease between us. I didn't feel like I was working but rather like I was part of the gang. It felt like they were embracing me as one of their own.

I looked around for Reese but couldn't see her anywhere.

"Where is Reese?" I asked Tyler.

"She just left."

"Oh, okay. I'm going to check on Paisley, then."

She was at the other end of the yard, sitting next to her father. "What are you two chatting about?" I asked as I approached.

"I was telling Daddy I want to watch *The Jungle Book* today." Tate gave me a meaningful look.

The corners of my mouth lifted. *So, this is where he draws the line.*

"Well, I think your dad might be a bit tired after barbequing for so many people, but why don't we watch it on Monday?"

Paisley lit up. "Okay. I'm gonna tell Great-Gran. Maybe she wants to watch it too." Sliding down from Tate's lap, she immediately headed to Beatrice.

"Thank you," he said with a sigh. "How could you tell that I couldn't find a good excuse?"

"You seemed a bit stuck and in need of my help."

"Thank you for coming to my rescue," he said with a twinkle in his eyes. "I've watched *The Jungle Book* so many times with her that I want to bust the screen when the theme song comes up."

We laughed for a moment, and then he asked, "Are you having fun?"

"Yes. I love your grandma."

"She's amazing," he said with admiration in his voice.

"Your whole family is lovely. It makes me miss my parents. They often have gatherings like these too. They love to invite neighbors and friends over for cookouts on the weekend. Well, they used to, before Mom had the surgery. But as soon as she's better, things will return to normal." I looked around with a smile, regretting that I had to leave. "It was a great day. I'm happy I stayed."

His smile faded. "You're leaving?"

"I'm meeting my friend, remember?"

"Okay. I'll walk you out."

"There's no need to. I can find my way," I said.

"I know you can. I want a few moments alone with you, without my brothers watching me."

My heart skipped a beat. I glanced around us as discreetly as possible, and yeah, everyone was looking at us, even Beatrice. "Why are they staring at us?" I asked.

"My brothers have… ideas."

That was clear as mud. And he was flashing me a mysterious smile. I opened my mouth before closing it again. I wasn't sure I *wanted* to know what he meant.

He walked me through the house, and the second we closed the door to the backyard, I felt a shift between us, like the air itself was different—hotter and full of tension.

As we reached the front door, he put a hand on my arm. My skin sizzled. He turned me around, holding my gaze. "We didn't talk about last night."

I bit my lower lip. I didn't want to talk about any of it, if I was honest. What good would it do? I knew all the reasons why this wasn't going to move forward.

Come Monday, we had to find a way for things to go back to employee and employer. But right now, my mind was pulling in one direction and my heart in the complete opposite.

"I don't know what to say," I said.

He came closer, bringing a hand to my face, touching my cheek with the backs of his fingers. "Thinking about you wearing my shirt all night had a very positive effect on me."

"Did it now?" I whispered.

"I barely kept myself from coming upstairs and knocking on your door. I thought about you all night."

A tremor went through my body. "I did the same."

He groaned, bringing his mouth close to my ear. I pressed my thighs together as heat pooled between my legs.

He groaned again, touching his lips to the side of my neck, moving them up and down. "What am I going to do with you, Lexi?"

"What are the options?" I asked in a lighthearted tone.

"Kissing you against this door or taking you upstairs."

I laughed nervously. "I don't think either is a good option. Your family is in the backyard, remember?" I had a visual of the whole family pressing their noses against a window, trying to see what we were up to.

He groaned again, pulling back. "Right. How could I forget? If we stay here any longer, I bet someone will burst through that door."

"Tate," I whispered, my voice soft. "We shouldn't."

"I know." His gaze instantly turned from playful to serious. But he kept touching my cheek with his fingers. The skin-on-skin contact was almost too much. He frowned, looking at my mouth. "You're dangerous for me, Lexi."

My eyes widened. "Why?"

"You make me feel." He pressed his thumb on my lower lip. "You make me want."

I swallowed hard, breathing in deeply.

He stepped back, letting go of me. "But you're right. We shouldn't. I'm not sure I have it in me to do the right thing. Not when it comes to you." He opened the front door, looking at me intently.

My body buzzed with adrenaline and a bone-deep yearning to close the distance between us. *Oh, sweet* heavens. In that moment, I knew I didn't have it in me to do the right thing either. How could I when he was looking at me with so much heat?

And that sexy smile? It made my underwear combust.

Panties? On fire.

Bra? Up in smoke.

And the most dangerous part? It also melted all my defenses, and I knew I had to do something about it.

I was going to think really hard about everything over the weekend, but I didn't think it was a good idea to stay on as Paisley's nanny.

NINE

Tate

*A*fter Lexi left, I made myself a promise: I wouldn't contact her until Monday.

I went back to the party, heading straight for the grill. Tyler and Declan exchanged a meaningful glance before looking at me.

"Not one word from anyone," I said as I picked up the fork, placing the corn on the grill and turning the five chicken wings I'd put on it before going inside with Lexi.

Declan glanced at Tyler again. "He didn't say anything about not talking to each other."

Tyler held up his hands. "I'm going to withhold my opinion."

"I won't," Luke said. "I like what I see so far."

"I already gave my opinion on this," Declan said.

Tyler rolled his eyes. "Can you stop being a lawyer for a minute here?"

"I'm just a concerned brother," Declan pointed out.

"There is no need to be concerned about me," I said, loud and clear. "Why don't we worry about the real problems in the family? Where is Reese, by the way? She wouldn't say what's going on, but I'm going to assume things with Malcolm aren't going well."

"She left earlier," Declan replied. "And no, things aren't going well. Malcolm insists on moving forward with the spa. The Halsey Group has a lot riding on this."

The Halsey Group was the company Malcolm worked at.

"What the fuck?" I exclaimed. My hackles rose. "Don't tell Gran. Not until we're sure of it."

"I wasn't planning to," Declan said.

No one was going to hurt my family. Not my grandmother, not my cousins, no one. I was going to make sure of it.

"Let's change the topic. Gran's coming this way," Luke said. "Don't look guilty or she'll know we're hiding something."

We'd perfected the art of the poker face over the years, but fooling Gran wasn't an easy feat. She picked up a chicken wing, glancing around the group.

"Whatever you boys think you're doing, it's not working," she said nonchalantly. "And before you ask how I know you're hiding something, remember I've caught you six scheming since you could barely walk."

"Gran, cut us some slack," Luke said.

She took yet another chicken wing. "I will. For now."

Tyler chuckled. Luke winked at Gran. Declan shook his head.

We hadn't perfected that poker face as much as I thought.

As soon as Gran headed back to the swing where Paisley was sitting, Tyler said, "Let's talk about this at the office. We got away once, but I don't think she's gonna be so forgiving a second time."

"Agreed," I replied, continuing to handle the grill because Tyler deserved a break.

Twenty minutes later, I remembered why it wasn't a good idea for my brother to have too much time on his hands. He got *ideas*. I only realized he and Paisley were up to something because they both had smug looks *and* held their hands behind their back.

"What is this—" I started to say, but before I could finish the sentence, both of them released firecrackers. I burst out laughing so hard I nearly cracked a rib, and so did Declan. Luke was looking with so much pride at the two of them that I wondered if he hadn't given them the idea in the first place.

Just another day in the Maxwell family.

My family left about two hours later. Paisley and I spent the evening at the lake before turning in for the night.

The next day, I took her to one of the vineyards I owned around Chicago. It was an hour away, not far from where I'd grown up. Maxwell Wineries owned vineyards throughout the country, though there was no need for me to visit them all; I had some very fine vignerons who knew the production process, and we were in contact often.

I always enjoyed being out in the vineyards. They relaxed me, and Paisley loved it too. She considered it a road trip, so I brought her out here every few months.

When we arrived, there was no one working the vineyard because it was Sunday.

"Daddy, the grapes look good. They're a bit small, though, aren't they?"

"Yes, they are. They're young like you, honey. Thankfully the storm the other night didn't damage them." That was another reason I'd suggested coming out here today. My crew assured me the storm didn't do any harm, but I wanted to double-check. So far, everything looked good.

For some inexplicable reason, I thought Lexi might enjoy being here with us. I'd been thinking about her constantly since yesterday. Usually, being in a vineyard cleared my mind completely, but I couldn't shake her.

Paisley walked slowly in front of me, stopping every few steps as we checked the grapes together. I envisioned the day when she would take over Maxwell Wineries, but I'd never tell her that. I didn't want to burden her with any expectations or pressure. My dad always told us that we could do whatever we wanted, that he didn't expect us to want to work at Maxwell Bookstores. Dad had stepped into his father's shoes without having had a chance to figure out what he wanted. He didn't want the same for us, and I respected him for it.

"Dad, can we come here during the harvest?" she asked once we sat down on a bench next to the vineyard's entrance. Paisley was taking out one of the peanut butter sandwiches I'd put in her backpack.

"Sure. We'll find a weekend." Depending on the weather, the harvest could begin as early as the end of August. It typically started later, though, and ended mid-October.

My phone beeped with an incoming message while Paisley ate her sandwich. I instantly tensed when I noticed the sender.

Nora.

Nora: Not sure I'll be able to take Paisley on vacation this year. Thought you'd want to know so you can prepare her. I MIGHT be able to, but there's a possibility I'll have to take a rain check.

I ground my teeth, not even bothering to reply. She was taking a rain check from Paisley's whole life.

"What's wrong, Daddy?" she asked, and I quickly schooled my features.

"Your mom says she might have too much work to go on vacation." I said this in a gentle tone, keeping any accusations out of it.

Paisley was silent for a few seconds before saying, "At least she's coming for my birthday."

"Yes, she is."

Paisley considered her birthday the most important day of the year, which might be because a few years ago it became the unofficial Yes-day. But birthday parties had always been legendary in my family growing up, and I liked continuing the tradition with my daughter.

She was suspiciously silent as she continued eating her sandwich.

"Paisley, everything okay?" I asked.

She looked up at me, frowning, as if carefully considering every word.

"Daddy, wouldn't it be nice if a lady was here with us?"

I blinked, jerking my head back. That was *not* where I thought this conversation was going.

"Maybe."

"I can find you a nice lady. The blonde one from the beach last year wasn't too nice."

I had no comeback for that. I'd always been careful to keep my dating life completely off my daughter's radar, but last year she'd met one of my dates through a mishap. We'd all ended up on the same beach, and I'd introduced them. Elizabeth, my date, had spoken to Paisley as if she were three years old, and at the end of it told me kids weren't really her thing. Obviously, I never called her back.

"You don't have to find me anyone, Paisley."

My thoughts went straight to Lexi.

I've already found one.

"We could all go out and have fun."

"Are you saying I'm not fun?" I winked at her.

"Not always." The smile she gave me was sheepish.

"What? Of course I'm always fun."

"Prove it." She stood up, a challenge on her face—my little competitive girl. I knew exactly what she was after.

"I'll chase you to the top of the hill. I bet I'm still faster."

"No, I am. Just wait and see." With a giggle, she turned on her heels and started running. I gave her a few seconds before chasing after her.

"I told you I'm faster!" Paisley exclaimed seconds before she reached the fence.

I purposefully let her win because I liked playing this game with her. It made her smile from ear to ear. That grin had me wrapped around her little finger ever since she was a few months old.

"Who isn't fun now?" I challenged, blocking her way, shifting my weight from one leg to the other and holding my arms wide to my sides.

Paisley giggled, holding her arms clenched to her sides. But when she glanced behind my back, probably to plan her escape, she let her guard down a bit, and I seized my opportunity. I went directly for her armpits, tickling her. She shrieked with laughter. "Okay, okay. You're fun, Dad."

I straightened up instantly, letting my hands drop. My daughter calling me Dad instead of Daddy was the equivalent of a parent calling their child by their first and middle name. I knew it was time to end the game.

I held my palms up in defense, and she gave me yet another toothy grin.

"What do you want to do? Go back to Chicago? Gran says she's expecting us for dinner, but I don't think she'll mind if we show up earlier."

"We can go now," she said.

On the drive back to the city, I kept mulling over our conversation. Ever since the divorce, I'd split my time between my daughter, my family, and Maxwell Wineries. I'd blocked out everything else. It had been as much a self-defense mechanism as a survival instinct. But Lexi was fun and sexy and made me laugh without even trying. And I wasn't going to let go of that.

I wanted Lexi.

I needed her.

We arrived at Gran's one hour later. After parking the car, I noticed the screen of my phone lit up with a message. I intended to ignore it, thinking it might be Nora again, but Lexi's name caught my attention.

Lexi: Hi! So I have an ear infection and I feel awful. I'm not sure I can make it tomorrow. And also... I think it might be a good idea for you to reach out to one of the others you interviewed for the job.

TEN

Lexi
---

*T*he pain in my ear was unbearable as I tried to turn from one side to the other on the pillow.

Oh no, why did I even try it?

Oh, that's right, my phone is ringing.

I blindly answered, putting it to my good ear.

"How are you feeling?" It was Tate's voice.

"Like I was hit by a truck, and every time I try to get out of bed, the same thing happens."

"What happened?"

"Apparently I didn't properly get the water out of my ear when I went swimming with Paisley. I nagged her into doing it, and I forgot to do it myself. And now I have an infection. At least that was the doctor's explanation."

"Do you have everything you need?" he asked, voice full of concern.

I was melting already.

"Yes, I have my medicine."

"Food?"

"I haven't eaten since yesterday. Swallowing hurts my ears.

Right now, I'm super proud that I had enough energy to answer the phone."

"Okay. I'll be at your place in half an hour."

My eyes widened. "What? No. You don't have to come here to check on me."

"Yes, I do. You're sick. I dropped off Paisley with Gran. I'm coming by your place."

"Tate."

"Lexi," he countered.

"It's really not necessary."

"I'm coming over."

Well, I couldn't argue with him when he went all alpha like this, even when I felt perfectly healthy. Now I had no prayer of resisting him.

"Okay, thanks," I whispered.

After hanging up, I got out of bed and headed to the shower. I'd only washed up in the sink yesterday since I'd been feeling a bit off-kilter, and I was a bit stinky. I moved at a slower pace than usual, but I was happy that I wasn't nauseous anymore, only a bit dizzy.

I barely had time to dress before the doorbell rang. I hurried to open it.

Tate stood in the doorway with a paper bag and a smaller plastic one, looking me up and down. "You don't look so well."

"Thanks for making me feel better," I said on a laugh. "But I need to sit. I only had enough energy to come open the door for you."

Dizzy again, I went straight to the couch to sit down and pull a throw over me. I loved cuddling in blankets on the couch, even in the summer. The kitchen counter was opposite where I was sitting, and I watched Tate with fascination as he took out containers of food from the paper bag.

He'd brought me food? Wow, I couldn't believe he was so thoughtful. That I was so important to him.

"I got you some stuff, okay? Easy things you can eat, like soup, so you can stay hydrated."

"Thanks. That's really nice of you. When did you even do this?"

"I stopped by a deli on the way here."

He moved with efficiency in my kitchen, putting everything in the fridge. He looked up at me from time to time. My body buzzed every time our gazes crossed.

Once he'd emptied the bag, he came and sat next to me. The couch sank under his weight. Even though I felt shitty from my ear infection, I couldn't help but notice his stubble and the way he smelled. It wasn't just his cologne; he smelled like the outdoors.

"Did you go to a doctor?"

"Yes. They gave me drops and antibiotics. They can't tell for sure when the pain will go away. Could be two days, maybe more. Apparently it depends on my body. I hate it when they say that."

He chuckled, but his gaze was hard. "What is this about you quitting, Lexi?"

I sighed, unsure where to begin. I avoided his gaze. It was too much to handle right now. It felt as if he saw right through me.

"Well, clearly I can't keep myself from flirting. You want to protect Paisley, and I totally understand that, and I'm a bit mad at myself because I stepped over my personal code of conduct, which is all the more proof that you're irresistible. And now I'm full-on rambling. And then you showed up with food, and… I mean, am I dreaming?"

I looked up at him because he was suspiciously silent. To my astonishment, amusement danced in his eyes.

"You're fucking adorable," he said.

"Because I'm rambling?"

"You just are." He tucked the blanket under my chin,

resting his hand on my shoulder. I liked feeling his warm hand over me.

"What did you and Paisley do today?"

"We went to one of the vineyards and walked around checking the grapes. Nora also wrote to tell me that she might not be able to take Paisley on the vacation she promised this fall."

"Oh no. How did Paisley take it?"

"In stride."

I could feel him putting up walls around himself. I couldn't explain how, but I felt it. But then a smile inched over his features, as if he was inwardly laughing at a private joke. "Paisley and I actually talked about me dating this evening. She says *she* can find me a *nice* lady."

"That does sound like her." I frowned, not understanding where he was going with this. My heart rate intensified. "So what are you saying?" I whispered.

He cleared his throat, looking straight at me and bringing his fingers under my chin again. "I don't want you to worry about anything. Take extra days off to get back on your feet. Tomorrow is the Fourth of July anyway, so stay home and relax. I'm taking care of you, and then we'll see."

"Tate…"

"Lexi…"

"You don't have to take care of me."

"But I want to. And I will. No discussion."

I rolled my eyes. "Well, okay, then, Mr. Alpha."

THE NEXT MORNING, I wondered if I dreamed that Tate was here last evening, being all swoon-worthy and stocking my fridge. I already felt better. The pain had dulled a bit, but my eyes still watered if I moved my head too briskly. The doctor said ear infections can affect the nose and eyes too, and I was definitely feeling it.

I went to the kitchen and opened the fridge to check if I had any yogurt. I gasped, seeing the containers of food.

Oh wow. I hadn't imagined it! Tate really had been here.

I pressed a hand to my chest, smiling. The man was definitely something else.

Taking out my phone, I texted him.

Lexi: Thanks again for the food. I actually thought I imagined your visit last night.

Tate: Feeling better?

Lexi: A bit, yeah. I'm thinking of having a smoothie... but it's green.

Tate: ???????

Lexi: I'm wary of green drinks.

He responded after a few seconds.

Tate: I've only ever heard Paisley say stuff like that.

Lexi: Probably why I like kids so much. How is she doing?

Tate: She's with Gran.

Figured. Early on he'd asked me if I could also work on the Fourth because he had clients in town.

Lexi: Is she upset?

Tate: No. Don't worry about anything. Focus on getting better, okay?

I did worry about disappointing her if I didn't go back, though. And after what Tate told me about discussing dating with Paisley, I was even more confused than before. What did it mean?

My heart thundered just thinking about him.

I braced myself to take a sip of the smoothie, and to my astonishment, it wasn't bad. It had a cooling effect on me, and swallowing didn't hurt my ear like it had before.

I felt much better than the day before, but not enough to leave my apartment, so I settled on the couch with Netflix.

Jenny and Ella texted me a pic of them at camp, with the caption "Happy 4th of July."

I sent them back a pic of me pouting, and they immediately called. I spent half an hour with them on the phone and then intended to rewatch *Reign*, but midway through the first episode, I realized I wasn't paying attention. I was thinking about Tate's conversation with Paisley again.

Grabbing my phone, I almost texted to ask him about it, but I deleted the message. I wasn't ready to have that conversation yet. I couldn't trust myself not to start rambling again. What if he started saying something swoon-worthy again? I'd ramble for sure.

I didn't know what to do. I needed advice, so I called my mom.

"Hey, sweetheart. How are you feeling?" she asked.

"Much better than yesterday."

"Do you have any food?" she asked in a crisp voice, making me smile, reminding me of the old version of Mom, when she was younger and stronger, before her heart problems began. I was happy that she sounded more like her old self.

"Yes, I do, actually. Tate stopped by with food yesterday."

"Tate, your employer?"

"Yes." I hesitated a bit. "Mom, there's something I need to tell you."

In a rush, I told her about my attraction to Tate, that it was mutual, and I wasn't sure what to do.

"And I don't know if it's even worth thinking about. I mean, I'm a teacher. Going out with a parent feels a bit wrong." Not to mention he was my employer, but that was temporary and didn't feel as daunting.

"Darling, I was a teacher too, so I understand where you're coming from, but Paisley's not a student at your school. I don't see why that should be a problem. You're too hard on yourself. Or is there something more?"

She could always see right through me. "I'm afraid I could fall for him, Mom. He seems a bit closed off. I think it's because of his divorce."

"There's no way of knowing what you can have without taking a risk, honey."

"I was afraid you might say that," I said. "Maybe I needed to hear it. How are you feeling? Is Dad spoiling you?"

"Oh, yes he is. He's been cooking up a storm lately."

That sounded like Dad.

I spoke a bit longer with Mom before hanging up. Glancing at my phone, I realized I had messages from both Jenny and Ella. They were asking how I was feeling.

I took a picture of myself with my smoothie and fully stocked fridge and sent it in the group chat I had with both of them.

Lexi: I'm feeling better today. My off-limits but irresistible employer stopped by with food.

Jenny: He did what? Girl, I'm liking this guy.

Ella: I second that. I really, really like him.

Oh yeah. So do I.

For the rest of the day, Paisley and Tate were front and center in my mind, along with Mom's words. It wouldn't be fair to either of them if I left right now. And deep down, I didn't really want to. But I had no idea where that left me with Tate, so I worked up the courage to text him that evening… after I received a food delivery. He'd sent me more soup.

Lexi: Hi. Thanks for the soup. I'm feeling much better. I can come back tomorrow morning. I thought about the job, and I'm staying.

Tate: Did you also think about me?

I chuckled. *That's his response?*

Lexi: How could I not, what with the soup and the smoothie?

My heart was beating fast.

Tate: You know what I mean.

I bit my lip, hesitating before typing back.

Lexi: Hmm… not really. You said we'll talk when I'm better. I'm better now.

I added three smiley faces before sending it.

Tate: I know, but I'd rather we talk face-to-face, and I can't come over now, or even call. I'm reading Paisley her bedtime story.

And just like that, my heart was in swoon mode again imagining him reading to his daughter.

Tate: But tomorrow evening, you and I will talk.

I took a long time before I answered, somehow feeling that if I did, it would turn over a new leaf.

Lexi: Okay.

Mom was right, and I was ready to take this risk.

ELEVEN

Lexi

_____

On Tuesday, Paisley and I decided to redecorate her bedroom.

"Are you sure your dad is going to be okay with this?" I asked, looking around her room. I'd shown her a few pictures of my apartment around Christmas, and she was obsessed with decorative strings of lights, especially after I told her that I keep a few all year round.

"Yes, he'll be okay with it," Paisley said, looking a bit too innocent.

I'd texted Tate half an hour ago, but he still hadn't answered. I didn't want to overstep any boundaries and preferred to check in with him before we started.

"You know what? Why don't we go and have a second lunch," I said, "and wait for your dad to answer. Then we can go to Home Depot and buy everything we need."

"Okay," Paisley agreed.

We went downstairs, and I made toast with her favorite cheese.

"These are so yummy," she said.

"Yes, they are, and I'm starving."

"Why didn't you come for breakfast today?" Paisley asked.

"I overslept."

She grinned. "Really? I didn't know adults oversleep."

I laughed. "Well, this adult does. Never happens to you or your dad?"

She shrugged. "I don't know. He's here every morning for breakfast. I've never had to go into his bedroom and wake him up."

Wow. That was one dad who was excelling at adulting. I never overslept during the school year because classes started at eight, but summers were my time to relax, so I usually didn't even set an alarm, which was exactly what happened last night.

It didn't help that I was dreaming about a certain sexy guy. This man was having a strange effect on me, but I chalked it up to the fact that I'd been intensely thinking about him.

When my phone buzzed with a message, my heart skipped a beat.

Tate: Sure. How are you feeling?

My pulse sped up.

Lexi: Great. My ear doesn't hurt anymore. I have to remember the drops and antibiotics.

After a few more messages with Tate, I announced to Paisley, "Your dad says it's okay."

She clapped her hands. "I told you."

"I know. I wanted to make sure. So let's finish the toast, and then we can go." Her excitement about decorating her room was contagious, and I was looking forward to seeing the end result.

Tate owned two cars, a Mercedes and a BMW, and I drove Paisley anywhere we needed in the latter. I was careful driving it because it was a brand-new SUV—much larger than the secondhand Mini Cooper I owned and rarely used. I relied on Uber and public transportation a lot.

I loved spending time with Paisley. She was a good kid and

didn't take advantage of situations, and I was impressed that she didn't ask for anything else except the twinkle lights. We bought a lot more of them than I knew we needed, but I figured they could use them elsewhere around their house during the Christmas season.

Once we were back, we headed directly to her room to set them up.

"Where do you want to hang them?" I asked, looking around.

"Everywhere," she exclaimed, making me laugh.

"Okay, so I have a few ideas. Why don't we put a strand around your windows? We do need a place to plug them in, so that's going to restrict us a bit."

Paisley pushed out her lower lip. "Okay."

"It'll still look like a fairy tale," I promised her.

It took us the whole afternoon to set up the twinkle lights, mostly because Paisley couldn't make up her mind where she wanted them. She had a lot of plugs in her room, so we had several options. In the end, she had one string around each window, one around her bed, and one on her toy shelf. We turned all of them on and stood in the doorway, surveying our work while I braided her hair.

"I think we've done a great job," I said.

"I love it. I'm like a princess," she said, running off toward her bed before I could finish her braid. It came undone immediately as she jumped on her mattress and grinned as she looked around.

I took a picture of her against the backdrop of lights. Her smile lit up her little face. I sent it to Tate, who replied instantly.

Tate: Someone's happy. Can I also get a picture of you?

Why would he ask that? And why was my heart flipping like that?

Tate had this effect on me. Just remembering his words and the way his lips felt on mine was enough to stoke the fire inside me.

"Let's take a selfie, Paisley," I said. "But wait, let me finish your braid first."

"Okay." She could barely stand still as I did it, and then she did mine. It was a bit messy, but I liked seeing her confidence grow as she braided my hair again and again, getting better at it each time.

I held the phone up, grinning at the camera as Paisley lifted my braid to the side so it was visible in the photo. Her toothy grin was priceless. She was so proud of herself. I sent it to Tate, along with a message.

Lexi: She's getting better and better at braiding.

He didn't reply, so I put my phone away, focusing on Paisley.

"Thank you for helping me with my lights," she said. "I'll take a picture with my phone and show it to my friend. She said only mommies could redecorate, and I told her you could do it too."

My heart sank. I looked at Paisley carefully. Her smile had dimmed a bit. I wasn't sure what to say. "Any time you want to do something that others get to do with their moms, you can ask your dad or me."

"I can ask you?" she said, looking up at me with a smile.

"Yes, of course."

"Okay. I'm going to talk to Mommy later today. I'll show her the lights. I know she doesn't have time for me, but I think she might like them anyway."

My heart ached for her. I had no idea what it must feel like to grow up without your mom. Remembering what Tate said about Nora canceling their vacation together made me angry. Wanting to lift Paisley's mood, I asked, "Do you want us to look up princess rooms online? That could give us more ideas about what to do with your room."

Her entire face lit up. She sat on her bed cross-legged. "We can do that?"

"Yes," I said hesitantly, wondering if I was opening Pandora's box. Browsing Pinterest led me to redecorate my apartment periodically. Was nine too young to have the redecoration bug? I hoped not, because I had a feeling Paisley was going to follow in my footsteps.

We sat side by side on the bed, and I opened my phone, pulling up the Pinterest app. Paisley fell hook, line, and sinker. She *oohed* and *aahed* at almost every picture.

"I want that," she said, pointing to a white bed with swans as the four posts.

"I'm not sure where you can get that, to be honest," I said.

Oh man, I *had* opened Pandora's box.

"And I want a pink room," she declared, standing up on her bed, looking around. Then she lay down on the bed, and I hurried next to her. She flashed me yet another grin before cocooning against me. I adored this little girl to bits. If I had a daughter, this was exactly how I'd spend all my free time: thinking up ways to make her laugh.

"I want to paint this wall and that wall, and maybe the ceiling too," Paisley exclaimed.

Oh, dear Lord. "We should talk to your dad about this."

———

Tate

WHEN I CAME HOME, I heard Paisley's voice upstairs. She was giggling. I headed straight up, but I didn't announce my presence immediately; instead, I stood and looked at them through the open door. They were both lying on the bed, looking up at the ceiling, and something tugged in my chest. Paisley was laughing so easily, and Lexi looked like she *belonged* here. I took a picture of them with my phone. Lexi was so damn warm and sweet that it was nearly killing me. She was special, and I had to convince her of that. That we needed her.

That I needed her.

I'd hired plenty of people to look after Paisley, but this was different because Lexi genuinely cared. She stirred things inside me that I'd long ago pushed to the back of my mind. I knew she felt the pull too, the attraction and the connection we had.

Ever since the divorce, I'd felt empty inside, and I'd been determined to stay that way. The alternative seemed too dangerous. It still did. Getting involved could only end up badly. My daughter was hurt once. I wouldn't risk it again. But I couldn't deny that Lexi made me *feel*, and that in itself was a damn miracle.

"We have to ask your dad," she said, snapping me to the present moment.

"Ask me what?" I said, stepping inside the room.

Paisley shrieked, jumping off the bed and coming straight to me. "Daddy, I want to make my room pink," she said, staring up at me with her toothy grin. "All of it."

I looked up at Lexi, taking my time as I glanced around the room. I tried to keep a healthy balance of what I allowed my daughter and what I didn't. I didn't want her to grow up being spoiled and entitled, but I couldn't see why she shouldn't make her room pink.

"Okay," I said. "I don't see why not."

She gave yet another shriek and then ran back to Lexi, jumping on the bed.

Lexi was avoiding my gaze. I watched her intently. She'd missed breakfast this morning. She'd texted to tell me she overslept, but I wondered if that was the only reason. The last thing I wanted was for her to feel uncomfortable, but fuck, just being with her in this room, my daughter's room—I wasn't able to keep my thoughts straight. Not when it came to Lexi, and not when I saw how easily she made Paisley smile. She also lit up an inner joy inside me that I didn't think I was capable of.

"Daddy, it's six o'clock. Can we call Mommy?" Paisley asked, eyes wide.

I sobered up instantly, feeling as if someone had thrown a bucket of ice over me. Monday evening was when we called Nora.

"Yes. Call her from your phone."

"I'll be downstairs," Lexi said, looking between the two of us. "I'll start dinner."

"You don't have to do that, Lexi. I'll take care of it after the phone call. It won't last long." It never did. Nora rarely seemed interested in details of Paisley's life.

"Okay, then. I'll wait downstairs and leave you two alone."

After Lexi left, I FaceTimed Nora's number. The call was for Paisley, not me, so I wasn't in the picture, but I did hover around while they spoke. It was a force of habit. I wanted to keep my daughter safe from everyone, including her mother.

"Hey, Mommy," Paisley said when the camera turned on.

"Hey, sweetheart," Nora said. "What's that behind you?"

"It's a twinkle light, Mommy. Lexi and I put it up today. She's helping me turn my room into a princess room, and Daddy said I could have pink walls."

"Sounds like you get along well with Lexi," Nora commented. Since Lexi had been in our lives, Paisley had mentioned her to her mother a few times.

"Yes. She's very friendly, and she's so pretty, Mommy. She has long dark hair, and she's teaching me how to braid it."

"Good for you," Nora said. Her eyes were already glazing over on the screen.

For fuck's sake. She had ten minutes with our daughter every few weeks. Couldn't she at least focus on her now?

"Nora, Paisley wants to tell you about her weekend," I said in a tone laced with warning.

She immediately trained her gaze on the camera. "How was your weekend, honey?" she asked.

My insides twisted. She always asked open questions so Paisley could talk by herself, and Nora would only have to answer with a yes or no or smile in the right places. It fucking gutted me, because my daughter deserved more. Every child deserved attentive parents who doted on them, who wanted them. Paisley was so young when Nora left, so I didn't think she knew how a relationship with her mother could be, but soon she would be a teenager, and she was observant.

She'd already asked me if I didn't want to date, for God's sake.

The phone call ended a few short minutes later, less than ten minutes total. I forced a smile on my face when I looked at Paisley. "Want to go down for dinner, pumpkin?"

"Yes, Daddy."

Annoyance coursed through me as I led Paisley downstairs, and also guilt.

The second I stepped into the kitchen, the negative emotions vanished into thin air. Lexi was dancing around the island. Her braid had come undone, and she was swinging her hips and mouthing along to the lyrics of the song she'd put on her phone.

Paisley shrieked with laughter, going straight to her. "You can dance. Please teach me, Lexi. Dad can't do it."

Her eyes widened, and then she blushed instantly, looking from Paisley to me. "Oh, I'm so sorry," she said, scrambling to pause the music. "I thought you'd be upstairs for a while."

"No, we're here. It's done," I said, rounding the corner and walking up to her. I wasn't going to be able to forget the image of her hips swinging any time soon. Everything about her was branded in my mind. The way she danced, the way she smiled, the delicious way she blushed when I even looked at her.

"You two do your thing while I make dinner," I said.

Paisley grinned, clapping her hands. Lexi turned the volume up, moving her body to the rhythm. Fucking hell, I had to look away from Lexi or I was liable to walk up to her and kiss her senseless right in front of my daughter.

Dinner wasn't complex enough to keep my attention from wandering to Lexi. I made mac and cheese with chunks of ham. It was ready in fifteen minutes. The girls weren't showing signs of slowing down even when I set the table.

Wait a second. They were looking at each other with meaningful glances. I immediately recognized Paisley's expression. It was the same one she had when she and Tyler threw firecrackers.

When they both looked back at me, I cocked a brow.

"Whatever you're thinking, don't," I warned.

Paisley jutted out her lower lip. Lexi's eyes widened. Her mouth was puckered in the shape of an *O*.

My daughter dropped her shoulders, motioning with her head toward me.

"No, we can't do it now. It doesn't work if he can tell we're planning something," Paisley explained to Lexi.

"I see. We have to surprise him," Lexi replied in a serious voice as if she was taking mental notes.

That impulse to kiss her grew stronger.

Behave, Tate. Your daughter is here.

We all sat down, eating the mac and cheese in no time. After dinner, Paisley went to the living room. Her favorite TV show was on.

"What were you and Paisley planning?" I asked Lexi as she helped me clear the table.

She looked over her shoulder, chuckling. "Right. Like I'd

tell you. We're still planning it. We have to time our *attack* better."

"Fuck, you're adorable, Lexi."

"I thought I was dangerous for you."

"That too. But I like living dangerously. I like *you*, Lexi."

Ever since the divorce, it had been just Paisley and me. The casual dates didn't count. I hadn't wanted to allow anyone near us. It happened almost on instinct, and now it was the opposite. I wanted Lexi here with us. But she'd almost quit because of this crazy attraction between us, and I needed to know why.

"Why did you want to quit?"

"My rambling explanation didn't make sense, huh?"

"I understood your concerns on the professional side, even though I can't really say I agree. Paisley doesn't go to your school."

She flashed me a small smile. "Mom said something similar."

"But that's not the only thing holding you back, is it?"

Her eyes widened. "Well, you seem like you don't really believe in relationships, and it's totally understandable after your divorce."

I stepped closer, watching her suck in a breath. "Lexi, I have scars, I won't deny that. But know this. These past few weeks, all I could think about was getting home to Paisley and you, and seeing you in the morning."

"Tate, God... the things you say."

I brought my mouth closer to hers, skimming my hands down her waist. She clasped my wrist.

"You can't kiss me here. Not now. Paisley is in the other room," she whispered urgently.

I groaned, gripping the counter instead.

"You're right. Not here, not now. You make me lose my head."

"Funny. You do the same to me."

I touched her cheek with the backs of my fingers, barely restraining myself. "Lexi, let's do something, just the two of us. Outside of the house."

She bit her lower lip. "Are you sure that's a good idea?"

"I have no fucking clue."

"I like the sound of it." Her expression morphed into a grin.

"You like that this might not be a good idea?" I double-checked.

"Yes. I think you need that. And I think I do too. My mom reminded me that some things are worth the risk. So here I am, taking a risk."

She kept surprising me.

She traced one finger around the button of my shirt. It made me want to hoist her up on the counter and bury myself inside her.

"If you do that, I will kiss you so hard that you'll forget we're not alone."

She dropped her hand, flashing me a sheepish smile. "I'll save that for when it's just the two of us, then."

TWELVE

Tate

---

*O*ne week later, on Tuesday afternoon, Declan strode into my office with a grim expression.

"I've got news. Malcolm is filing a lawsuit."

"On what grounds?"

"Loss of business opportunity. Since the Halsey Group also planned to lease the adjacent building to open the spa, they're now claiming that if Gran doesn't go through with the lease, it's going to be damaging for the business."

"Goddamn it. That fucker!" I exclaimed, rising from my chair. "So, what are we doing about it?"

Declan cocked a brow. "*You* are doing nothing. *I* am taking care of the lawsuit."

I groaned, tipping my head back. "I can't do nothing, Declan. Telling me that is a recipe for disaster."

"I'm on top of it," Declan said. "The question is, how do we tell Reese? I just got the paperwork."

I glanced out the window, taking in the skyline. "I'm going to put Luke on this."

He was the closest to Reese and Kimberly. Growing up, they were in completely different camps, with Luke considering girls the enemy even though they were close in age. During summer vacation, when Reese and Kimberly were staying with us, they ran away from home. Shortly after that, we realized Luke had disappeared too. He'd gone to find them, and he'd succeeded. They just hadn't found their way back. When the police discovered them, we were all relieved. The three of them were inseparable for a month afterward, and they remained very close.

"I'll be in my office if you need me, but be careful how you break the news to the others. Don't egg them on," Declan said.

"What do you mean?" I asked impatiently.

Declan grinned. "You have this way of rallying everyone to follow you even when your ideas are shitty."

"That happens very rarely," I pointed out.

"What? That people do what you tell them to do?"

"No, that my ideas are shitty. Most of them are good."

"Remember that one time when you convinced us to put fart bombs under the biology teacher's seat? Just because you wanted to be the one with the ideas for once instead of Luke."

Okay, so that was not my proudest moment.

I pointed at him. "Exactly—in school. I'm much wiser now."

"Right. Whatever you do, don't involve Tyler."

"I won't," I said with a straight face. Our brother had a hockey career to focus on. But I didn't promise I wouldn't get involved.

Declan caught on immediately. "There's no warning you, is there?"

"You can try, but it won't work."

I needed to look that fucker in the eye. He thought he could push us around, did he? Malcolm was in for a nasty surprise.

I was restless after Declan left my office, so I called Luke immediately, and he answered right away. I didn't often make

personal phone calls from the office, but every member of my
family picked up at once whenever I did.

"Hey, are you coming up to headquarters today?" I asked.

"No, I'm visiting construction sites. Why?"

"Declan told me that Malcolm is suing Gran and Reese."

"Fucking hell," he exclaimed. "I'm gonna punch that
moron."

Luke was so much like me—no wonder Declan was
concerned. In fact, all five of us were stubborn and hotheaded.
Declan was the only odd duck.

"I haven't ruled that out," I said honestly, knowing Luke
wasn't going to judge me. Quite the contrary.

"Good, whatever you're planning, I'm in. I don't care what
Declan says."

"For now, I want you to talk to Reese about this."

"Come on, man. Why are you making me the messenger?"

"You're closer to her than I am." That was only partly the
reason.

"Try again."

Damn, my brothers could see right through me. Luckily, I
did a better job with negotiations in business matters.

"Fine. You're better at… talking to people than I am."

"That's more like it. I'll speak to Reese."

"Make sure she knows we have her back, okay? And in case
she wants to confront him, we can both go with her."

"Duly noted," Luke said.

"Thanks. I'll tell the others."

Declan's warning rang in my ears. I knew why he'd explicitly mentioned leaving Tyler out of it. The rest of us owned
our business. We could take PR shit if it came to that. It was
different for Tyler. He belonged to a team. His career
depended as much on his talent on ice as it did on what was
written about him in the press.

I didn't want to share this with my brothers to get them

riled. I wanted to hear their views on the matter. We always fought back as a group.

I spent a good chunk of the afternoon on family matters, so I ended up working late enough that I had to ask Gran to go home and stay with Paisley so Lexi could leave. It bugged me because I didn't like missing out on dinner with my daughter. And I'd been looking forward to seeing Lexi. But I had bottle designs and social media campaign budgets to approve.

When I finally left the building, it was 11:00 p.m. Luke hadn't gotten back to me, and Declan didn't have any more news. The idea of meeting Malcolm face-to-face was still nagging at me. I wanted to look him in the eye and tell him to fuck off. Intimidation was a strategy that served me well with assholes—but it was a face-to-face kind of thing. I was determined to protect Reese and Gran. I didn't even care how much it would cost. It didn't matter.

When I got home, Paisley was already asleep. After a driver picked up Gran, I went to Paisley's room but only watched her from the doorway; she was a light sleeper, and I didn't want to wake her. Then I went to my bedroom, but I was filled with too much adrenaline to go to sleep.

I hated that I'd missed dinner with Paisley… and with Lexi. I wondered what she was up to. Was she already asleep? Was she out on the town with friends? Male friends? The thought did not sit well with me.

Damn it, how could I already feel so possessive of her?

Sitting on my bed, I punched in her number. I needed to hear her voice, and I wasn't used to needing anything or anyone. I hadn't allowed myself to in a long time. But I was powerless when it came to this woman.

"Hey," she answered in a breathy voice. "Is anything wrong?"

There was commotion in the background, as if she were outdoors.

Promise Me Forever

"No, why would anything be wrong?"

"It's late. I thought maybe something happened to Paisley."

"No, she's fine. She's asleep. I just came home. I don't like missing out on my evenings with her."

"Did anything happen to make you stay so late?"

"Yeah. Reese's ex is a jackass. He's trying to make Gran's life difficult, and I'm not going to allow it."

"What are you going to do?"

"Declan is already working on the legal aspect."

"It sounds like you're working on the illegal one," she said with a chuckle.

I propped a pillow on my headboard, leaning against it and putting my feet up on the bed.

"No, I want to meet with him and tell him to stop fucking around with my family."

"Intimidation. I can see that working, Mr. Maxwell."

"You think I'm intimidating?"

"Hell yeah. When I came in for the interview, I was a mess. No, wait. That was because you were too damn hot. My bad."

I laughed, running a hand across the pillow next to me. "I wanted to surprise you today," I said honestly.

"Oooh, how?"

"Can't tell you. But the day got away from me."

"Don't worry. Do whatever you have to do. Family's important."

Something twisted in my chest. How was it possible that someone I'd just met understood me so completely?

"I think so too. I've always wanted to give Paisley a childhood like the one I had."

"You're a great dad, Tate."

"Thanks."

Fucking hell, hearing her voice intensified that need to see her.

107

"Tate, we're going to…" Her voice faded, and I heard her whisper, "No, thank you. I still have some beer left."

"Let me know when you want a refill," a male voice said.

Adrenaline spiked in my veins. "Are you out in town?" I asked.

"Yes. I'm at the lake with a group of friends."

"Male friends?" I couldn't keep my tone even.

"It's a mix. We're a group of teachers. We hang out in the summer."

"Any of them interested in you?" I asked, still failing to keep my voice even.

"Mr. Maxwell, what's this? Are you trying to stake your claim on me? After one kiss?"

"Yes," I said roughly. "Yes, I am."

"Tate…"

"I have half a mind to come where you are and make it clear to everyone that you're off-limits."

She drew in a sharp breath. "Oh, wow. Well, just so you know, no one is interested in me. Better?"

"Yes." It wasn't, though. Not really. I felt possessive of her in a way that consumed me. But all I said was "Good night, Lexi. Have fun."

THIRTEEN

Lexi
—————

$\mathscr{F}$or the rest of the week, I didn't see Tate at all. He was always out before I arrived, and I left before he came home. Beatrice was sleeping at the house and spending the day with us. I wasn't sure why, but I certainly didn't mind; having this extra time with her was a gift.

I found an excuse to stay later than six every evening, and not *just* because I hoped to get a glimpse of Tate. Beatrice seemed in way over her head watching Paisley, who was full of energy even after spending the whole day outdoors.

Besides, Beatrice was a *hoot*. She was like the grandma I never had, giving me advice for everything, be it food or dresses. She even taught me how to make apple pie.

Now it was Monday, and I was buying cherries for yet another pie.

On the drive to the house, I also checked in on my parents. They weren't big on phone calls, but we had a WhatsApp group where we shared random pics, mostly of food. Snapping a photo of the cherries, I sent it to them along with a message.

Lexi: I'm learning to make cherry pie today.

Mom: Yum. Good for you. Send me the recipe, and I'll try it too. I'm feeling great today.

Dad: I'll help.

Mom: No you won't. You'll be in my way.

I chuckled at their banter without interfering. They had a healthy relationship.

When I arrived at the house, Beatrice and Paisley were in the kitchen.

"Tate already left?" I asked, looking around.

"Yes. About half an hour ago," Beatrice said, relieving me of the bag of cherries. "How is your mom feeling, Lexi?" she asked as we prepped them.

"She's recovering, slowly." And despite Mom insisting that I didn't have to help with the medical bills, I could hear the relief in both their voices whenever we spoke. That meant the world to me.

"That's good to hear. By the way, I wanted to ask you—are you dating anyone?"

Out of the corner of my eye, I saw Paisley perk up.

"Uhh... no, I'm not."

I wasn't lying, technically. Tate and I had just kissed. And flirted.

Beatrice eyed me speculatively. "Haven't found the right one yet? It's good to be picky. Two things in life you never have to chase: buses and men. There's always another one waiting just around the corner."

I burst out laughing. This was exactly the grandmotherly advice she liked to dish out.

She glanced at Paisley, who was perched on a chair at the island coloring in her book. "Don't tell your father I said that."

Paisley grinned. "I won't, Gran. I promise. But you and Grandpa were together for a long time, right?"

"Only twenty-five. He was young when he passed." She looked away, but not before I noticed the sorrow in her eyes. I wanted to hug her. I hadn't known she'd lost her husband so early on. "But I had to kiss a lot of frogs until I found him. Was like that in my time, and I can't imagine it's gotten easier. Also something you shouldn't mention to your father."

Paisley's grin widened.

Midway through the baking process, my phone beeped with a message. Washing my hands off, I took the phone out of my back pocket.

Tate: Morning, beautiful. This week is getting out of hand too.

Lexi: ☹

Last week we'd barely texted, even on the weekend.

Tate: I want to see you. Can you stay until later this evening?

My heart rate sped up.

Lexi: Yes.

Tate: Great. I'll tell Gran she can go home in the evening.

Lexi: Oh, so whatever you have in mind requires us to be alone?

Tate: Yes. Fuck, yes.

———

THAT EVENING I experienced Paisley's bedtime routine for the first time. I'd never been here for it. When I spent the night at the house after the thunderstorm, she'd fallen asleep right away. She liked to wash her hair and wear her fluffy teddy bear coat, and she needed some persuasion to change into pajamas afterward. She also wanted to have someone read her a story.

"Does your dad do this with you?" I asked.

"Oh yes, every evening," she said, comfortably snuggling against me as I started reading her the story.

I was only three pages in when the rhythm of her breathing

changed. It was more even now. I glanced down at her, and her eyes were closed, but I still continued. I loved the feeling of her small body next to mine, nuzzling against me like she'd found all the warmth and security she needed. I loved this little squirrel and was already missing her, even though we still had the rest of the summer ahead of us.

I'd always hoped to be a mom by this age. I wanted to have someone to read stories to every night and watch fall asleep, console when they scraped their knees, and hug when they were afraid. *She's not my girl*, I told myself, but sometimes, like now, it was easy to forget that she wasn't really mine even though I knew her favorite color and her favorite toys, and she'd confided in me that she was still a bit afraid of the dark. I needed to remember that I wasn't part of her life in any meaningful way.

I read for ten more minutes but then stopped because I was afraid my voice would wake her up. I slid out of bed carefully, tiptoeing out of the room, and then stood in the doorway for a few minutes watching her sleeping peacefully before closing the door. I nearly checked my phone, but Tate didn't say anything about already being on his way, so I assumed his dinner with the clients was going to take longer.

He said I could make myself at home and even go to the wine cellar, but it felt wrong to be there without him, like I was snooping. So instead, I went to the kitchen. I didn't want to have wine while I was technically still working, so I poured myself a glass of orange juice.

I was a bit restless, and I knew what I needed. I was about to start the music, and then I remembered Paisley was sleeping. I didn't want to risk waking her up, so I put in my earbuds and turned the volume loud, and then I danced.

Oh yeah.

I loved dancing. It was such a playful way to get rid of

excess energy. I even did dance workouts sometimes. I shook my booty and my hips, lowering myself to the ground, then pushed myself back up to the kitchen counter, all the while focusing on keeping my mouth shut. Yep, I was one of those who felt the need to sing along every time.

But I danced and danced, twirling my hips, doing a pirouette, and then a second one until I slammed against something. Against *someone*.

Oh shit.

Blinking my eyes open, I realized that someone was Tate.

"Oh my God, I'm so sorry," I exclaimed, scrambling to take out my earbuds and dropping them on the counter. Only then did I realize Tate had an arm around my waist. His pupils had dilated a bit.

I was flush against him, and I didn't want to pull away even one inch. In fact, all I wanted was to get even closer.

"I didn't hear you come in," I whispered.

"Clearly. I called your name a couple times." A smile was playing on his lips.

I felt every word reverberate in his chest and against my breasts. I smelled his cologne, and all I wanted to do was lean in some more to kiss that spot where his neck met his shoulder.

"You do love your dancing, huh?"

"Yeah, but I was wearing my earbuds because I didn't want to wake up Paisley."

"You're so fucking beautiful," he exclaimed. With a start, I realized my pelvis was pressing against his erection. "You drive me crazy, Lexi."

I swallowed hard, looking up at him. "You do the same to me."

He feathered his mouth over mine, leaned in, and fully kissed me. My body was covered in goose bumps by the time he pulled away.

"Tell me to stop," he said.

"Don't stop," I whispered.

"Lexi, tell me to take a step back."

I shook my head again. "I don't want you to."

He groaned, sealing his mouth over mine in a fierce kiss that obliterated every thought. My mind was blissfully blank. I couldn't think at all. I could only feel his mouth on me, his lips on my own, his tongue coaxing mine.

He moved his hands from the small of my back to my waist. One slid toward my ass, cupping it and pushing my hips even closer into him. I groaned when his erection nudged me. Little tremors shook my body as the aftershock of pleasure reverberated through me. He groaned, deepening the kiss. I was desperate for him, for all the things he could make me feel.

I opened the top button of his shirt, needing to feel skin-on-skin contact, trailing my fingers down to the next button. He covered my hand with his, and I stilled. Heat rushed through me when he pulled back and looked directly at me.

"Are you sure, Lexi?"

I nodded, too desperate for words. I leaned back in to kiss him.

My lips barely brushed his when he took control over the kiss again. This kiss was surreal. It was like learning to breathe again, learning to live, as if I'd been in a sleepy haze until now and this was the first time I truly felt alive. Desire pulsed through my veins—a desperate need for him.

Before I knew what happened, I felt my toes leave the floor. He was lifting me by my bottom. I immediately nestled my feet and ankles under his rear, pressing my inner thighs against his torso. He kept kissing me and kissing me, and I lost all sense of time and space, except that we were going up and up.

I tore my mouth from his, looking around us before grinning down at him. "Someone's super strong, carrying me up the stairs like this," I whispered, stroking his arms. "It's sexy."

"You're sexy," he whispered back. His eyes were hazy with lust, just as I imagined mine were.

I realized we'd headed to the same bedroom where I'd slept last time. I lifted a brow. "Why are we here?"

"Because it's farther away from Paisley's room. You don't have to be quiet."

I licked my lips at the promise in his voice. "I'll try anyway."

"You won't be able to, Lexi. I'll give you so much pleasure that you'll lose track of everything—where we are, who you are."

I pulled him closer to me, undoing the second button of his shirt and then the third one. When he groaned, I looked up in desperation.

"What's wrong?" I asked.

"I only have condoms downstairs."

Jutting out my lower lip, I let my hands drop. "Go," I said. "I'll wait for you here."

With a wolfish grin, he said, "I'll be quick."

As soon as he left, I turned to look at the bed, taking off the covers. After a brief minute, I decided to take off my clothes too. He wouldn't expect it, and I grinned, imagining the expression on his face when he saw me butt naked.

I lay down on the bed in what I hoped was a seductive pose. I was lying on one side, with one leg straight and the other bent. My breath hitched when I heard him come up, and I realized this was it. After tonight, there was no going back. And even though I had no idea where we were heading, I knew I wanted this. I wanted him.

"Lexi, fuck," he whispered when he came into the room and saw me naked and on display. "You're so damn beautiful."

"And you're still wearing clothes," I said in a taunting voice.

He came up next to the bed, pulling me up until I was on my knees. He lowered himself with one knee on the mattress, tilting my head up because he was still towering over me, and sealed his mouth over mine, dominant and demanding, leading the kiss just as I knew he would lead everything tonight.

"Know one thing, Lexi," Tate said in an authoritative tone. "After tonight, you're mine."

FOURTEEN

Lexi

"Tate…," I whispered.

His hands skimmed down my naked body slowly, torturing me while I kept undoing his shirt. Pushing it down his arms, I let it drop to the floor as I brought my hands to his belt. He cupped my ass cheeks with both hands, pushing me against him. My eyes rolled back in my head when my clit collided with the fly of his pants. I moved back just a nudge.

"No, no, you're going to be naked when you seduce me," I warned him.

He took a step back so he was out of my reach. I pouted, but then my face broke into a smile when he took off his belt, then pushed down his pants along with his boxers. I sucked in a breath when I took in the size of him. *Oh wow.*

I was still on my knees, watching him hungrily. Leaning forward, I grasped at his thigh, pulling him closer to me until he was within my reach. I clasped my fingers around his cock, moving my hand up and down. He groaned, tipping his head back. I swiped my tongue over the tip, making him moan again. It filled me with satisfaction that I could please him and tease him at the same time. I moved my mouth up and down, along with my hand. When my mouth reached the tip, I clasped my hand around the base. I glanced up at him and found him staring straight down at me, a hungry look in his eyes. Wrapping a hand in my hair, he guided my movements, moving his hips slightly too. I couldn't get enough.

"Touch yourself, Lexi. I want to see you," he commanded.

Hearing those words alone made me wet.

His tone was always brimming with authority, but now it sounded downright dominating. I parted my thighs wider, bringing my hand to my clit. A shudder of pleasure went through me, and I groaned against his cock. He pulled back the next second, lifting me until we were eye to eye.

I blinked, confused. "Why did you do that? I wasn't done."

He didn't say anything, just curved his mouth in a half smile before kissing the side of my neck. He slid his hand down between my breasts, straight to my pussy, and when his finger nudged my clit, I bucked my hips forward, slamming into him, trapping his erection between us. A groan tore from his throat.

My inner muscles were pulsing, hungry for him. Then he kissed me again, even deeper, even faster than before. His erection rocked between us. He cupped himself, driving it up and down my clit, sending shiver after shiver through my body.

"This is too much," I whispered while he kissed down my neck. Pushing me down on my back, he continued kissing the side of my body as if he intended to explore every inch of me.

"I need you to be ready," he growled. He moved upward, and then he reached my breasts and clamped his lips around the peak. I was so sensitive that I felt the flick of his tongue over my nipple as if he'd licked my clit. I threw my head back, and a groan reverberated through me.

"I'm ready," I said.

He looked at me with a lazy smile. I braced myself as I felt his hand rest on my folds, rubbing up and down. When he pressed his thumb against my clit, my thigh shook. An intense pulse of pleasure rocked me. The next thing I knew, he slid two fingers inside me, moving them in the same rhythm as his tongue around my nipple. If I thought he was driving me crazy before, it was nothing compared to now. I couldn't breathe past the tension forming inside me. I was going to explode. I was sure of it.

He brought his lips to my ear. "I'm going to make you come like this, and then I'll give you my cock, but not before you come, understood?"

"Yes," I said. My voice was so breathy that I wasn't sure if he heard me.

Then he clasped his mouth over mine again and curved his fingers inside me at the same time that he flicked my clit with his thumb. I came so hard that my whole body shuddered. A loud groan tore from me, but he silenced it by holding his mouth over mine, kissing me through my orgasm. Pleasure rippled through me, and the small aftershocks of the orgasm lasted longer than a few seconds.

Fluttering my eyes open, I found him looking at me.

"Now I want to make you mine, Lexi. All mine."

He leaned sideways, taking the condom from the night-stand. Ripping the foil, he put it on before settling between my legs. I gasped when I felt his tip push inside me. My inner muscles were still pulsing. I felt like I was going to fall apart from so much pleasure, just from feeling him slide inside me inch by inch.

"Fuck, you feel amazing," he moaned into my ear, moving his hips faster and faster, burrowing his head in my neck.

I'd never felt this way—utterly and completely owned. He didn't just have my body and my pleasure. He had all of me.

Without warning, he turned us around so we were lying on our sides, legs intertwined. I pushed myself up a little, meeting his thrusts with mine.

I loved this position. I felt him so deep that I wasn't sure I could bear it. He captured my mouth, flicking his thumb over my clit, making this even more intense for me. I'd never felt pleasure like this. It was overwhelming feeling him inside me, his cock pulsing, his tongue caressing mine, his thumb over my clit. I wasn't going to last. I needed my release, and I knew without a doubt that it was going to be shattering.

I felt him pulse inside me even more as I succumbed to my orgasm. Once again, he captured my mouth, drowning my sounds of pleasure and giving me his own too. We climaxed hard, a roaring sound reverberating from his chest and through his body. We both thrust and undulated our hips until we were spent.

When I blinked my eyes open, I looked at him lazily, taking in those sexy muscles. Pushing myself to one side, I propped my head on my hand, glancing from his shoulder down to his ass, then back up. He attempted to come closer, but I scooted even farther back.

"What are you doing?" he asked.

"Adding some distance. It's the only way I can take in this holy hotness."

He threw his head back, laughing and revealing his neck. I took advantage of the fact that he was unprepared and leaned forward, kissing his Adam's apple before retreating to my original position. He straightened up, looking at me with a playful twinkle in his eyes. I liked seeing him like this, completely relaxed with a huge smile on his face.

"Last time you had me here in your shirt, and now I'm naked. You have a strange power over me, Mr. Maxwell."

The playfulness in his eyes turned to scorching-hot intensity as he came closer, and this time I didn't pull back. He put an arm around my waist, pulling me flush against him. "Next time, I'm going to do even more," he said in a delicious voice full of promise.

My heart somersaulted. *Next time. There's going to be a next time.* I swallowed hard, trailing my fingers from his shoulder down to his arm. "I should go. It's late."

"Lexi, whatever this is, I don't want to end it." He brought his hand to my jaw, cupping it and tilting my head so I was looking straight at him. He trapped my gaze with his.

My heart was beating faster. "Well, when you get all bossy," I whispered playfully, "how can I not agree with you? I don't want it to end either. "

I wasn't sure I could pierce this armor he had around himself, but even so, I couldn't say no to him. I wanted to explore whatever this was.

His lips tilted up in a smile, but his gaze was still intense.

"Good." Getting out of the bed, he took off the condom and went to the bathroom.

I sighed, staring after him. Who could resist the sight of those sexy buttocks? I definitely couldn't.

He came back with a wet cloth. I blushed, taking it from him and cleaning myself up as he sat down on the bed next to me. "Sleep here."

"I don't think it's a good idea. It could get confusing for Paisley."

"Then stay for a while longer."

I smiled, lying back on the bed. "I could stay a while longer. It all depends on you."

He wiggled his eyebrows. "Challenge accepted."

"Are you sure? You're the one who's got to be in top shape in the morning. Paisley and I can have fun even if I'm sleepy."

He groaned. "Don't remind me about tomorrow. Let's focus on tonight. It's all about you."

I lay back down on one side, smiling up at him but feeling a bit self-conscious that I was naked, which was ridiculous. But now that the hormonal craze was out of my system, I remembered that my thighs and ass were a tad too big for my liking. I tried to pull the bedsheet up to my middle.

Tate cocked a brow. "What are you doing?"

"Covering up my ass," I blurted.

Oh my God. Why did I say that? Body insecurities were not sexy.

He tilted closer, a deep sound reverberating in his throat. "Lexi, you're fucking beautiful. Don't doubt that."

I pressed my lips together, giving him a small smile.

Narrowing his eyes, he peeled the sheet off me, skimming his lips up my belly.

"What's the plan, mister?" I whispered.

"I'm going to show you how sexy you are to me."

"And how will you do that?"

"I'll worship every inch of your body." Goose bumps broke out on my belly. I smiled, trailing my fingers along his right shoulder. His voice was in a lower octave when he added, "Every. Single. Inch."

IT WAS NEARLY two o'clock in the morning when I finally arrived home. I was smiling from as I stepped inside my apartment. Not even bothering to take a shower, I dropped my clothes next to my bed and slid under the covers. I reached for my phone before I forgot to set the alarm again. To my surprise, he'd texted me.

Tate: Tell me when you're home. I want to know you're safe.

Grinning, I replied.

Lexi: I'm home. I slipped under the covers.

Tate: I wish I were there with you.

My heart gave a mighty sigh, and I knew he'd only just begun making me swoon.

Tate: I can't stop thinking about you.

My body was sizzling again. My heart rate intensified.

Lexi: I can't stop thinking about you either.

It was the truth, and I didn't like playing games. Tonight had been incredible.

Tate: I can't wait to see you tomorrow morning.

Lexi: I hope I won't oversleep.

Tate: Then I'll stay longer and wait for you.

Lexi: That's how much you want to see me?

Tate: Oh no. I want to do a lot more. Kiss you, take your clothes off, but I also like seeing you. My mornings are better after that.

I laughed, intending to tease him, but then I stopped because what if he was serious? His gran had said something similar, so there had to be a seed of truth in it.

I dropped the phone to one side, pushing the pillow against my face. My belly was full of flutters, and I couldn't believe it.

I didn't know what to do with this longing I had for him. It wasn't purely physical either. I liked talking to him, being with him, laughing with him. But he still had scars from his divorce, and I wasn't sure he could do anything more than a fling.

I pulled the covers up to my chin. *Enjoy how he makes you feel, Lexi.* I placed a hand over my chest, smiling. Even if I could forget that he was hot as sin and kissed deliciously, I couldn't ignore the way he made me feel.

Oh, Tate. What are you doing to me?

FIFTEEN

Lexi

$\mathscr{T}$he next morning, I was in a frenzy. I hadn't heard the alarm clock, but I somehow woke up anyway. Only it was fifteen minutes too late.

I got ready quickly, choosing a red dress that brushed my knees and had a generous V-cut. It was hot as hell outside and told myself that was why I was wearing this.

I had a huge grin on my face as I left the building, and it hadn't toned down one bit when I arrived at Tate's house. But that was okay. I didn't think Paisley would be able to tell if anything was different about me. Kids weren't inherently suspicious.

I knocked at the door, bracing myself for the sight of Tate. To my astonishment, Declan opened it.

"Morning," he said. "Gran and I stopped by for breakfast."

"Hi," I squeaked.

Oh wow. Is that my voice? What's wrong with me?

I tried to dampen my smile as I stepped inside.

"I'll come in the kitchen and see if I can help," I said.

When I entered the kitchen and greeted Beatrice and Paisley, I realized I had no clue how to act around Tate. I stole a glance at him as I sat down in front of the plate Beatrice indicated was mine and found him looking at me.

One corner of his mouth tipped up in a smile. As he brought the coffee cup to his lips, he muttered, "I'm sorry," darting his eyes at his brother and then at his grandmother. I took that to mean he didn't know they would be stopping by.

I smiled to myself as I dug into my breakfast, which was an omelet today.

Midway through breakfast, I felt my skin heat up for no reason at all. I stole another glance at Tate. With a jolt, I realized he was watching me. It was as if my body was tied to him on a different level since last night. I could feel his presence and his gaze on me, even if I couldn't see him.

Declan cleared his throat, and I realized he was looking between the two of us. Oh God, was he able to tell there was something different between us? Men could be oblivious to such details, but I didn't know Declan well enough to know if that was the case with him too.

He wasn't the only one watching us. Beatrice was also looking at me with a sort of knowing smile. I could practically feel her reading my thoughts. How was that even possible? I glanced back down at my plate.

"So, what brings you both here this morning?" Tate asked Declan and Beatrice. I mentally thanked him for shifting the focus.

Beatrice narrowed her eyes. "Declan told me last night that Malcolm is suing for the right to use my building."

Tate stared at Declan, who held up his hands in defense.

"You try lying to Gran's face when she asks you point-blank what's going on."

She shook her head. "You two are acting silly. I spoke to Reese. I guess you forgot to warn her to keep it a secret from me."

Tate groaned. "I didn't *explicitly* warn her."

"Tate, I don't appreciate being kept in the dark."

"Gran, we're taking care of it," Tate said in a strong voice. He sounded so reassuring, like nothing could happen if he were in charge.

"Oh, I'm not worried," Beatrice said. "With Declan representing me, I know this will go away."

"It will," Declan said in a voice that was as strong as Tate's. "We're not going to let anyone get away with anything or harm you. Or Reese." His voice was cold now. It also had a menacing note, and I was hoping that whoever was causing trouble for them was cowering in their boots. They deserved it. I couldn't deny I was melting a bit, seeing how both of them were so protective of their grandmother.

"That isn't what this is about. It's about how disappointed I am that you two didn't tell me anything. Is this what you were so secretive about at the cookout?"

"Yes," Tate admitted.

Beatrice pressed her lips together. "I don't want this type of treatment from either of you ever again. Understood?"

Both Tate and Declan nodded. I barely held back laughter. These two were used to always getting their way, yet they now looked thoroughly schooled.

Paisley seemed to pick up on the same vibe I did, because the corners of her mouth tipped up in a smile.

"Good," Beatrice said. "Now, I'll just spend some time with my lovely great-granddaughter while the two of you sort it out."

"Are you hanging out with us the whole day?" I asked.

"Yes. Gran's staying with us, and next weekend I'm staying with her."

"That's right," Beatrice said. The two of them looked a bit guilty, and I was sure Paisley would be spoiled nonstop while she was at her great-grandma's.

"That's awesome. Paisley, you still want us to go on a picnic today?" I asked, and she nodded vigorously. "All right, then. I'm going to go prepare the backpack we'll take with us." It was a perfect excuse, as I didn't want to intrude on their family time any longer. "Thank you for breakfast, Tate."

"My pleasure," he answered, and I swear my lady bits tingled at the sound of his sexy voice. Was there a double entendre there, or was my imagination out of control? I couldn't tell. I'd barely been able to keep my thoughts straight around him before I had those sexy hands on me and his body over mine, but now it was downright impossible.

I headed to the back entrance of the house. The backpack was there in the mudroom. I was already making a mental note of everything I was going to put in it. I needed an extra change of clothing for Paisley, towels, a blanket.

I was about to unhook the backpack to take it upstairs when I felt someone behind me. I drew in a sharp breath as Tate's hands gripped my waist, and before I even had time to turn around, I felt his lips on my neck.

"Good morning." His breath landed on a sensitive spot on my neck. Goose bumps broke out on my arms and then my legs. I wasn't sure how I would resist his proximity if my body reacted this way every time.

"Morning," I said in a chipper tone, wondering if he could tell the effect he had on me.

"I'm sorry about the ambush. I had no idea they were planning to stop by until they were here."

"Hey, it's your family," I said. "You don't have to apologize."

He growled against my neck, sending delicious tingles through me. "No, but I had a plan for this morning."

"Oh? By your voice, I'm guessing it was a sexy plan?"

He turned me around to look at me intently. "Yes," he replied seriously, making me laugh.

My heart was thumping in my chest. My entire body

heated up. "Well, keep it in mind," I whispered. "I'm sure you'll have an opportunity to put it in motion."

From the dangerous glint in his eyes, it was clear he disagreed with me. He parted my legs with his knee, spreading his fingers on my neck. This bad man wanted to put whatever sexy plan he had in motion right now. That spelled disaster. He tilted closer, and I sucked in a breath.

The next moment, Paisley called for him from the other room. He groaned, pulling back and dropping his hand. I immediately missed having him near.

"I want to talk to you before I leave," he said.

I nodded. "Okay, but go. You don't want her thinking there's something between us."

"Right," he said, his expression tightening before he turned around.

All in all, I was proud of myself. I didn't think Declan or Beatrice could tell anything was happening between the two of us. It wasn't that I necessarily wanted things to be a secret, but it only made sense that if we didn't want Paisley to know, it would be easier if the rest of the family didn't either.

Tate and I didn't get a chance to be alone again because Paisley was determined to tell me all the decoration ideas she had. After he and Declan left, Paisley declared that she wanted to watch *The Jungle Book* for a bit before we headed out. She had strict screen time, so I opened my mouth to suggest watching it later in the evening, but Beatrice said, "Let her watch it. Nothing will happen. I will never understand why young people have so many rules for their children."

I pressed my lips together to hold back a laugh. Spoken like a true grandmother.

"Let's you and I drink a coffee," Beatrice said after Paisley moved to the living room with her headphones and the iPad. "And you can tell me all about what's happening between you and my grandson."

I nearly swallowed my tongue as my hands froze in the act of making coffee. I turned around. How could she tell?

"I'll take a guess and say that physical attraction won over," Beatrice said in a relaxed tone, as if she were talking about the weather forecast.

All I could do was nod.

"Paisley doesn't know," I added hastily. I couldn't admit it was more than physical attraction. Saying it out loud felt dangerous. Like the idea would take hold of my heart and not let go.

Beatrice was studying me but didn't say anything.

I turned around, twiddling my thumbs after pressing the button that made two coffees at once. Once they were ready, I took them to the kitchen island and climbed on the bar stool.

Beatrice was watching me intently. "How do you feel about my grandson?" she asked, again in that relaxed tone, as if she were asking me what I thought about our picnic today.

"I… Well, I haven't known him for long," I mumbled. I'd met the man a month ago, after all.

She laughed, covering my hand with hers. She radiated warmth and motherly energy. "It's too early. My bad. I shouldn't have asked."

I felt like I was talking to Mom. Over the past few years, most of the conversations with my parents centered around her health. I couldn't remember the last time I talked to Mom about a guy I liked. Of course, I hadn't been attracted to someone in a long time, not the way I was to Tate.

"Beatrice, I'm not sure what to say."

"You don't have to say anything, darling. I'm happy that my instincts weren't wrong. I could tell the minute you entered the kitchen that something has changed. He couldn't take his eyes off you the entire time."

He'd looked at me that much? I'd caught him a few times, but I hadn't realized he'd been watching me the whole time. My face split into a grin again.

"I know my grandson. He's been different lately. He'll disagree with me on this and say he likes his life as it is, but I know deep down he longs for a relationship. He doesn't allow himself to admit it."

Her words stirred something in my chest. *Oh, Tate...*

Beatrice went to the living room and sat next to Paisley. I seized my chance and texted Tate.

Lexi: Beatrice knows. I have no clue how this happened. I didn't tell her.

He replied immediately.

Tate: Don't worry. I was sure she caught on. She was giving me funny looks this morning. Can you get somewhere alone? I want to call you.

Lexi: Sure. Give me a minute.

I headed upstairs to one of the bathrooms. There was no chance of Paisley or Beatrice finding me here.

Lexi: I'm alone.

He called the next second.

"Hey," I said, leaning against the closed door.

"Hey. We didn't get to talk again before I left."

"I know. What did you want to talk about?"

"Seeing you. Out of the house. Every time I make plans, something gets in the way, so I'm going to be spontaneous."

"Why do I have a feeling that's not your thing?" I asked with a grin.

"It usually isn't."

"So I get special treatment?"

"Yes, Lexi. You do. You fucking do."

My breath caught, and I only managed a whispered "Okay."

"Do you have time for a date tonight?"

I shimmied my hips, barely restraining the urge to break out in a happy dance.

"Yes, I do," I exclaimed. "I do."

"Good. I can't wait for tonight, Lexi."

"Back at you."

I hung up, and my face exploded in a huge smile.

I had a date with Tate Maxwell.

A date.

I was the luckiest woman on the planet.

SIXTEEN

Lexi

---

*W*hen I came back downstairs, Paisley was still watching *The Jungle Book*, so I went ahead and packed everything for our picnic. Twenty minutes later, I was done. Poking my head in the living room, I realized Beatrice and Paisley hadn't moved one inch.

"We're ready to go," I said.

Predictably, Paisley asked, "Can I stay and watch some more?"

The corners of my mouth tugged up. "You can watch more another day. Let's go out and enjoy the sun."

Beatrice nudged Paisley. "Your dad messaged me, asking me to spend the evening here. We'll watch more tonight."

"When did Tate message you?" I blurted.

"Now," she answered, looking at me with a very knowing smile.

Oh sweet Lord. The man moved fast.

I smiled nervously as we all got ready to go out.

The day was perfect for sunbathing and relaxing, but I couldn't wait to get home for the first time since I became Paisley's nanny. It wasn't that I didn't enjoy spending my time with her and Beatrice. But I was too excited about the date, and that feeling multiplied once I received a message in the early afternoon from Tom, the owner of the small deli next to my building, telling me I had a special delivery that I had to pick up from him.

Lexi: What is it?

Tom: I am under strict instructions not to tell you.

I stared at my phone.

Lexi: Who is it from?

Tom: Tate Maxwell. That's all I'm allowed to tell you.

I laughed at my phone, shaking my head. Tate had bribed him not to tell me what he sent me? Well, well. And I thought I was on good terms with Tom. I had to take my bribing game to another level.

The day rolled by fast—probably because I spent half the time daydreaming about the evening.

"Why don't you go ahead?" Beatrice asked sweetly at five o'clock when we returned to the house after a day of sun, snacks, and laid-back fun. "Paisley and I are good."

I couldn't help but blush. Could she tell what was on my mind? That all I could think about was Tate and what the evening would bring?

Who was I kidding? Of course she could tell. That explained the knowing smile.

"Are you sure?" I asked, not even bothering to pretend that I didn't want to go home as soon as possible.

"Yes, yes. Paisley and I can entertain each other."

Oh sweet Lord. By the way Paisley looked at Beatrice, as if she walked on water, I knew she was going to spoil the young girl nonstop. That was fine. That was a great-grandmother's prerogative. I'd only had a few years with my grandparents— they passed away when I was pretty young—but the one

LAYLA HAGEN

summer I spent at their house was one of my happiest
memories.

Once I arrived at my building, I went straight next door to
Tom's deli, impatiently drumming my fingers on his counter.

"Okay. I'm here. I want my present."

"Girl, whoever this guy is, he's a keeper."

"How exactly did this happen?"

"A delivery guy came. He gave me his phone, and I spoke
with Tate Maxwell, who made a very convincing case for why I
shouldn't tell you what you got." Bending at the waist, he
disappeared for a few seconds under the counter and then
came up with a box of my favorite kind of chocolates—they
had cherries inside.

Wow. I couldn't believe it. My mouth was already watering
as I took my box of chocolates.

I was lucky that the elevator wasn't too crowded. I was
getting the side-eye from my neighbors, probably because I was
smiling like a kid on Christmas morning. Once I got inside my
apartment, I texted him.

**Lexi: I got the chocolates. And they are my favorite
kind!!!!**

Tate: I know. You told me you loved them.

Oh, sweet heavens. He remembered? Who is this guy?

Lexi: How did you do this?

Tate: That's my secret. But it involved Gran too.

**Lexi: So family conspiracy for the perfect
date, huh?**

Tate: All the best for you Lexi. Only the best.

I sighed, planning to look absolutely gorgeous for this date. I
washed my hair and styled it in waves with my large round
brush. Then I applied makeup, carefully following the steps,
using face cream and then foundation. I played with eye color
until I got it right; I was wearing a white dress and black sandals,

so I could get pretty creative with eyeshadows. Choosing a few shades of green, I put a lighter color starting from the inner corner of the eyelid and going darker toward the outer corner.

Once I finished the makeup, I put on my white dress. It was strapless with sewn-in bra cups so my nipples wouldn't show. It was made of a stretchy fabric that highlighted my curves. I turned around, looking in the mirror, and decided to pair it with some fun earrings.

In my spare time, I liked to make jewelry. It was nothing fancy; I liked crafts, having done it a lot with the kids at school, and it became a habit that relaxed me more than even being outdoors. I put on huge hoops with all sorts of trinkets on them. I liked wearing neutral colors because it allowed me to play with accessories and makeup.

Turning around again in the mirror, I smiled at myself, happy with my work. I still had two minutes left until Tate arrived, so I quickly put on my shoes, which were pretty high and made my legs look endless. I couldn't wait to see Tate want to devour me the second I opened the door.

I even sent my friends a pic of the chocolate box after I'd updated them on my night with Tate.

Jenny: He's a keeper.

Ella: Holy shit, girl. Where did you find this guy?

I grinned at their responses. One and a half minutes later —yes, I was counting—my doorbell rang. I opened it without even checking the peephole.

Wow. Was Tate even hotter tonight? He looked absolutely delicious, with a five-o'clock shadow, the top button of his shirt open, and his sleeves rolled up. He was pure muscle, and I loved every inch of him.

"Good evening, Lexi."

"I'm ready." I felt a bit ridiculous as I posed in front of him, jutting one hip out to the right and placing my hand on it.

I stayed like that for a few seconds before picking up my black clutch.

Tate didn't take his eyes off my face. He seemed oddly still.

Okay, this is not the reaction I was hoping for. I'd hoped he would at least look at me up and down, but he was staring firmly at my face.

We walked back out to the corridor, and I locked the door, before we headed to the elevator and pressed the button. It came quickly, as it usually did in off-peak hours. It took forever to catch an elevator very early in the morning or in the evening when everyone left or and came home. Everyone seemed to leave and arrive at the same time.

The elevator was empty, and the second we stepped inside, I felt a shift in the air. When the door closed, I noticed Tate's appearance in the mirror. He was standing behind me. The hunger in his eyes made my skin turn to goose bumps.

He pushed my hair to one side, kissing my naked shoulder.

"Lexi," he whispered. "Fuck." Then he promptly turned me around and covered my mouth with his, kissing me hungrily, tangling our tongues, taking his time with his deep-and-dirty kiss. He buried one hand in my hair and rested the other one on my waist.

I was so turned on that when he parted my legs with his knee, I nearly rubbed myself against his thigh. Holy shit, he could make me lose my decency in record time.

I gasped, and he pulled back with a groan.

"Damn it. I thought I could hold back." He was looking at me up close, dragging his thumb across my lips. "But like I told you once, you make me feel too much. Want too much. There is no in-between with you."

I took a step back as the elevator doors opened, laughing nervously. "Can I point out that you had excellent restraint back in the apartment? I was wondering what was up with that. You were looking at my face and nothing more."

Tate looked incredulous for a few seconds before bursting out laughing. "That's because I knew if I looked too closely, I was going to lose it."

I grinned, wiggling my eyebrows. "That was exactly the reaction I was hoping for when I got dressed," I said as we walked down the hallway toward the exit.

Tate put an arm around me when we stepped outside, feathering his fingers up and down my left arm. It was such an intimate touch. I loved it. I wanted more of it. I wanted everything.

We walked to the edge of the street, and I only realized he was calling a cab when I saw him lift an arm. I was so used to Ubering everywhere that I didn't even pay attention to cabs anymore. Still, they were quite convenient and circulating a lot in the summer in the evenings because people spent a lot of time outdoors.

"Where are we going?" I asked when he opened the door of the cab for me. I slid in, moving to the center of the seat so he could get in on the same side.

"Navy Pier," he told the driver, who simply nodded, and the car lurched forward.

"I haven't been there in a long time," I said, fidgeting in excitement. "What are we doing?"

"We're going on the Ferris wheel."

I squealed like a teenager. "Oh my God, really? That's so awesome. I've never been on it."

"I know. You told us that when we made the waffles."

My eyes widened. "I did. That's right."

I smiled, and he smiled right back before bringing his mouth to my ear and veering left at the last second to where my jaw met the neck. I thought he might tell me something, but instead, he placed a kiss there. It was innocent at first, just a brush of his lips, but then I felt the tip of his tongue, and I instantly clenched my thighs. Desire poured through me, especially between my legs.

Then Tate straightened up, and I caught his smug smile before he turned to look out the window.

This man had some serious seduction skills.

SEVENTEEN

Lexi

———

I'd wanted to go on the Ferris wheel since I came to Chicago, but I never got to do it for some reason, and now it was turning into a romantic date.

Which turned out to be even better than I thought. When I imagined traveling on the Centennial Wheel, I always thought I'd get squished between a bunch of tourists. But Tate didn't buy normal tickets—he booked a VIP gondola with plush seating and a glass floor. The most important thing was that we were alone inside.

"This is so romantic!" I exclaimed as I sat down, touching the seats and looking outside. Chicago was beautiful all the time, but it seemed almost magical with glittering towers everywhere at sunset. I couldn't wait for us to move higher.

"All the best for my girl," he said with a cheeky smile. "I didn't want to share you with anyone tonight."

I lay back in my seat, looking around as the lift spun and we rose in the air. "Are you sure that's a good idea, considering how dangerous the elevator ride was?"

"Yes. We have to keep to a simple rule," he said.

"And what's that?"

"No kissing, or we're going to have a repeat of the elevator scene."

I shimmied in my seat, crossing and uncrossing my legs. That sounded like a delicious promise.

He trained his gaze on me, hard and unrelenting, and I felt on fire. He looked so different now from when I showed up for the job interview one month ago. He seemed carefree and had this smile on his face that filled my heart with joy. The lake was dark at night, but now we were at that magical time after sunset when the sky was a beautiful orange color. We might not kiss, but I was acutely aware of his presence and the fact that our legs were intertwined. He looked at me more than he looked at the scenery. I was at a loss for words, so we just enjoyed the view like this, commenting only on which landmarks we recognized. Unfortunately, the ride only lasted fifteen minutes.

"And what now?" I asked once we stepped out.

"Now I'm taking us somewhere I think you'll like very much," he said, putting an arm around my back and resting his fingers on my upper arm.

"Let's see what you have in store for me," I teased, feeling giddy and like the luckiest woman in all of Chicago.

Tate brought me to a rooftop bar not far away from the lakeshore. It was unlike any other bar I'd been to. There were wooden walls around the perimeter with lush green plants climbing all over; it almost seemed like we were in a garden. They'd intertwined twinkle lights between the plants, and it looked magical. I snapped a few pictures with my phone right away.

"What are you doing?" Tate asked.

"Paisley loves twinkle lights." I slipped the phone back into my clutch. "She'll want to see this."

Tate didn't reply, and when I looked up from my bag, the emotion and intensity in his gaze took me by surprise.

Before I had a chance to ask if something was wrong, the host greeted us. He showed us to a table in a corner with a cozy couch and armchairs. I also spotted a dance floor in the opposite corner.

A dance floor? Hmm. I could see some potential for fun. I wondered what I would have to bribe Tate with to get him to agree to dance with me.

We each ordered cocktails and a food platter, and they were delivered almost right away. We had salami, different types of cheese, marinated olives, sun-dried tomatoes, and grilled mushrooms with oregano sprinkled on top.

"This is delicious," I said after stuffing a mushroom in my mouth.

"I'm glad you like it."

We were sitting side by side on the couch, and if I thought I was acutely aware of his presence on the Centennial Wheel, it was nothing compared to now. The setting was so intimate that it was almost sensual. Potted plants separated our corner from the rest of the bar, creating a nook with a lot of privacy.

"How did you find this place?" I asked him. "It's really pretty."

"A friend of mine owns it, and I told him I wanted the best table they have."

"Of course you did. The question is, how could he give it to you on such short notice?"

Tate leaned in slightly, bringing his mouth to my ear. "I know how to persuade people."

"Oh, yeah. Tom, the guy who got the delivery, said something similar."

"I've had lots of practice in business."

Tate Maxwell was in a league of his own when it came to making me swoon. I could imagine him in his office, looking all dominant and businesslike and negotiating like a shark.

Was it odd that I felt honored he was using the same skills

to romance me? Because that was exactly what it felt like, and I loved it. How was I ever going to date anyone else? The thought made me sad.

As I sipped my cocktail and slid up a bit farther away from him so I could take a good look at him, I was surprised to find his gaze on me once again. *Is he always watching me?* My heart fluttered.

"I can't believe you organized all this in one day. I wonder what you could do if you had more time?"

"Try me," he said, and then he wiggled his eyebrows, which was so out of character for him that I couldn't help but laugh. "I knew about the Ferris wheel for a while, though."

"You still get full points for all of this."

His gaze was playful now. "Points? Okay. I like this game."

And he was so good at it. Why was he still single?

"Tate, can I ask you something?"

"Sure."

"Have you always been single after your divorce?"

He nodded, drumming his fingers on his glass. "I've been with women, but nothing serious, and I didn't want Paisley to get confused."

My heartbeat accelerated. It was on the tip of my tongue to ask if he wanted to tell Paisley about us, but I couldn't work up the courage to ask it. So instead, I started rambling nervously.

"Dating isn't easy. I've been dating for, I don't know… fourteen years. Ever since I was in high school."

A weird noise popped up. It seemed to come from Tate, but maybe the cocktail messed with my senses. I kept rambling. "I had a few relationships over the years, but I don't think I've ever been in love."

The admission surprised me, and by the way his eyes widened, it surprised him too. Maybe he wasn't ready to hear something so deep from me yet, or perhaps it wasn't something he wanted to know at all, but I didn't feel the need to hide from him. I wanted him to know who I was. But what if he didn't like it? This was too much information for a first date.

I licked my lips before adding, "So, yeah, I would think that now in the age of Tinder, it's easier to get dates, but every time I swipe—" That weird noise came again. I turned my head to him. "Did you make a sound at the back of your throat?"

He tilted closer. "Lexi, I don't want to hear about you seeing other men now or in the past, ever. It drives me crazy."

Oh my God. That *had* been him earlier. I swallowed hard, acutely aware of the heat of his body, his forehead pressing against mine, his fingers sitting in the small of my back possessively.

"You're mine," he growled. An honest-to-goodness growl.

"Okay. Fair enough," I responded, breathless. His presence was all-consuming. For a few seconds, I completely forgot people surrounded us. We might not see them through the plants, but we could hear voices and the sounds of laughter and clinking glasses.

"Tate," I whispered, my voice uneven.

His fingers were pressing into my back even more, and the corners of his mouth tilted up.

"You're doing something to me, Lexi, and it's even more dangerous than I thought."

"Hmm," I murmured, keeping my tone playful. "I like the sound of that."

He leaned back, taking his hand away.

"And you think not touching me will make it less dangerous?" I teased.

"I sure as fuck hope so, because I'm close to throwing you over my shoulder and walking out of here with you."

Oh. My. God. That sexy, determined voice was going to be my undoing.

I shifted even farther away on the couch. A twinkle of amusement popped in his eyes. I loved it.

"My mom always says that when a person makes you feel everything intensely, it's a good sign," I said before pressing my lips in a tight line. Oh sweet heavens. I'd only had one cocktail and I was already reciting Mom's advice. I'd managed to scare off a lot of dates like this, and I hadn't even shared half the things I just told Tate. I didn't seem to want to hold back.

"You're close to your parents, right? I mean, I know you're helping them, but that's not the same thing."

"Mom is my best friend. I tell her everything. Growing up, she was the best mother I could want. She listened, and when I asked for advice, she gave it to me, but it never felt stifling or overly pushy or like she was taking away my freedom. We had a bit of a rough time when I was a teenager because, well, all teenagers seem to want to piss off their parents."

"I'm sure Paisley won't be like that," he said stoically.

I couldn't help but chuckle. "Right. Keep thinking that if it helps. Just prepare yourself for the worst." Sighing, I added, "I miss being able to talk about everything with Mom. In the past few years, life has changed a bit, especially this last year with the surgery. I spoke more to Dad, but even so, most of our conversations were about health or bills. I'm sure it's going to get better. Mom is already feeling loads better than before. I sent her a box of sweets last week from Le Chocolat, and she sent me, like, a dozen silly pics. That's a good sign."

Tate looked at me intently but didn't say anything.

"You freak me out when you do this," I said honestly.

"What?"

"You don't say anything, just look at me."

"Trust me. If I say everything that's on my mind, it'll scare you even more."

I swallowed hard, whispering, "Try me."

His eyes flashed. "Not tonight, Lexi. Not tonight."

"Hmmm... this is a two-way street, mister. I want to know stuff about you too."

"You can ask me anything. Except what you just did."

Chuckling, I racked my brain for something I wanted to know. "I haven't met your parents. Do they live far away from here?"

"No, they live in the city, but every summer, they go on a long vacation. They'll be back in two weeks."

"Okay. And you're as close to them as you are with Beatrice?"

"We're all very tight. Tyler jokes that Gran is the glue that keeps us together because we take turns finding stuff for her to do so she doesn't get too bored."

"But she still has the bookstore, right?"

"Yes, but she's not actively involved. She's had someone managing it for years. It's more of a keepsake." Chuckling, he added, "She was even more excited than my parents when Paisley was born."

"She told me that she lost her husband when she was young."

"Yeah, my dad had graduated college, and his brother had started his freshman year. My uncle took a bit harder and lost his way for a while."

"Oh. Is that the reason Kimberly and Reese spent so much time at your home growing up?"

He shook his head. "No. My aunt passed away when the girls were young. My uncle didn't cope well. He buried himself in work, traveling nonstop to expand the bookstore chain. Gran and my parents practically raised them. Since they lived close to us, my cousins were at our place a lot. Then, once we were all grown-up and doing our thing, she went through a few years of depression. She went to therapy, but she was truly only back to her old self after Paisley was born."

I wanted to hug Beatrice even more. Now I understood

why they were so overprotective of her. However, something told me they would try to keep bad news from her anyway.

"The therapist told her that keeping busy is important, and I try to arrange for her to spend as much time with Paisley as she wants. She just can't keep up with her anymore."

"You're a great guy, Tate."

His expression changed from serious to playful in a split second. I loved that I had such an effect on him.

"Okay, I have an idea. Why don't we play a get-to-know-each-other game?" I asked playfully.

He leaned closer. "Does it involve clothes?"

"Yes, it does. We're in a bar."

He laughed. "I know. I didn't say we had to play it here."

"Oh, you bad man. I knew you would get at this sooner or later."

"I'm honest about what I want, Lexi. And what I want is you, all the time."

My breath caught when I realized he was serious. "I was thinking about something more like 'What's your favorite color? What's your favorite food? Book?'"

"Your favorite color is green. Your favorite food is a veggie burger."

I jerked my head back, blinking rapidly before looking down at my cocktail.

Holy shit, did I already tell him that and forgot? Am I that drunk?

"How do you know that?" I asked suspiciously.

"Paisley talks about you a lot, Lexi. But I don't know what your favorite book is."

"It's *The Adventures of Anne Delaware*. It's out of print, unfortunately. But wait, what do you mean, Paisley talks about me?"

"She does—a lot. And I take advantage of it. I keep asking her for details."

The thought of him talking to his daughter about me was

making me melt. I wanted to be a fly on the wall and listen to that. What would she say if she knew I was dating her father?

Would Tate even want to tell her?

Despite feeling more at ease around him than anyone I've ever dated, I *still* couldn't work up the courage to ask him. But I didn't have to know the answer tonight. I could have this one amazing evening and focus on reality tomorrow.

Licking my lips, I pointed a finger at him. "But I don't know all this stuff about you. So, what is your favorite color?"

"Blue."

"And what do you *love* to eat?"

His eyes glazed over, and at first, I thought he hadn't heard my question. But then he brought his mouth to my ear. "Right now, you. I want my mouth on you until I make you squirm and come and cry out my name."

A shudder went through me. The skin on my whole body turned to goose bumps, including on my pussy, if that was even possible. I swallowed hard, jerking my head back so I could look at him.

"Damn, you're good," I whispered. "I wanted to ask if we could dance, but now all I want is to get out of here."

"Your wish is my command."

"Does that mean I can get a kiss now?" It was more of a tipsy challenge, but I needed him. "Since we're leaving anyway?"

"Fuck yes."

The second his lips brushed mine, my skin sizzled everywhere. I had no idea how he could light up my body with a single touch. He already had so much power over me that it scared me. But every kiss made me feel even more alive than the one before, every touch even more wanted and worshiped.

Tate Maxwell was mine. Nothing else mattered—at least not tonight.

EIGHTEEN

Tate

----

*T*he rest of the week was just as intense as the one before. The only thing keeping me sane was going home to Paisley... and to Lexi. I decided to track down her out-of-print book—or rather, I'd put Gran on it. Since she still ran the bookstore, she had access to the market. If anyone could find it, it was Gran; she had an immense talent for finding rare items and convincing people to hand them over.

One week later, Gran called me.

"I found it. I have it right here. The previous owner was a book murderer, but it's better than nothing."

"A what?"

"Book murderer. Edges are folded. Some pages have ink stains."

I chuckled at her description. Who came up with these things?

"This is for Lexi, right?" she asked.

"Yes, ma'am."

"Oh, Tate. You're finally giving yourself a chance to be happy. That's all I ever wanted—for you to take a chance and stop thinking that you shouldn't have someone in your life until Paisley is older."

My daughter had essentially told me she was okay with me dating, but who knew if she really would be? I had to tread carefully. I couldn't let Paisley down again. But that didn't mean I couldn't spoil Lexi and make her happy. I could imagine her reaction when she got the book.

"Gran, I have to go. I'll send someone for the book—"

"Nonsense, I'm going to your house anyway. I'm going to give it to her."

"Thanks."

One hour later, Lexi sent me a picture. She was holding a book next to her face.

Damn. I'd never seen her smile like that. The pure joy on her face brought me to my knees.

Lexi: I can't believe you got me this. THANK YOU THANK YOU THANK YOU.

Tate: You're welcome. I like your smile.

I leaned back in my chair, looking at that picture for a long time… right until Declan stomped into my office.

"The owners of the buildings next to The Happy Place have joined the lawsuit," he announced.

"Fuck."

I wasn't surprised, but I was pissed.

I was used to fighting off morons, but usually the fights weren't personal. Competitors were predictable—they were after profits—but this was different. It was personal. Malcolm and the Halsey Group weren't acting purely out of business interest. Well, the Halsey Group might have been, but not Malcolm.

He'd thought that by marrying into the Maxwell family, the doors to Chicago would open to him—and they would have. There wasn't much we didn't do for the family. But he shot himself in the foot, and his continued interest in Gran's building smelled of revenge more than a business decision.

"We'll fight them with all we have," I said. "Spare no expense. Take whatever risk necessary. I don't care. The company is doing well enough. I know it, and they know too."

"I think they're hoping we don't want the hassle," Declan said. With a smirk, he added, "I guess they're going to learn the hard way what it means to go against the Maxwells."

"That's right. They will. A display of force from time to time is necessary."

Declan grimaced. "You scare me when you talk like that."

"I mean it," I said.

"I know you do, hence the scaring part. Who would have thought that having all this would require having to fight for it every day?"

I scoffed, sitting down. "It's worth it."

We lived by a code: protect the family at any cost. With money and power came jealousy, and we had people who wanted to take us down. I wouldn't allow it.

Gran's building was part of the Maxwell Trust, and no one was going to strong-arm us into anything. Gran once told me that going to the bookstore, The Happy Place, was what kept her alive. I wasn't going to allow anyone to mess with it.

I had an extreme measure in mind… but I was going to let Declan try the *gentle* approach first.

"Do you want to tell Reese about the newest development?" he asked tentatively.

I looked up at him. "No, not yet."

"She's going to be pissed if we keep this from her."

I groaned. "We're not keeping it from her."

"What do you call not telling her?"

I smirked. "Protecting her. We don't have all the facts. I don't see why we should worry her."

"Maybe because it's her shithead of an ex-fiancé who's pulling all this, probably to get to her."

I groaned again, dropping my pen. It was no use trying to multitask, not when I was this pissed. "Of course it's to get back at her. The guy thought he was going to have the world at his feet, and now he doesn't."

I still remembered the day Reese called to tell me the wedding was off and that she didn't have the strength to cancel everything.

Maybe it was wrong to keep things from her, but I still remembered how fragile she was those days. Even though it was months ago, I was sure this would affect her, and I wanted to protect her from it as best as I could.

"No word to Reese for now," I said.

Declan nodded. "Okay, but for the record, if she finds out, I'll say it was your idea not to say anything."

"Fine. I don't care."

He cocked a brow, knowing I did care. I hated it when my cousins were mad at me, but I was sure Reese would understand. We'd always protected them. We told everyone we were their brothers at school so no one would mess with them, and no one did. No one wanted to pull a prank on someone when you had six angry Maxwells ready to pick a fight.

After he left my office, I tried to distract myself and not think about Reese's reaction if she found out, but it was no use. While I made the calls all morning to stave off the fire the Halsey Group was stoking, all I could think about was what Reese would say when she eventually found out. I knew I had to tell her. I just didn't have to do it today.

Maybe I'd ask Luke to do it.

I ASKED Declan to report to me as soon as he had anything, and I only heard from him twice during the day. I knew that was normal in a lawsuit, but I was still in a bad mood. I wanted to get this over with before it escalated more. Before it could hurt my family.

In the afternoon, I stopped in Declan's office without knocking.

He looked up at me, cocking a brow. "Why do you look like you're about to pick a fight?" he asked.

"I'm not. I wanted to check on the status of the lawsuit."

He leaned back in his chair, brow still raised. "I don't have any more news than what I sent already. I thought my ignoring your last five emails clarified that."

I swore, pacing in his office.

"Oh, so I was right. You do want to pick a fight. Why does it have to be with me?"

I turned around, grinning. "Because you're here."

"True, but I think Luke is in his office too, and Travis is coming back later today, just in case you want a fight on a bigger scale involving all of us." His tone was conversational.

I was being an ass. It wasn't his fault that things were moving slowly. But when I had something on my mind, I wanted it solved on the spot. It frustrated me that it wasn't possible.

"Dude, you need to relax," Declan said.

"How?"

"Don't look at me for answers. I'm even more of a workaholic than you are."

I groaned. "I know."

"Hey, you know who does know how to relax? Luke. Why don't we head up to his office? I'll tell them I—"

"No, I'm not in the mood for that."

A knock at the open door startled both of us. Luke poked his head in.

"Good. Just in time. Tate was about to blow up for no reason," Declan said.

"You know me. I have a sixth sense. Especially because you two looked like you had sticks up your asses this morning."

"I didn't," Declan said breezily, nodding in my direction.

Luke rubbed his hands, looking around with an exaggerated tilt of his head. "Lucky for you two, I'm only a few doors away to balance everything out. Let's go up to the bar once we're done. Or, you know, right now."

I cocked a brow. "It's early."

Luke walked up to me and put a hand on my shoulder. "Brother," he said in a dead-serious tone, "I don't know if anyone's told you this, but you are the CEO of a huge-ass wine company. You're your own boss. If you want to leave earlier, you can."

"Don't waste your time, Luke. He's a lost cause. But I'm not. Let's go up for a break," Declan said before turning to me and adding, "if you change your mind, you know where to find us."

I didn't change my mind.

After the two of them left, I went back to my office. And then the day got away from me, as usual. Preparing the launch of an exclusive collection was no small feat, and I wasn't too proud to admit that I'd underestimated the effort it would take. But it was going to be worth it.

When I'd started Maxwell Wineries, I wanted to build something my family could be proud of for generations to come. It was still what drove me to this day, even on the busiest weeks.

At five o'clock, I was restless. Out of nowhere, Lexi's voice popped into my mind. Usually I avoided distractions, but I welcomed this one. In fact, I wanted more of it.

Taking out my phone, I brought up Lexi's number, and I was surprised to see I had a few unread messages from her.

Lexi: We're going on a picnic today. Beatrice is

with us. **She seemed a bit off, but Paisley and I have a plan to cheer her up.**

The next message was from a few hours later.

Lexi: We're still on our picnic. We're going to be late for dinner, and I'm not sure how much Paisley will want to eat because she's snacked the whole day.

Tate: Are you still at the lake?

Lexi: YES we are. At Oak Street Beach. I don't think I can convince anyone to leave 😊) Paisley and Beatrice are dangerous when they're together.

She sent me a picture of the three of them. They were sitting down and smiling at the camera. Paisley was sticking out her tongue.

I felt lighter for the first time today and made a split-second decision. Rising from my chair, I headed straight out of my office and poked my head into Declan's. He and Luke had returned a few hours ago from their break.

I'm leaving," I announced.

Declan jerked his head back. "It's 4:15."

"I know."

He narrowed his eye". "Are you sick?"

"No. Lexi, Paisley, and Gran are at the lake. Lexi sent me some pictures."

"Wait a second. So, when Luke and I asked you to take a break, you gave us the evil eye, but Lexi texts you a few pics and you're off? I'll mark this day on the calendar."

"You're an ass," I said.

"I'm just remarking that this isn't exactly your usual behavior."

I flipped him the bird before leaving the office. He was right, obviously, but if I admitted it, I'd never hear the end of it. I typically had enough work that I could stay at the office until late into the evening, but I made it a golden rule to be home for dinner. I sometimes worked later after Paisley fell asleep, but not often. But I'd never left early, not unless she had an emergency or a recital at school.

Seeing all my girls out at the lake, I couldn't help myself. I asked Lexi to send me their location, and she replied with what felt like a million emojis, making me laugh. She wasn't capable of hiding her emotions.

I arrived at the lake half an hour later. My three ladies were sitting under a huge oak tree. Gran was reading on her Kindle. The picnic area was vast, but there were so many people that it still felt cramped.

"I want to wear this to my birthday," Paisley was telling Lexi.

It was on the twenty-fifth of September, but she always started talking about it two months before. "Do you think a red dress would clash with my freckles?"

I blinked at the weird conversation. *Clash?*

"What? No, I don't think so, but try on the yellow one as well. It's so luminous. I think it would make your eyes stand out too."

They're talking about fashion? Damn.

"What are my ladies up to?" I asked, appearing behind them.

Paisley shrieked, jumping to her feet and then straight into my arms. "Daddy, what are you doing here? Did something happen?"

Fuck, that anguish in her voice slew me.

"No, pumpkin, I just thought I'd join all of you and have some fun. I don't want you all to have fun without me."

"But it's early," Paisley said as if she couldn't possibly comprehend what I was doing here.

"Yeah, I decided to leave the office earlier today," I said.

Gran was watching me with a knowing look.

Lexi rose to her feet, smiling from ear to ear. The desire to pull her closer and kiss the living daylights out of her slammed into me.

"We were making a list with summer dresses," she said, turning her iPad around and holding it for me to see. "They're all-natural fabrics like cotton and silk. Pastel colors are in this summer. Well, they are almost every summer, but I chose a few that are more powerful for Paisley too."

It all sounded like gibberish to me, but I was happy Paisley had someone to talk fashion with besides Reese and Kimberly. I'd once asked her why she didn't talk about it with Gran, and her reply had been, "Gran is ancient. I can't wear what she wears. Everyone would laugh at me."

I'd avoided the subject since then.

"We're also making lists for her birthday," Gran said.

"What do you want to do?" Lexi asked, looking at me. "Want something to eat?"

"Yes. I'm starving," I said. "I only had lunch."

Lexi pointed to a huge hut on the other side of the sitting area. "They're selling delicious fries with chicken wings. We already had a few portions throughout the day."

"I'm going to buy something for myself. Lexi, are you sure you don't want anything to drink?" I looked at her in a meaningful way.

"Oh no, I'm—" She broke off midsentence, laughing. "You know what? I do. I'm not sure what I want to drink, but I'll come with you and look."

Gran looked up from her Kindle but didn't say anything. That knowing smile deepened. Next time I was alone with Gran, she'd talk my ear off, I was sure of it, but right now, I didn't care. I wanted to be alone with Lexi, even for just a few minutes.

We walked on the crowded beach, and she was talking nonstop. "I love it here. It's such a fun vacation-like feeling."

I nodded, looking around as we joined the huge line. I hadn't been here in a while, but she was right.

"Paisley is so excited about her birthday. She also mentioned her mom is coming."

My jaw tightened. "Yes, Nora visits once a year on her birthday."

"That's a good thing, right?"

"Honestly, I'm not even sure. Paisley gets all excited, and then she's sad after Nora leaves. But this year, she seems more... cautious."

"She's a bit older, so I think she understands everything better. By the way, I'm not sure what's wrong, but Beatrice wasn't her usual self today. She was more withdrawn."

The fact that she was worried about Gran made something twist in my chest.

"The anniversary of Grandad's death is coming up. She's always feeling down around this time of the year. She might hang out more often with you and Paisley."

"Poor thing! Okay, I'm going to ask Paisley what cheers Beatrice up and make a plan next time she's with us."

How is this woman real?

"You're doing that thing again, where you look at me and don't say anything," she whispered.

"You're changing me, Lexi."

Her eyes widened. "How?"

"Today, when I saw your message, all I could think about was that I wanted to be here with you, enjoying the afternoon, and not cooped up in my office, even though I had a million things to do."

"Oh. Now I understand why Paisley acted that way."

I grunted. "Declan gave me shit too. It's been a tough day."

"Why?"

"Because the lawsuit against Gran and Reese is escalating. The owners of the adjacent building are also suing."

"Oh no. Beatrice didn't say anything."

"She doesn't know about this recent development. Neither does Reese."

She pressed her lips together. "Did you learn nothing from keeping things from Beatrice?"

"We're gonna tell them... eventually. Anyway, both Luke and Declan were giving me shit about leaving the office earlier."

She wiggled her eyebrows. "I'll try to lure you out of your cave more often, then."

"Cave?"

"Yep. You're a Neanderthal, and the office is your cave. I just realized that."

"I'll show you how much of a Neanderthal I am."

She bit her lower lip, driving me crazy. I had been dying to kiss her ever since I got here, and now I couldn't help myself anymore. With my last drop of self-restraint, I took her hand, drawing her out of the line. I felt more relaxed just because I was here with her. Nothing about the lawsuit was moving forward, but I felt carefree right now.

She giggled. "Where are we going? What are you doing?"

I didn't say anything, just grunted, keeping her hand firmly in mine as we rounded the back of the hut. It was empty, as I was hoping it would be. Without any warning, I turned her around, pinning her against a wall. "I want to kiss you. I've wanted to do it ever since I saw you this morning. I thought about it all day. Now I can't help myself anymore."

"Then do it," she whispered.

I claimed her mouth the next second, kissing her hard and deep, keeping my hands on her waist and pressing her hips against me, wanting her to feel exactly what she did to me. She made me lose control, and I wasn't used to it. It was something I used to hate, but with her, I couldn't help myself, and I wasn't sure I wanted to.

I deepened the kiss, skimming a hand up the side of her torso and touching her breasts. A groan tore from my chest as I realized she wasn't wearing a bra. She was going to be the end of me. I knew it.

I brought my hand over her nipple. I could barely feel it through the fabric, but I moved my thumb in small circles, knowing it would earn a reaction. I was growing more desperate for her the longer I kissed her, and I wanted her to be just as hungry for me.

When I felt her nipple turn to a hard nub, I groaned, rocking my hips into her.

With a gasp, she pulled back, breathing hard. The contour of her mouth was red. Her eyes were wide. "Oh my God," she whispered. "How can you kiss me so shamelessly?"

"I can't kiss you any other way."

"I'm starting to gather that. But I'm a teacher, Mr. Maxwell. I'm used to being on my best behavior when I'm in public." Her tone was sassy, but she looked around nervously. She was goddamn adorable. She seemed to relax when she realized we really were hidden from view.

"You're not wearing a bra," I said. "And yes, I know one thing has nothing to do with the other. But it's all I can think of."

"Well, no. I had a bathing suit on earlier but changed out of it. The dress has some cups that are sewn inside them. Nothing should be visible." She glanced down at herself, and when she looked up, her blush intensified. "Unless, of course, someone turns me on."

"Not someone," I growled. "Me. Only me. Lexi, you're mine. You're in my thoughts all the time. And I want to be in yours."

Her lips parted. I cupped her face, moving my thumb across the red skin around her lips. We hadn't defined this thing between us. It went past pure physical need. I didn't know how

159

to describe it, but I knew I needed more than stolen kisses here and there and half nights spent together. I knew that with the surety I knew my name was Tate Maxwell. I wanted her just for me for a couple days.

"Let's go somewhere the weekend when Paisley's at Gran's," I said.

Her body went rigid.

Fuck.

"Where?" she mumbled.

Is she buying time to say no? Maybe she didn't want more than this.

"I want to show you the vineyard where I grew up." I felt her soften under my touch, and some of the tension left my shoulders, but I wouldn't relax until she said yes. "Friday to Sunday," I said and could hear my pulse thrum in my ears, the thumping of my heart against my rib cage. I'd never felt anything like this.

"Okay," she whispered, and relief washed over me like my bones were turning liquid. "But on one condition, Mr. Workaholic."

"What?"

"We leave Friday while it's still sunny outside so we can enjoy that afternoon too. So, something like three o'clock?"

There was a delicious challenge in her voice.

"I see. So, first you corrupt me to leave the office at four thirty, and now three?"

She held up a finger. "First, you're the one who decided to leave today. I didn't even suggest it." Bringing the finger to her temple, she tapped her head. "But I'd hoped you would. I probably sent you vacation vibes. And as to corrupting you to leave at three, yes—yes, I am. I get you for a weekend, so I want it to last as long as possible. Whatcha gonna do about it?"

"I'll tell you what I'll do." I tipped my head closer, and she widened her eyes before quickly looking to her right and then the left as if thinking I'd kiss her again. She wasn't far off.

"I'm gonna fulfill that condition. And when we get there, I'm going to lay out *my* conditions."

"Oh, sneaky. First you get me there, *then* you share them with me." Her lips spread in a smile that lit up her face. "We're going to have so much fun."

NINETEEN

Tate

*P*atience wasn't my strongest suit, but waiting for the week to pass was testing me in ways I hadn't experienced before. For the first time since I started Maxwell Wineries, I couldn't wait for the week to be over.

At lunch on Friday, my brothers strode inside my office. Declan came first, followed by Tyler and Luke.

"So, since you're off the hook this weekend, are we going out on the town?" Tyler asked. That was usually what we did when Paisley was with Gran or my parents. "It's off-season," Tyler went on, "so I've got a lot of time, and I'm still in a celebratory mood. Man, winning the Stanley Cup never gets old."

I hadn't told my brothers my plan to go away with Lexi, but this was the right time to do it. I couldn't wait to see their reactions. "I'm going away for the weekend."

Declan cocked a brow. Tyler jerked his head back. Luke frowned as if he wasn't understanding.

"You mean for a break?" Luke asked.

"Yes. With Lexi."

"Where are you going?"

"The vineyard," I replied smoothly. Mom and Dad lived in the city, and we all used the vineyard as a vacation home.

My brothers weren't just stunned now. They were downright shocked. Declan opened his mouth and closed it again. I'd never seen him speechless, and that was saying something. As a lawyer, he always had a reply for everything.

Tyler narrowed his eyes. "Wait, so he took off one afternoon," he said slowly, counting on one finger.

Declan turned to him. "After blowing Luke and me off, I want to point out."

So, he'd found his voice again.

Luke was glancing around with a grin. "No one's jumping to conclusions? No? Just me?"

Tyler grinned. "Oh, I'm not just jumping to conclusions. I'm diving headfirst. Anyone want to hear my theories?"

I groaned, standing up. "I don't have time for this. I have to pick up Lexi."

Declan whistled. "Yeah, you do have time. You don't want to hear us."

I shook my head, announcing, "I'm leaving now. I'll see you all on Monday."

As I drove to Lexi's, I mulled over everything. Nothing else had changed, yet I was in a better mood than ever before.

I pulled the car in front of her building and headed straight up to her apartment. I'd only been here twice before, but I'd been so focused on Lexi that I didn't properly inspect it. This time, I looked around with a critical eye. I liked that the building had a doorman, even though there were always strangers going in and out as they pleased. Did she have a security system?

I took the elevator up to her floor and knocked on the door. She immediately opened it, eyes wide.

"I'm almost done," she said before I even had the chance to say hello. "I need to find my toiletries bag, which I packed with great care, and I have no idea where I put it." She dashed away from the door.

"Hey, I don't even deserve a kiss?" I called after her.

"After I find my toiletry bag," she called from inside the apartment. "Come in. Make yourself comfortable."

I was preparing myself to wait for a while. Whenever Paisley said she needed a bit of time, it took forever. So I went to the living room, sat down, and looked around. It was a comfortable apartment but on the small side. Remembering my security question, I glanced at the front door. It didn't look like she had an alarm.

"I'm done," she said, coming in a few minutes later holding the toiletry bag in front of her like it was a prized possession before stuffing it in the luggage next to the front door. She grinned, looking up at me and making a come-here motion with her finger. "I'll give you that kiss now if you're still up for it."

I strode straight to her, pinning her against the wall. I needed to kiss her just as much as I needed my next breath. I couldn't explain it, but my need for her was buried deep inside me. As soon as I kissed her, I knew it wouldn't be enough. This wasn't going to satisfy me, not even close. I pressed my hips against her, deepening the kiss. My cock stirred, hardening by the second.

Lexi moaned, rolling her hips before pulling her head back, laughing. "Wow. That's what I call a kiss. But I meant what I said, mister. I want us to get to the vineyard while it's still sunny outside so you can give me a tour."

I took a step back, rocking from my heels to my toes, legs wide apart, hands in my pockets. "Okay, then. Let's go."

She looked at me suspiciously.

"If I come any closer, Lexi, I'll kiss you again, and this time, I won't stop at that. I need to make you mine. It's a need I don't understand, but I feel it every single time we're together."

Her breath caught. She pushed a strand of hair behind her ear, taking two steps back. "Okay, then we'd better go before I tempt you too much."

"You're a walking temptation for me, Lexi, no matter what you do." She grinned, moving to grab her bag, but I was there first, clapping my fingers around the handle. "I'll take this."

"Oh, such a gentleman. Thank you. Let me lock up. Now, where is my key? Oh, here it is."

"Do you have a security system?" I asked as we went out of the apartment and she locked the door.

"I think I do."

"What do you mean, you think you do?"

"I've never used it. I have this fancy box next to the door, but I don't know what functions it has."

I groaned. "Lexi, you're killing me. Open the door so I can look at it."

She laughed, and instead of opening the door, she finished locking it before turning around. "You, sir, said it's my job to make sure we get out the door on time. So let's go. You can look at my alarm system another time."

"Lexi, I want you to be safe."

Her eyes softened. "Fine. I promise I will let you look at it at some point, but now we should go. Come on. I'm eager to start the weekend."

I agreed reluctantly, and we took the elevator down. Once we were in the car, she buckled her seat belt and started chattering. "How is Paisley?"

I loved that she thought of my daughter so often. It proved how right she was for me.

"She's over the moon. She loves spending the weekend at Gran's since she's going to be spoiled from early morning until late in the evening."

Lexi laughed softly. "Yes, she will. I'm glad you're aware of that. So, tell me a bit about the house."

"Well, it's been in my family since I was a kid. I grew up there. We rebuilt it a few years ago, so it doesn't look anything like the original house."

"And it's on a vineyard, right?"

"Yes, but that's a small one, one acre. I bought other vineyards in the area that are much bigger."

"And you also have quite a few in California."

I grinned. "You've done your research."

She shrugged. "My favorite wines come from there. So, does anyone live at the house?"

"No, but every once in a while, we go there for a weekend escape too. I have to admit I haven't been in some time."

"What made you decide to, now?"

I reached for her hand, and she put it in mine. "I want to spend time with you, and I want to share with you where I grew up. That house means a lot to me. It inspired me to go into the wine business."

"So, what is the plan for the weekend?" she asked.

"I didn't make one. We can do what you want. I just want to be with you."

She flexed her fingers against mine as she looked out the window, but I caught her smile.

"You certainly know how to turn on the charm and make me feel special," she murmured.

"You are special," I assured her.

She glanced at me out of the corner of her eye before turning around to face me. She didn't say anything.

"What?" I asked.

"I was thinking about things that I'm not gonna share with you."

"Why?"

"To give you a taste of your own medicine."

I burst out laughing. "I'm not doing it to tease you, you know."

"But I am. You have this sexy edge when I challenge you. Makes me want to jump your bones."

"Lexi!" My voice was almost a growl.

"Ooops. Not what I intended to say. Ignore me." Dropping her voice to a whisper, she added, "Just until we get out of the car."

This woman. She was sexy and seductive even when she was trying to be playful.

She was going to be the death of me.

———

WE ARRIVED AN HOUR LATER, and I brought her straight inside the house to give her a tour. The house was dead center in the middle of the vineyards. It had three bedrooms and panoramic views everywhere.

"This is beautiful," she said, looking around the living room.

"The original house was actually up the hill, close to the edge of the property, but I wanted the new one to be in the middle of it all."

"I can see that. It looks beautiful. So serene," she murmured. "Thank you for bringing me here." Turning around, she said, "I saw food in the fridge. I'd love to cook something."

That caught me off guard. I'd expected that she'd want to go to a restaurant. There were several expensive ones around us. "We can go out," I suggested.

"But I want to cook something for you and make a cozy evening for us. Take care of you a bit and hear lots and lots of stories about this place."

Her words tugged at my chest. I liked being here with Lexi, talking to her about the things that were important to me and that meant something. They were all part of who I was. And she seemed to want to hear about it all.

I wrapped my arms around her, kissing her neck. "Funny, I was thinking to do the same: take care of you."

She melted into my embrace. "I love the energy of this space. It's so calm. Is that why you like it here?"

"Partly. It also reminds me of where my love for wine-making began. I have very fond memories of this place."

"Oooh, do tell."

"Later." I kissed the back of her neck, tilting her head so I had better access on one side. Her skin was inviting, her sweet floral scent intoxicating.

Her stomach rumbled, and she chuckled. "I think that's our cue to make dinner. How come there's food here?"

"We have someone who takes care of the house. I asked him to stock the fridge."

I let her go reluctantly. She opened the fridge, taking out chicken and potatoes.

"What if I make pan-fried chicken and baked potatoes?"

"Everything sounds good to me."

"Awesome. You can start by peeling the potatoes. It'll be a team effort," she said with a wink.

"And by pouring your wine."

"Oh, I love it when you talk dirty to me. What kind of wine do you have?"

I wiggled my eyebrows. "Chardonnay."

"Yes, please."

"Your wish is my command."

"You can't keep your mind out of the gutter, can you?" she asked, shimmying her hips.

I instantly stepped right into her space, groping her ass.

"Not if you do that."

"You, sir, are being shameless, and I'm only warning you once. I need food to have energy for any sexy stuff."

"I can do all the work."

She burst out laughing. My ego took a hit.

"Why are you laughing?"

She tilted her head, glancing at me out of the corner of her eye. "I'm going to tell you as soon as you let me finish dinner."

"Fine by me," I said. "I'll grab a bottle of wine and then stay here, making sure your lovely ass doesn't get cold or anything. I love this dress, by the way."

"Why?"

"It gives me access." I fondled it with both hands, making her laugh again.

We had a cellar here too, of course, and I went down to grab a bottle of Chardonnay.

After pouring for both of us, I started peeling the potatoes. Next to me, Lexi kept fidgeting, and it took me a few minutes to realize she was dancing to a song she was humming while she was rinsing the chicken.

This moment was so simple and mundane, but it was so damn perfect. This was how life could be. Coming home to Lexi, cooking dinner with her, and drinking a glass of wine— enjoying *her*.

I couldn't even believe I was entertaining these thoughts. I'd tried the marital life once, and it was anything but bliss. It left me with scars, and worst of all, it left Paisley with them as well. I didn't even have the luxury of dreaming about a life with Lexi, but damn, if that wasn't all I wanted to do right now. For the first time, I could see how a relationship *could* work.

———

DINNER WAS ready one hour later, and we ate at the small table in the kitchen. Lexi usually ate her breakfasts much slower than I did, but tonight, she was scarfing down food, and we were both done at the same time.

"You were hungry. I've never seen you eat so fast," I commented.

"I want to take a walk through the vineyard. I want you to tell me all about its history and why you love it so much."

I couldn't believe she was so interested in my life and my past.

We cleaned up quickly and headed outside. We still had plenty of time for a walk; the sunset was at eight at this time of the year.

I kissed her shoulder, eliciting a giggle from her.

Fucking hell, I loved that sound. And I liked having her here in this place that had always grounded me.

Taking her hand, I led her through the vineyard. It wasn't huge, but you could walk through it for about forty minutes.

"So this is where your love for wine started, huh?" she asked.

"Yes. Dad always loved making wine. It's how we bonded when I was a kid. He didn't produce much. It wasn't something he could do as more than a hobby. He didn't have time."

"The bookstores kept him busy?"

"Yes. He and my uncle ran the company my grandfather started, Maxwell Bookstores. He never loved it, but he felt it would be disrespectful if he gave it up. And it was probably the only thing keeping his brother alive."

"But they sold the chain of bookstores a long time ago, right? And Beatrice kept The Happy Place."

"Yes, exactly. They sold off the company ten years ago. I was in college. They got a good offer, and both of them decided it was time to let go."

"Where is your uncle now?"

"He lives in Europe. Travels a lot."

"How come he's not running The Happy Place?"

"It wasn't a challenge for him. He ran a whole chain before. Besides, the manager is doing a great job. And Reese is around now too."

She looked around curiously. The desire to kiss her slammed into me. Turning her around, I captured her mouth, exploring her like a man possessed. Lexi belonged here, in this place that made me into the man I was today. The vineyard usually grounded me, but tonight, it was more than that.

I wasn't just feeling balanced or grounded. I was whole in a way I'd never, ever been.

And that was all Lexi.

TWENTY

Lexi

_____

"*W*atch it, mister," I whispered when we paused the kiss to breathe. "This is a dangerous kiss."

He smiled against my lips. "Not shameless?"

"It's always shameless, but this is next level. It's a so-hot-we're-gonna-rip-each-other's-clothes-off kiss."

"And what's the problem with that?"

"We're not done with the tour yet." I wiggled out of his grasp, taking a step back just to be safe.

I loved, loved, *loved* finding out more about him. The way he spoke about his family warmed my heart.

"So, you were saying about your dad?" I prompted.

"I watched Dad work all his life at a job he didn't like," he replied as we resumed our walk. "It took a toll on him, and this was his escape. He spent most of his free time working the vineyard and with us. Now he and Mom are retired, so they have time for other hobbies too. I hope I'm making him proud."

My heart gave a mighty sigh. How was this guy even real? The way he treated those around him was something I hadn't seen in anyone else. Looking over his shoulder, he winked at me before kissing my hand. Heat spread through me from the point where his lips touched my skin.

The air was so different here than in Chicago. It was even hotter and more humid.

I checked my phone quickly as we started walking. I'd messaged back and forth with my parents today after they sent me a huge heart emoji—they'd gotten my wire transfer from my latest paycheck. It made me immensely happy that I could help them out.

"I'm sure you are. Did your gran also live with you?"

"Not officially, but she was here a lot when my parents were at work. I learned from them the importance of discipline and grit. They both gave their best to their jobs and to all of us all the time. We had a happy childhood."

There was something in his tone I couldn't quite pinpoint. It was melancholy and something else, perhaps sadness that he wasn't giving Paisley the same. I really hoped he didn't think that, because Paisley was such a happy child.

I had a few kids in my class who didn't have happy home lives. It broke my heart whenever they shared that with me. Sometimes they didn't outright say it, but I could tell they were missing affection by the way they always sought out hugs.

With a jolt, I remembered that school was starting in a month, both for me and Paisley. What would happen then?

"How come none of your brothers are involved in the wine business? Or were they involved in the book business before?"

"No, my parents also encouraged us all to pursue our passions. I think it was because they felt like they couldn't pursue theirs. We all had different interests. Declan was already in law school when they sold the company. Tyler always knew he wanted to play pro hockey. I was the only one with the wine bug. How about your parents?"

"Dad was a carpenter and Mom a teacher, like me. I always wanted to be like her. I liked that she had time in the summer for me, although she did take some odd jobs. A lot of teachers do. Sometimes it's just random work that has nothing to do with teaching or children. This job is a godsend. I'm so happy I found it. No clue how I would've helped my parents otherwise. Camp jobs don't pay as well."

He stopped walking, and I looked up at him questioningly. The look in his eyes was so intense that it startled me. He came closer, putting both my hands on his chest.

"Lexi, anything you need, tell me."

"What? What do you mean?" I asked.

"If your parents need more care, I want to know. I want to help."

My heart thundered in my chest. "Why?"

"Because I care about you, Lexi. You're important to me. I want you to be happy. I'll do anything to make that happen, understood?"

"Thank you," I murmured, too emotional to add anything else. Obviously, I could never do that. Our relationship wasn't at the level where I'd feel comfortable asking for financial help or anything. Honestly, I didn't think I could ever do that, no matter what. It wasn't the Langley way.

Tate was still trapping me with his gaze. Could he tell how much his offer meant to me? Regardless if I'd ever take him up on it, my heart was about to burst with happiness at the thought.

A suspicious sound caught my attention. My heart jumped to my throat. I glanced behind me, inspecting the grass.

"What's wrong?" Tate asked.

"Umm... are there snakes here? I heard something that sounded like slithering."

He laughed, kissing my cheek. "I'll protect you from them."

"Oh my God. That's a yes." I instinctively moved closer and slammed into him. He didn't lose his balance, though. He was rock solid and put a hand on my waist, slipping it down until it was right on my hip.

I glanced down and back at him, chuckling. "That's supposed to protect me?"

"Hell yes. You see a snake, I'll lift you into my arms."

"Hmm. I can't decide if you touching me will distract you or make you react faster."

He leaned into me, brushing his lips to my cheek, sending another wave of heat through me. "I guess we'll find out."

———

Tate

SHE WAS SO DAMN CUTE, looking around at every sound. I kept an arm firmly around her shoulders while talking about the particularities of the wine from this region, but she was only half listening. Rarely did we come across snakes in the vineyard, but we did have a few rodents that ran around.

"Why are you so afraid of snakes?" I asked, steering her back to the house.

She winced. "When I was a kid, I found one under my bed once. We lived in a house on the outskirts of Boston, and my bedroom was on the ground floor. We kept the doors open in summer, and I got the scare of my life. It didn't bite me or anything, but I was afraid to go to sleep for years after that. I kept checking under my bed until I was a teenager. And yes, you can laugh. I know it's silly."

"Fear isn't silly. It's just fear." I brought my mouth to her ear, tugging at her earlobe with my lips. "Don't worry about anything when you're with me."

She giggled, elbowing me slightly as we went inside the house. "Oooh, want to be my protector, Mr. Maxwell?"

"Yes," I informed her, taking off her coat. I wasn't kidding.

I didn't want her to worry. I wanted to know her fears and fight them with her.

I had this burning desire to make her happy.

Wrapping my arms around her from behind, I walked with her into the living room, burying my face in her hair.

"You smell delicious," I murmured.

"Tate…," she whispered as I trailed my lips from her earlobe down her neck.

"I want you. All the time."

She giggled, but I felt her body shake in my arms. I was turning her on. "I see. So, this is a sexcapade weekend, not just to relax."

"We can do both. I have confidence in us."

She giggled again, smacking my thigh. "So do I."

I was starved for her. I needed to make her mine, and I was satisfied that we finally had a whole weekend stretching ahead of us and didn't have to rush. "I can take my time to explore you now," I whispered in her ear, kissing down her neck. "I can make you come as many times as I want."

She gasped, and I felt the muscles of her belly clench.

I trailed my fingers down her abs. "With my fingers, my mouth, and my cock."

She moaned, bracing her hands on my shoulders, pulling back. I looked her in the eyes before leaning in to kiss her. The kiss unleashed something inside me. Despite having the whole weekend ahead of us, I wanted her immediately. I needed to be inside her right now. I couldn't wait any longer.

Taking her hand, I led her to the master bedroom on the ground floor and pressed her against the door, kissing her deep and wet and long until I felt her legs shake. She rolled her hips back and forth against my leg, needing the friction.

I led her farther inside the room, taking off her short blue dress. She was wearing black lace panties, and it was driving me crazy. I traced the contour of her bra straps with my thumbs and then curved my hands around the edges of the cups. She groaned as if the skin-on-skin contact was too much, even though I'd barely started. Leaning down, I trailed my mouth along where fabric met skin, keeping my hands on her thighs and buttocks.

She ran a hand through my hair, tugging at it. "Tate, please," she whispered. "I need you."

Hearing her say my name in that tone made my control snap. I yanked her panties down. She gasped before stepping out of them. I trailed my hand between her thighs and up to her pussy. A shock of pleasure went through me when I realized she was wet. Kissing her mouth, I moved my fingers in a circle over her sensitive spot, feeling her come apart with every passing second. The need to bring her pleasure was stronger than anything else, even the instinct to chase my own satisfaction. She gasped, rocking against my hand while she fumbled behind her back. I realized she was unclasping her bra. She let it drop to the floor, and I brought my mouth to one of her nipples, sucking it in.

"Tate... Tate, oh, Tate," she chanted while I worked her clit with my hand and her nipple with my lips. I was holding her firmly by her ass and smiled against her breasts when I felt all her muscles contract. She came apart so spectacularly that I barely fought the instinct to step back just to watch her succumb to the pleasure. But I moved my fingers over her clit until her shudders subsided. Her body was so soft now. Looking up, I saw her eyes were soft too.

"That was amazing," she whispered.

I laid her on the bed, taking my clothes off at record speed before pushing her farther into the middle of the mattress and kissing her inner thigh.

"That was the first one," I said against her skin. She shuddered. I skimmed my thumb over her clit, looking up at her.

"The one I gave you with my fingers. Now I want to feel you explode on my tongue."

Her legs clenched as if on instinct, but I pressed them back open, kissing up her inner thigh until I reached her pussy. I could thrust inside her now—she was so wet that she was definitely ready—but I wanted to feel her pleasure against my mouth.

The second I put my tongue on her sensitive flesh, she cried out my name, pulling the sheets with her fists. Her back arched. Fuck, she was beautiful. So sensitive, so ready for everything I wanted to give her.

I circled her clit with the tip of my tongue, only briefly touching it at first, watching her squirm and flinch as if the torture was too much. She straightened out one leg, parting her thighs even wider and allowing me better access. I took a condom from the side of my bed where I'd put them when we arrived and dropped it on the mattress next to us.

I moved my hands over her thighs and her upper body, wanting to touch as much of her as possible, to feel the pleasure coil through her body. I knew she was close; I felt a slight shudder in her legs. She was moving her hips back and forth, and I followed her rhythm, wanting to give her exactly what she needed.

This time, I had my eyes on her when she came apart, thrashing on the bed and moving her head from one side to the other. She was looking for a pillow, but they were farther up by the headboard. She couldn't muffle her cries, and I heard them in all their glory.

I was hard before, but now my erection was almost painful. Moving up her body, I sheathed my cock with the condom. She was flushed and so damn beautiful. I hovered over her, nudging her clit with the tip of my cock before pulling back a bit and turning her around.

Her eyes were wide as she lay against the mattress. I spread her legs and pushed inside her, feeling her tightness adjust to accept me.

"Fuuuuck," I exclaimed, dropping my head back. I was going to lose my mind. She was pulsing around me and felt so damn good that I could barely breathe. I was sure I could come like that, just feeling her inner muscles clench around me, but I'd promised her three orgasms, so I was going to give them to her.

I kissed her back while I rocked my hips, exploring a side of her I hadn't before, moving my mouth downward near her spine and then back up on her shoulder blades. The sound of our bodies slapping against each other filled the room between her moans. She gave herself to me with an abandon I hadn't seen in her before. She was putty in my hands, her body soft from the two orgasms but still filled with tension, demanding another release. She thrashed and cried out my name, spurring my need to hear her. I needed to make her come right now or I'd explode inside her before she reached another climax.

I brought a hand to her pussy, skimming three fingers over her clit. She squeezed her inner muscles so tight that she nearly pushed me out.

I smiled against her skin. "Let go, beautiful," I said.

"I don't think I can take it anymore," she whispered.

"Yes, you can. I promise you fucking can. Give me that third orgasm, Lexi. I want to hear you. I want to feel you come around my cock."

My words had the exact effect I wanted. I felt the moment her climax exploded through her. She was so damn beautiful I couldn't look away. Her back arched, her fingers gripping the sheets, her toes curled, and she pushed her pelvis back into me, bringing a hand over mine on her clit, pressing down and intensifying the sensation.

The sight of her like this, wild with pleasure and full of me, spurred my own orgasm, and I came so hard that I couldn't

LAYLA HAGEN

even breathe. For a few seconds, my vision blurred and I couldn't even see. The air caught in my throat. My lungs were on fucking fire. All my muscles seemed to be spasming at once.

I toppled us both onto the bed. Lexi was lying on her belly, ass up on display, her feet up in the air. Sitting on one side, I trailed my fingers up and down her back and over that gorgeous curve of her ass.

"You, sir, have excellent skills," she said in a teasing tone. "I can't make up my mind which orgasm was best."

Laughter burst out of me. "You're rating the orgasms?"

"I'm trying to, but I think I might need a few more to make up my mind."

I leaned in closer. "My pleasure. We have all weekend ahead of us."

Even as I was saying it, I was already dreading Sunday evening. I didn't want our time together to end.

TWENTY-ONE

Lexi
_____

*T*he next morning, I woke up to the sound of a sexy voice.

"Morning, sleepyhead."

I blinked my eyes open slowly. The room was inundated with light. Tate was sitting at the edge of the bed, looking so sinfully hot that he simply jolted me awake.

Oh yeah. Who needs coffee when I have this sexy guy? I wondered if I could convince him to be my own personal alarm clock every morning.

"Hell yes," he said.

I winced. "Did I say that out loud?"

He grinned. "Yes, you did."

"Oh, shucks. Please ignore me. I'm too groggy."

"That means everything you say is true."

I blinked several times, pushing myself up on my elbows. "When did you wake up?"

"An hour ago."

"Wow. I didn't hear you."

"You were sleeping soundly. You're not an early riser, are you?"

"I need coffee. Until I have at least one cup, I don't even notice anything around me."

He smirked. "Clearly."

I narrowed my eyes, not really understanding, and followed his gaze to a spot next to me.

I gasped. He'd brought breakfast. A wooden tray lay in the middle of the bed, and I saw ham and cheese and a hard-boiled egg along with sliced avocado and tomatoes.

"Wow. Oh my God. This was here before?" I asked unnecessarily.

"Of course it was. Clearly you didn't notice it."

"Hey, I did notice you," I said, exaggeratedly blinking, trying to bat my eyelashes. I wasn't sure it was working. I probably looked ridiculous.

"Fuck, you're cute." He leaned in and kissed my forehead.

He brought the tray next to me. We split everything, except the hard-boiled egg, which I ate all by myself.

"You are the greatest guy. I like everything about you. How can I not find even one fault?" I mumbled, putting the tray back to one side.

"Not even one?" His tone was playful, but something in his gaze told me he was doubting my words.

"Oh yeah."

"I have scars, Lexi."

His wife had cheated on him and wasn't a big part of their daughter's life. Of course he had scars. I'd have plenty if that happened to me.

"You told me that. But I happen to like those too."

"You do?"

I nodded, trailing my fingers up his arm. I was startled by the deep vulnerability in his gaze. I wanted to mend those scars. If I was really honest with myself, I was already falling for this amazing man. And that was frightening because this was new, and I wasn't sure what the start of the school year would bring. We'd never spoken about the after.

Was there going to be an after?

But I didn't have to figure that all out now. I just had to drink enough coffee to spur my neurons into working.

I kept my voice playful as I said, "You're like one of those superheroes. They all have scars, you know?"

"Superheroes? That's your point of reference?"

"You know what I mean."

"Not really, but if it makes sense to you, I'm good." He chuckled, flashing me a genuine smile that reached his beautiful eyes.

I shimmied on the bed, doing a small happy dance. I was getting through to him, even though I was still half asleep. What better way to start the day?

"And I came up with the perfect way to describe you. And just so you know, I usually don't have a single ounce of inspiration in the morning."

"I inspire you?"

"Absolutely."

"So, how would you describe me?"

Rolling my shoulders back, I exclaimed proudly, "Fantastic Tate."

His eyes bulged, and he pressed his lips together.

I pointed at him. "What are you doing?"

"Nothing." His answer came too quickly. I was even more suspicious now.

"I work with kids. I'm an expert at interpreting nonverbal cues. You're holding back a reaction. Out with it."

"Lexi, that's a sucky way to describe me."

I blinked, taken aback, considering it. "Okay, maybe. I'll drink coffee and think some more."

He burst out laughing so wholeheartedly that I couldn't

help but join him. Hey, this was a win. I'd gotten him to laugh at the crack of dawn, shitty description and all.

The mattress caved as he shifted his weight. For a split second, I thought he wanted to grab food. Nope, he just wanted to grab me. He pinned me to the mattress, pushing my thighs wide apart with his knees.

"You're rewarding me for coming up with *fantastic*?" I teased, rolling my hips into him.

He groaned, kissing down my chest. Pushing up my pink pajama top, he trailed his mouth around my navel. At the same time, he skimmed his fingers up my inner thigh.

"I want—" he began but stopped midsentence. At first, I didn't realize why, but then I heard sounds from the living room.

Someone was inside.

Tate frowned, immediately rising to his feet.

"What's going on?" I asked.

A masculine voice chuckled from the living room, and a female voice said, "Someone must've aired the place out. It's not stuffy."

Tate groaned. "My parents are here."

Holy shit.

I was instantly awake. Adrenaline spiked my blood. I leaped off the bed, running a hand through my hair.

"What do you mean, your parents are here?"

"We take turns coming here, and there was nothing on the calendar. They probably assumed it was vacant."

My chest heaved up and down. Sweat dotted my forehead. I took a mental inventory of myself. Yeah, I was a sleepy mess. No way could I meet them like this.

"Can you keep them occupied and give me a few minutes?" I asked.

Tate chuckled. "Lexi, it's gonna be fine. Don't stress out."

I made a strangled sound low in my throat. "It usually takes me forever to get ready."

He stepped closer, cupping my face in his hands.

"Lexi. Relax."

"Go, go," I urged. "Before they barge in here and see me like this. They'll know what we've been doing for sure and… and… oh my God! And I'm Paisley's *nanny*!"

He flashed me a smile before dropping his hands.

"Lexi, you're making too much out of this." He tried to comfort me, but I shooed him toward the door.

After he went out in the living room, I darted to the bathroom. I was in panic mode. I glanced from the shower to the bathtub and decided to forgo the shower altogether. It would take me too long, and I—

No, damn it. I *had* to shower.

I went into the stall and cleaned up very quickly. No way was I going to wash my hair. That always took forever. I'd put it up; no one would ever know.

Stepping out of the shower, I brushed my teeth and clumsily applied foundation. *Oh my God. Oh my God. His parents are here.*

I knew why this had me so out of sorts. It was because I felt like a kid caught doing something wrong at camp, except we weren't doing anything wrong. Still, something about meeting his parents had me all in knots.

I put on a long green dress and pulled my hair into a messy ponytail. I hoped it would look bohemian to them, because I couldn't unknot my hair without washing it in the morning.

I groaned, dropping my chin to my chest. *The day I meet Tate's parents, I'm a total mess.* But I couldn't make it any better, so I decided to face the music.

I cracked the door open. The voices were muffled and far away, so I supposed they were in the living room. I hurried down the corridor, my stomach knotting even more.

I am Lexi, hear me roar.

"There she is," a woman exclaimed. I assumed she was his mother. Tate looked a lot like her, with those intense eyes and chocolate-colored hair, but he got his height and build from his dad. He was smiling brilliantly, the way he did when he was around his daughter.

"Lexi, these are my parents, Emmett and Lena. Mom, Dad, meet Lexi."

"Good morning," I said, moving to them and shaking their hands. I self-consciously patted my head, feeling the knots in my hair. Oh my God, I was a mess.

Tate was looking at me with amusement in his eyes.

"We're so sorry for imposing," Lena said, sounding a little formal to me. "We had no idea there was someone here."

"We checked the family calendar. We have this Google log where everyone puts their name if they come here. It was empty," Emmett replied.

Why were they apologizing to me? This was their place. They were the Maxwells, for heaven's sake.

Oh crap, why did I have to remember that? My nervousness escalated tenfold.

"Yeah, my bad," Tate exclaimed. " I completely forgot about it."

"That's because you haven't been here in almost a year. Even though you love this place," Lena said.

Tate shrugged. "I'm here now."

"Well, we're glad you're here, son, and we won't keep you two any longer." Emmett turned to his wife and said, "Lena, let's head back to the city."

"What? No, no, no," I said hastily, feeling a bit like the intruder. "Why leave? You came here for a getaway—"

Lena shook her head. "Darling, we just got back from our vacation. We came here to check if everything was okay. I know we have a caretaker, but I don't like leaving this place unattended for too long. And the last time someone was here was months ago."

"Why don't you stay for lunch?" I asked, looking at Tate for confirmation. I couldn't have them leaving when this was *their* place.

He nodded. "That's a good idea."

I let out a sigh of relief. I had been afraid I was overstepping by asking his parents to spend some time with us.

"Yes, let's do that," Lena said. "That way, you and I can talk a bit, Lexi. All I've heard so far is secondhand information from Beatrice."

The tips of my ears felt hot. They *had* talked about me. Shouldn't have been a surprise, of course. My nerves accelerated. Tate seemed to sense my apprehension and stepped in. "Mom, don't scare Lexi away. Let's have lunch."

"Tate! I would never do such a thing." Looking at me, she added, "I don't think my son and granddaughter have ever been in better hands, Lexi. You have no complaints from me."

As we all walked into the kitchen, my fears subsided a bit. And then when she cheerily said, "What shall we have? Put us to good use, Lexi," I knew everything would be all right.

Looking in the fridge, we found ingredients for roast beef and mashed potatoes. It was only ten o'clock, but roast beef needed time in the oven, so we started cooking lunch right away.

Lena was peeling potatoes. I was washing thyme and rosemary. Tate was crushing garlic while his dad oiled the beef. We all worked around the kitchen island, and the collaborative effort was so coordinated that it was obvious they'd done it before.

"You cook together often?" I asked no one in particular.

"When the kids were young, we did almost all the time. There's no other way to feed so many people," Lena said. "We made it a point to be home at dinner, but we often came late, so we only had time to whip something up quickly. Dinner with the kids was a tradition. I called it tornado time because all the kids had an energy boost in the evening, driving us crazy."

I glanced at Tate. That explained why he wanted to cook dinner for Paisley as often as possible. I focused on chopping the herbs, smiling to myself.

It was easy to be around Lena and Emmett. They chatted about wine and a special collection Maxwell Wineries was bringing out this year. To my astonishment, I relaxed pretty quickly. Tate's parents had welcomed me with open arms, making me feel like I was at home. Since leaving for college, I'd never felt like I belonged anywhere—until now.

"Okay, nothing more for us to do," Lena said once the beef was in the oven. "Who wants to take a walk through the vineyard?"

I nodded while Tate and Emmett answered, "Yes," at the same time.

With one last look at the oven, we all headed outside. The air was even chillier than last night, but I didn't want a jacket as the sun was keeping me warm. Lena led the way, and I realized she and I were probably going to walk alone because Tate and Emmett had already stopped, inspecting the new crop.

"Those two always get like this when we're here. They can talk about wine for hours," Lena said, looking at the two of them fondly.

"It's awesome that they have this in common."

"They've always bonded over it. Emmett was over the moon to share his passion with one of the kids, and Tate was always interested. He's got a talent for finding common ground with anyone. And he's always been so full of energy. I'm not sure where he gets it from. He used to wake up the earliest and was the last to go to bed."

"So before, when you meant that everyone had a burst of energy at dinner, you actually meant Tate?"

She chuckled, and something in her facial expression reminded me of Tate. "Mostly, but Tyler and Luke were also balls of energy. Luke was always the one with the bright ideas. He had no problem talking Tyler and Tate into his shenanigans. Luckily, Declan balanced them out. Sam was caught in the middle all the time, and Travis changed sides according to whatever he was up to at that moment."

"And Reese and Kimberly? Beatrice told me they were here a lot."

"Those two were a godsend. The first few years after they lost their mom was hard, especially because my brother-in-law wasn't in a good place. Poor man was brokenhearted. Reese and Kimberly were here daily after school for years. Kimberly resembled Declan the most. And Reese is a lot like Tate. They're both fierce and strong, but they also hold themselves to high standards."

"What do you mean?" I asked as we slowly started to move through the vineyards.

"Tate has been very hard on himself since the divorce."

"I wondered about that."

"I'm afraid he thinks that happiness isn't meant for him anymore. That it's not in his grasp. Maybe even that he doesn't deserve it."

My heart sighed at that. I'd wondered if that might be the case but questioned how an amazing man like him could think that.

Lena winked at me. "But I think you're starting to change his perspective."

"Really?" I responded, not sure what else to say.

"Yes. The fact that you're here, that he brought you here, speaks volumes. And Beatrice told me that he's left work early a couple times to be with you."

"Oh, he likes spending time with Paisley," I said, because that sounded like a reasonable explanation.

The corners of her lips twitched. "He always did, but until you, he never came home from work early."

Lena's words stirred something powerful inside my chest. Hmm… so he really was changing his old ways because of me? That made me *so* happy.

"What are you two gossiping about?" Tate asked, startling me. He and Emmett were heading toward us with quick strides.

"About you two, of course," Lena replied in a sassy tone. "I thought you were going to let us walk alone."

"No can do." Tate came up next to me, putting an arm around my shoulders. "Need to protect Lexi here from snakes and all that."

"All what?"

Lena chuckled as she and Emmett started walking a few feet in front of us.

Amusement danced in Tate's gaze. I narrowed my eyes, inspecting him. "You're keeping something from me. What other animals are around?"

"Nothing I can't protect you from."

I pinched his shoulder. "Tate! I'd almost forgotten about the snakes until you brought them up."

"Why don't I kiss you until you forget about them again? And everything else?"

Oh my God. His gaze was so intense that there was no doubt he meant it. Heat skittered along my skin, especially between my thighs.

"And you say that with a straight face when your parents are only a few feet away. You truly are shameless. In fact, I think I've found a better description. Forget Fantastic Tate. You're just Shameless Tate."

TWENTY-TWO

Tate

---

*E*ven after returning to the office the following week, I couldn't stop thinking about our outing. Being with Lexi out in the vineyard had been incredible. She was incredible. The way she seemed to embrace me, scars and all, was more than I expected. I was itching to do something for her, like lift the burden of her parents' medical expenses off her shoulders—anything that could make her life better. But for now, I wanted to do something for her that showed I cared for her.

On Friday, I was still out of ideas, so I decided to call my mother while I went to pick up Paisley from a playdate. Mom answered immediately.

"Honey, what a surprise. You're calling during your work hours. You never do that."

"I'm actually leaving the office. I'm picking up Paisley. She, Lexi, and I are going to watch a movie." Mom said nothing to that, which was suspicious, but I continued anyway. "I have a personal question that keeps nagging at me."

"I'm listening."

"I want to do something for Lexi, something meaningful, and I'm out of ideas."

"And by the way, you're on loudspeaker," Mom said.

I groaned. "Really? You couldn't have told me that two seconds ago?"

"We asked her not to," Tyler said.

"Who else is there?" I inquired.

"I am," came Reese's voice.

"And I'm here too," Travis added.

I groaned. "Great."

"I have so many ideas," Tyler said in his typical overexcited voice. "One: expensive gifts. Two: more expensive gifts."

"Really? That's your suggestion?" I asked sardonically. *Wait… does he have someone in his life?* Last I knew, my brother was enjoying the perks of being a star hockey player. Had that changed?

"Well, that's my advice. Take it or leave it. Though that might work for me because I'm so good-looking."

"And humble," Mom teased.

"Oh, Tyler. That's such bullshit. It doesn't matter how expensive they are. Do something romantic," Reese added.

"Thanks, Reese. Do you have anything more practical?" I asked.

"Well, no. I mean, I do, but if I voice them all, you'll think I'm crazy."

"We think that regardless," Travis said conversationally. "But we love you anyway."

"Yes, but there are several types of crazy," Reese said, "like 'Oh, she's crazy but I'll go with it,' or 'She's crazy. Let's call the police,' and if I tell you all my ideas, I think it will be the latter."

Everyone burst out laughing.

"Travis, do you have any ideas? Everyone pitched in anyway, even without my asking."

"I'm not the right person to ask. For the past three years, I've just had time for one-night stands. Oh fu—Chuck. Sorry, Mom."

Mom groaned. I could practically see her rolling her eyes.

"I'll pretend I've heard nothing," she said.

"Anyway," Travis cut back in, "I vote to listen to Reese. She always has good ideas, unlike others in the family."

And by others, he clearly meant Tyler.

"Hey, don't diss it until you try it," Tyler said in a smug tone. "You know my motto. I'll try everything once, and the good things twice."

"That motto's gotten you into trouble a lot of times, young man," Mom said sternly.

"Yes, but you know me. I like to focus on the good things," Tyler pointed out.

That was true.

"Why are all of you together so early on a weekday?" I asked.

"Well, I just finalized the sale," Travis said lazily.

"Congratulations, man. That's epic!"

"And I thought I'd treat the ladies to a dinner out in the city," he went on.

"And me. There can't be a party without me," Tyler added. "Someone's got to spice things up."

"Talking about parties, I am actually going to throw a huge one next week, and everyone's invited. I'm sorry for the short notice, but I've been too focused on the sale until now."

"No problem, man. Send me the details," I said. And all of a sudden, I had an idea about what to do.

———

BY THE TIME I picked up Paisley from her playdate, I had a plan in mind.

"Dad, where is Lexi?" she asked first thing as she secured her seat belt.

"She's meeting us directly at the shopping center. She went to take your favorite dress for dry cleaning, remember? But we'll all watch the movie together."

"I changed my mind. Can we go shopping instead?"

I groaned. Why didn't I foresee this?

"I thought you wanted to see that robot film. What happened to that? And you always say shopping with me is frustrating," I reminded her, glancing at her in the rearview mirror. She was in the back, as usual, because it was safer.

"But Lexi will be with us too."

"True." I hesitated a moment. "Paisley, you like Lexi, right?"

"Yes, Daddy. A lot. Lexi told me it doesn't feel like work when she's with me. That she really likes me and we're friends. And she's so pretty, isn't she, Dad?"

"Yes, she is," I agreed.

Paisley narrowed her eyes, looking at me intently without saying anything. I focused on the traffic as we approached the parking lot of the shopping center. My daughter was silent until we entered the underground garage.

"Dad, do you know what kissing is?" Paisley asked as I parked. I nearly bumped into the car in front of us.

My eyes bulged as I wondered where this was coming from.

"What?" I said, looking straight at her in the mirror. "Why are you asking?"

She shrugged. "No reason."

What the hell? There was always a reason.

Once I parked the car and turned off the ignition, I turned to look straight at my daughter.

"Do *you* know what kissing is?" I asked her.

She rolled her eyes. "Obviously."

"You're nine years old," I exclaimed.

"Yes, I'm nine years old, not nine months. Some girls in my class have a boyfriend."

"Boyfriend?" I sputtered.

Why didn't Lexi tell me anything about this?

This was wrong. A boyfriend at nine years old? What was happening with the world? I was completely out of my depth in this conversation.

My mind raced back to what Lexi told me about boys. It was a good thing we were meeting her, because I needed her advice on this. I felt the irrational need to lock my daughter in her room until she turned eighteen, but somehow, I didn't think that was the answer.

The shopping center was extremely crowded, but luckily Paisley only loved one shop and we went straight there. Typically she tried on one hundred outfits and chose five. I dreaded the experience usually, but Lexi joining us made it better by a factor of one million.

I took out my phone, messaging her.

Tate: (Im)patiently waiting for you. We're at Paisley's favorite store…

Lexi: I'm on my way.

Tate: Since we're clearly not going to the movie, do you want to have dinner with us?

Lexi: Are you trying to lure me back to the house for "a glass of wine"?

I chuckled, because that was the code I used to convince her to stay over every evening after Paisley went to bed this past week.

Tate: Yes.

Lexi: Was that DIRTY TALK? Because my panties combusted. Spontaneously. Of their own accord.

I grinned at the phone. Since our trip last weekend, I'd been looking forward to every moment I could spend with her, but the few hours after Paisley went to bed weren't nearly enough. I wanted to hijack *all* her time.

———

Lexi

WHEN I ARRIVED, Tate was sitting in an armchair looking pretty miserable. I didn't blame him. This store was all about teenage life, from the weird music to the weirder outfits, but it was a hit with many kids Paisley's age.

Even sitting in that ridiculous pink armchair, he looked sexy as hell, as usual. He was wearing jeans and a polo shirt, and I wholeheartedly approved of the outfit. If I wasn't mistaken, they were his sex-bomb jeans. Yeah, I had a ranking of his jeans, and these were at the top of the list.

His expression suddenly lit up when he noticed me. I had flutters in my belly, and my already combusting panties seemed to vanish into thin air.

Paisley came out of the dressing room a second later, essentially throwing an ice bucket over me.

She noticed me right away and squealed, "Lexi, you're here! Please help me. Dad isn't even paying attention."

"Yes, I am!" Tate said, sounding indignant.

Paisley rolled her eyes. "Dad, you looked right through me the past four dresses."

I laughed, glancing between the two of them. "Well, I think this dress looks great on you, Paisley. The one thing I don't really like is the color. This shade of yellow is too pale. Do you have it in any other colors?"

"Yes, I also have it in pink."

"Okay. Let's see it. You want me to come inside and help you?"

"No, I'm okay."

"All right, I'll wait right here," I replied, smiling at her display of maturity.

Going back to the changing room, she drew the curtain. I remembered being her age and not wanting anyone to see my body. In a few years, she was going to need a bra. I wondered if Tate or one of his cousins was going to take her, or maybe the future nanny.

A lump suddenly settled in my throat. I wanted to be there for every milestone.

Tate was right behind me the next second, putting an arm around my waist and kissing my cheek.

"Hello, beautiful," he whispered in my ear. Hmm… his voice had a naughty edge that turned my skin to goose bumps. "Thank you for coming to my rescue."

I turned around, putting my hands on his arms and feeling those hard muscles under my fingers. "Any time. I love shopping. How did she manage to drag you here?"

"Ambushed me."

"Clever."

He touched my bare shoulder with his fingertips. An unexpected wave of heat shot through me.

"Dad!" Paisley exclaimed, startling both of us.

Holy shit! She was standing right next to us.

I instantly let my hands drop, taking a step back. My pulse quickened.

Her eyes widened, looking from me to Tate, who seemed as taken aback as I was.

Shit, shit, shit. I had no clue if he ever intended to tell her about us, but this wasn't the best way for her to find out.

I bit my lip, wondering if I should try to distract her. Did he want her to know? I sucked in a breath, waiting for his reply.

"Paisley, Lexi and I would like to tell you something." He cleared his throat, stepping closer to me. My pulse calmed down a bit. "Remember when you asked me a while ago if I ever wanted a lady in my life? Well, Lexi and I are dating. We're—"

"Yes! Yes! Yes!" Paisley's face exploded in a grin. She clapped her hands and then started shimmying her hips, the way I did when I was happy about something. Then she hugged Tate around his middle, staring up at him before looking at me.

"I'm going back to try more dresses."

She did a little dance as she went back into the changing room. She'd even forgotten to ask our opinion on the dress she had on.

Tate trained his gaze on me, and the air between us instantly charged. He took me a few feet away from the dressing room to the back of the store before stepping right into my personal space, tilting my chin up.

"Are you okay?" he asked.

I nodded. "Yes. Why?"

"We never spoke about telling Paisley."

"It was your call, Tate. She's your daughter. I... didn't even know if you wanted to tell her at all."

"Fuck yes, I did." His gaze intensified. "For weeks, it's all I've been thinking about."

Oh man. Those flutters in my belly were out of control now. And so was my grin.

"Really?" I definitely felt like dancing, but we were in a store, so I stayed put.

When Tate brought his hands to my waist, I felt the touch of his fingers, even through my cotton dress.

"Yes, Lexi. You're in my life, and I want everyone to know it. I was serious when I said I want you all the time. And I don't mean in bed. I like spending time with you. Pouring you wine in the evening. Watching you pretend to look for the TV remote when you're raiding the stash of chocolate."

"I don't do that *every* evening," I countered, even though I kind of did. And he'd noticed!

"Today, I wasn't thrilled about coming to this place, but knowing you were going to be here made everything better."

I couldn't help myself and shimmied a bit. "Oh, good. I like this arrangement. I give my opinion to Paisley. You make me swoon and fan myself when she's in the changing room. Everyone's happy."

I wasn't just happy. I was over the moon.

He wanted Paisley to know.

Even though his parents and siblings knew about us, sharing this with his daughter meant so much more.

When Paisley called my name, I nodded toward the changing room. We headed that direction, and when we were within earshot, I said, "I'm here."

"I don't like the pink one, Lexi," Paisley called from inside the changing room, "but they also have one in green."

"I can go get it for you," I said. "Where is it?"

"Right next to the entrance."

"I'll be right back," I said.

Tate groaned, but I slapped his hand, and he reluctantly dropped it from my waist.

I went to the rack with clothes near the entrance and quickly found the green version of the dress Paisley was trying on. When I returned, the sales associate was there as well, checking in with her through the curtain.

"No, it's okay. Lexi is bringing me the dress," Paisley was saying.

"Okay." She stepped back, looking at me and smiling at the dress. "I think that one is going to look great with her eyes."

"I think so too," I said. "I'm her nanny, and we talk about clothes and fashion a lot." I gave Paisley the dress, poking my head inside. "You want me to take anything back?"

"No, I'm good," Paisley said, pushing me back out.

When I turned around, to my astonishment, the sales associate was flirting with Tate, who was standing next to the pink armchair. She was playing with her hair between her fingers and looking up at him between her eyelashes.

"Anything you and your daughter need, let me know."

"We're good," Tate said, coming up to me. A second later, he put an arm around my shoulder, kissing my temple. "Lexi's a genius when it comes to finding clothes for Paisley, but we'll let you know if we need any help."

Her smile dropped. She looked at me, eyes cold. "Right, okay. I'll wait at the front, at the cash register." She stepped away quickly, but Tate still didn't let go of me.

"I can't believe I turned my back once and someone's already flirting with you." I knew I sounded jealous, but damn, she moved fast. Of course, with the way Tate looked, it was no surprise.

"Why did you tell her you were the nanny? You know you're more than that, Lexi. I'm more than happy to tell everyone that we're together." He turned me around, looking straight at my mouth. "*Everyone*, Lexi."

"But I *am* Paisley's nanny."

"If you want, I'll fire you now, just so we're clear." Amusement danced in his eyes. "You're also my girlfriend."

Oh man. I was swooning again.

"I don't want you to fire me. I love the job. But we probably should talk about you paying me. It doesn't feel right if I'm your girlfriend."

He stared at me incredulously. "You're one of a kind. We can talk about that another time. Now, I have an idea."

"Do tell."

"My brother Travis announced that he's throwing a party in two weeks."

"Oh, I haven't met him yet. It's his birthday?"

"No. He finalized the sale of his tech startup, and he wants to celebrate 'in style,' as he calls it. I want you there, with me."

"Sure. Will there be any more kids besides Paisley? I can probably watch about six or seven."

He pressed a thumb at the corner of my mouth.

"Stop that, Lexi. You're not going as Paisley's nanny. I want you to go there with me as my date, my woman. I told you I want everyone to know. I mean, my family knows. But I want us to go there together."

Something crept up inside me, filling me with a burst of joy. The impulse to shimmy my hips and break out in a dance right here in the store was stronger than ever.

"Together," I repeated, then murmured, "Tate, I would love to." I couldn't deny it. My feelings for him were deepening. And with that, the chances of getting heartbroken were also growing, because I knew Tate still hadn't healed from his divorce.

"Now, keep your hands to yourself while I help Paisley, mister."

He grinned. "Your wish is my command."

"Really?"

"For now."

I raised a brow. "Oh, you have ulterior motives? Care to share? Is it part of your plan to convince me to come home with you?"

"Yes."

"Ha! You don't have to work too much to sell me on that. You and Paisley are there. And the not-so-secret stash of excellent chocolate too."

TWENTY-THREE

Lexi

_____

Two weeks later, on Saturday afternoon, we arrived late to the party. Paisley wanted an intricate braid, and I fell down the YouTube rabbit hole searching for the right twist. Then she changed her outfit from a white dress to crop pants and a tee. I was wearing a simple cotton summer dress in a peach color. We also packed an overnight bag for Paisley because she was spending the night with her grandparents. One thing led to another, and then Tate had to chase us out of the house.

My phone beeped as we entered the yard. I had messages from Jenny, Ella, and Mom. I'd sent everyone a pic of me, Paisley, and Tate.

Jenny: Girl, that is a very dreamy pic.

Ella: Wow. I'm jealous.

Mom: You three look wonderful. Like a small family.

My heart tugged at that.

I'd spent a few nights at the house ever since we told Paisley we were dating, and she was starting to tell everyone I was her dad's girlfriend, her best friend, *and* her roommate. It was adorable how much she'd embraced me. It made my heart happy, but I couldn't deny that I was still on edge whenever she talked about her first day of school, which was in two weeks.

Tate and I still hadn't talked about what was going to happen once school started.

Travis rented an entire restaurant at the lake for his party. I'd never been on this section of the lake. The restaurant was nestled between huge oak trees, and the garden was large and full of all sorts of flowers in bloom. It looked heavenly. The weather was hot and so humid that my hair was already curly, but the breeze between the trees was pleasant. It felt amazing against my skin.

I was on pins and needles because this was the first time I was at a family event strictly as Tate's girlfriend and not Paisley's nanny. In fact, that description hadn't been used after me calling myself nanny at the store, making me feel even more a part of this family than I'd ever hoped for.

I couldn't help but smile when Paisley ran off to Lena the second she saw her.

Tate whispered conspiratorially, "I'll bet anything we won't even see her until the party ends. It's the same every time Mom and Dad are around."

"Hey, she missed them. They were gone for quite some time."

"True."

"Where is Beatrice?" I asked, not seeing her anywhere.

"She's got a cold. Mom and Dad checked on her this morning."

"Oh, okay. Poor Beatrice. I'm sure she didn't want to miss this."

"It's not serious, but Dad thought it best that she rest up." He grabbed my hand. "Come on. I want to introduce you to Travis. And then to Sam and Kimberly. They both flew in for the party."

I knew Kimberly and Sam were both overseas, working. They'd flown in for the occasion? Wow, that was sweet.

"I can't wait." The three of them were the only ones I hadn't met yet.

I racked my brain, trying to remember the last time I'd met the family of anyone else I'd dated, but I came up blank. Then again, none of the guys I ever dated were in Tate's league. No one had ever made me feel the way he did.

"I want my whole family to know you and how important you are to me."

I swooned. This was Tate to a T. All he needed were words —or sometimes one look—to make me feel so happy that I could barely contain it.

I'd seen pictures of the family in the house and on Paisley's phone, so I immediately recognized Travis. He was a carbon copy of his father, even more so than Tate or Declan, but his hair was longer than it had been in the pictures Paisley showed me.

He grinned as Tate and I approached, holding his arms wide open.

"Brother, congratulations on not letting her slip through your fingers." Focusing on me, he added, "If he acts like an ass, call me. I'll talk sense into him. By the way, I'm Travis."

"I know. I'm Lexi. Nice to meet you."

"You act like you have your shit together. You're not exactly the sensible brother," Tate teased.

Travis patted Tate's shoulder. "But I'm so good at pretending I am. Besides, I like having different skill sets. I've been working on becoming more sensible. And I'm proud to say that I'm making progress."

Reese and a woman I assumed was Kimberly approached us, and by the amusement in their expressions, it was obvious that they'd eavesdropped.

"So that's why you rented out this huge space and are going to have fireworks?" Reese asked.

Kimberly nudged her shoulder before moving over to Travis, lacing her arm through his. "Hey, it's a big reason to celebrate. A huge party is more than warranted. I'm proud of you, cousin."

Travis kissed her temple, putting an arm around her shoulders. "Finally, someone who doesn't give me shit."

"I'm Kimberly, by the way," she said to me.

"I thought you might be." She looked very similar to Reese.

I liked watching their interactions, and I *loved* how everyone liked to tease everyone. And I realized Lena was right: Tate did like to egg everyone on.

"Lexi, what's your stance on this?" Tate asked. He had a hand at the small of my back, tipping me so our hips touched like he couldn't bear to let go of me.

"I agree with Kimberly. Travis just sold his company. If this isn't a reason to celebrate, I don't know what is."

Travis winked at me. "I like you even more, Lexi."

"Back at you," I replied, looking at Tate and wiggling my eyebrows. He made me feel like part of the family so effortlessly.

"I can't believe everyone's on time," Kimberly exclaimed.

"Except Tyler," Reese pointed out. "He says he's coming with a surprise. I'm very curious what it's about."

"Probably a present for me," Travis said, looking very self-assured.

"Yeah, you wish," Reese teased him.

"Come on, let's say hi to Mom and Dad," Tate said, looking around the huge garden for them.

Lena and Emmett were at the edge of the lake with Paisley. Emmett was skipping stones with her, and he was quite impressive at it. He managed to throw them at such an angle that they bounced two or three times on the surface of the water before sinking to the bottom.

As we walked toward them, Tate kissed my temple, and his hand went so dangerously low on my back that I swatted it away. A low growl reverberated in his throat as he slid it back down again, though not as low as last time.

"You can't behave, can you?" I whispered.

"Not today. Not when you look like this. Not when I want you this much," he said into my ear.

Heat coursed through me. *Holy shit, how can he do this to me with just a few words?*

"Since when are you so shameless?"

He looked at me with a stern expression, "I'm Shameless Tate. I've got a reputation to live up to."

"Yes, but you're being extra shameless right now. Before, you were kissing me behind corners. Now you're shameless out in the open."

"I want everyone to know you're mine, Lexi. I don't want them to have one fucking doubt."

Oh wow, the way he spoke made me feel like I was the only woman on the planet for him. Emotion grew in my chest, snowballing. I couldn't let it out now, though, or I was going to make a spectacle of us.

I tilted closer, kissing his cheek. "All that talk about Travis not being sensible, but you aren't either."

"I'll show you sensible." Pulling back, he looked straight into my eyes. They'd darkened a notch.

I backtracked a few steps before bursting into giggles. "You want to greet your parents, remember? Can you behave long enough to do that?"

"I'm not sure, Lexi. You might have to keep me in check." His eyes traveled down my body, lighting me up even more than before. It was as though now, after we openly told Paisley we were together, it was even harder to keep our hands off each other, but we had to try.

We headed toward his parents at the same time as one of the other Maxwell brothers—the only other one I hadn't met—Sam.

In contrast to Travis, he looked exactly like the photos Paisley showed me: dark hair cropped short and blue eyes standing out against tanned skin. He straightened up at the sight of Tate and me.

"You're the mythical Lexi, yes?"

"Yes, I am," I confirmed.

"I've heard so many good things. I wondered if you were real."

"She's very real," Tate said. "And mine."

"Yes, brother. I think everyone saw that by the way you're glued to her."

I felt my face get hot. *Oh my God. Did anyone else see the possessive way he was holding me against him?* I'd given him shit, but in truth, I thought no one was paying enough attention. I'd underestimated the Maxwells.

Lena joined us right away, leaving Paisley and Emmett by the lake.

"This is a glorious day. Travis had such a good idea to bring us all here. It's beautiful," she said.

"Yes, it is," Sam agreed, kissing his mom on the cheek. "By the way, I think Tyler arrived. And what the f—Chuck?" His eyes bulged. "Hey, I think he brought a woman."

Tate, Lena, and I all turned at the same time.

"That must be the surprise he mentioned before," I murmured.

The woman on his arm was stunning. Her hair was fiery red, and she was as tall as Tyler in her heels. Her body was slender, and she looked like a supermodel in her short white dress.

Tate chuckled. "And Travis thought he was going to get a present. He's always overly optimistic."

"Sam," Lena said, sounding uncharacteristically sharp, "don't tease your brother."

Sam slowly turned to his mother. "For what? Coming with a woman?"

"Exactly," Lena said. Her voice was even more stern.

Sam held up his hands as if not comprehending it. "You're joking. He hasn't said one word about dating anyone, and now he's bringing her to the party. You can't expect me to behave."

The corners of Lena's mouth lifted up. She was trying to fight a smile.

"I really can't, can I? I don't know why I was even trying."

"It's good to try, Mom. Sometimes it works," Tate said, but he was on the verge of laughter too.

"I give it ten minutes before everyone circles Tyler to razz him," Sam said.

It turned out they didn't even need half of that time. I was pretty surprised that Tate was staying put, and that surprise turned to suspicion. I glanced at him intently.

"What's this? Trying to prove you're sensible?" I teased him.

"Nah, merciful. Half the family is going to pounce on him."

"And you won't?" I asked skeptically.

"Of course I will, but not right now. I'll save it for later. You know, keep the best for last." He took my hand, strolling with me farther along the edge of the water.

"So, we're just staying here to bide our time? I can get on board with that," I said.

"That, and I want to enjoy this moment with you," he said simply, making me swoon. "I'm so happy you're here," he murmured.

"Why? Because you can fondle me anytime you want, even in front of your family?"

He chuckled again. "Sam was bluffing."

"How do you know that?"

"Because he's my brother, and I've seen him do it more times than I can count."

"Okay, that is a good argument. So, back to why you're happy that I'm here. Even if you don't admit it, fondling is a big part of it."

"I won't deny it," he said, stopping in his tracks. "I love sharing my life with you, Lexi." He looked at my mouth before making eye contact. "I love you."

Wow! My heart stopped. Breath whooshed out of me. My knees weakened.

"Tate," I whispered, tugging at his shirt, bringing him closer. "You love me?" I asked, for some reason needing to hear it again.

"Yes, I do. I love you, Lexi."

It was a moment in time I'd never forget. Although I'd felt it for a while, I'd been afraid maybe he didn't feel the same— that he couldn't.

"I love you too."

Tate looked at me for a few seconds, then glanced around.

What is he doing?

A few seconds later, I realized exactly what—he was looking for a place to hide.

Hmm, what does this man have in mind? He couldn't possibly make me swoon any more than he already had.

A few moments later, I realized he could. He pulled me off to the right of the shore, in between a few trees and some huge pink hydrangea bushes, and then he brought his mouth over mine, kissing me hard and deep.

My knees truly became so weak that I placed my palms on his shoulders to ground myself, and still, he didn't stop kissing me. It felt as if I was the very air he breathed, as if he needed me more than anything else. And I kissed him back with everything I had. He buried one hand in my hair and parked the other one on my waist, pressing his fingers deeply into my flesh.

We only paused because he groaned, pulling his head back a few inches. "Damn it. I'm going to lose my head." His voice was almost a growl.

"You're *going to*?" I whispered. "I thought you already had."

"Trust me, you'd know if I had." He was looking at me intently, hand still in my hair. "I wish the party was already over so it would be just the two of us."

"Hey, don't say that. Travis has been waiting for this party for some time."

"I know. But I can't help wanting what I want. You and me. Alone."

"We just have to wait for a few hours," I whispered.

"And then I won't be holding back anymore, Lexi. Not one bit."

TWENTY-FOUR

Tate
___

*A*s the day went by, I watched my woman enjoy my family. She wasn't just making small talk or smiling politely; she seemed genuinely happy to be here and to meet everyone.

Lexi mingled with everyone in the family, even Tyler's girl-friend, Blair. I only exchanged a few words with her before she took out her phone and posted a photo of her cocktail on Instagram, tagging Tyler. Unlike Lexi, she didn't seem very happy to be here. In fact, she reminded me of Nora, who always complained during every family gathering that it was too much, that everyone was so high-energy and always had something going on. She'd liked the idea of being married into the Maxwell family, but not the reality of it.

In the afternoon, Tyler approached me.

"Should I be worried that you're not teasing me?" he asked.

"Why, are you expecting me to?"

"Obviously."

"I thought I'd go easy on you. Everyone else already pounced on you and your woman. I can do it another day."

He nodded. "Very generous of you, thanks."

"How long has this been going on? Why didn't you say anything to any of us?"

"Bro! I thought you weren't going to pounce."

"I'm not. I'm just curious."

"We only started going out recently, but I like her, and I thought, why not? A party is a good opportunity to introduce her to the clan. Besides, I knew Lexi was going to be here today and she would be the main attraction."

I scoffed. "Don't let Travis hear that. He still thinks he's the center of attention today."

"He really does, doesn't he?" Tyler asked in an amused tone. "Where is your girl, by the way?"

"She was with Reese around here somewhere." I looked around, locating both of them next to the entrance of the restaurant. I instantly realized something seemed off. Reese had her shoulders slumped, and Lexi was patting her back.

Next to me, Tyler straightened up. Clearly, he realized the same thing.

"Know what's going on?" he asked me, voice tense.

"No. Let's go find out."

Lexi and Reese stopped talking abruptly when Tyler and I approached.

"What's wrong?" Tyler asked.

Reese looked from Lexi to me, then to him and said, "There's no point keeping it from you. I'm a basket case."

"I know. You look upset. That's why we came over," Tyler said.

"Malcolm is here. He kept bugging me about wanting to talk to me, and I kept blowing him off. I'm guessing it's about the fact that the neighboring building also joined the lawsuit. Something neither you nor Declan shared with me." She gave me a halfhearted glare.

I closed my eyes, feeling guilty as hell. Why did I never learn? Protecting them always backfired.

"Reese—"

"It doesn't matter. I know you meant well. But I feel a bit stupid for giving him the address."

"You're not stupid," Tyler said in a strong voice.

"He won't make a scene knowing everyone is here. I'll meet him in the parking lot and talk to him so he won't bother everyone else."

"Alone?" I asked. "Hell no. We'll be there."

"Exactly," Tyler said. "Anything he wants to tell you, he can say in front of us too."

"You don't need to come out. Stay here and enjoy the party," Reese said.

Lexi patted her shoulder again. "I don't think it's a bad idea if they come with you. It's good for him to see that you've got the support of your family. Just be firm with him, okay? Don't let him put you down again."

"Put you down again"? What the hell? Reese never told me that. It was the first time it dawned on me that perhaps she didn't tell me everything in detail. But clearly she trusted Lexi, who looked concerned for my cousin. This woman never ceased to surprise me.

"Okay. Okay. Maybe that makes more sense," Reese said. "I bet he won't stay too long."

"When is he coming?" I asked.

"He must be arriving right now." Reese's voice was a bit high-pitched.

"Come on. Let's go out and see," Tyler said.

"Okay. But don't tell anyone else. I didn't want to ruin Travis's party. He's worked so hard for months, and now I want him to be happy on his big day instead of worrying about my bad choices."

Tyler and Reese headed toward the gate. I deliberately didn't follow them, waiting until they were out of earshot to ask Lexi, "What's going on? I haven't seen Reese this out of sorts in a while."

"I think she's probably feeling overwhelmed and tired of fighting. And I think that, deep down, she might still care about him, and that makes everything even harder."

"That thing about him putting her down. What was that about? I've never heard of it until now."

Lexi shook her head. "That's not important right now. Just be with her, okay? Being with family will give her strength."

"I'll protect her from that moron."

Lexi flashed me a heartfelt smile. "That's right. Be my hero. You're so damn sexy when you do that."

"Hold on to that thought," I said before following Tyler and Reese.

We walked outside the restaurant, heading to the parking lot. Since Travis rented the whole space, there were only a few cars there.

Malcolm stepped out of a Mercedes. There was another guy in the car, but he stayed inside. Malcolm looked from me to Tyler, clearly not pleased to see us. Well, tough luck. I was not fucking happy to see him either.

"I asked to speak to you alone," he told Reese. "Without these two or anyone else."

Reese stood ramrod straight. "I don't have to listen to your demands. Not anymore, Malcolm."

"When the fuck did I get anything I wanted? It was always you, you, you."

"Yes, of course. It's my fault you cheated on me. Everything is my fault," Reese said. And for the first time, she sounded beaten, like she didn't want to continue this fight with him anymore. That wasn't a problem, because I could finish for her. This schmuck didn't know who he was messing with. I could do nothing about his cheating, but I sure as hell wouldn't let him talk down to Reese or take over Gran's building.

"Whatever you have to say, I suggest you do it quickly," I said coldly. "Our lawyers are in contact. All information is being passed between them. There is no need for personal meetings."

"That's why I didn't want to meet with you," he spat. "I wanted to talk to her."

"Why?" Reese said. "You thought you could intimidate me into reaching an agreement?"

Malcolm looked again from me to Tyler, who was completely silent. That wasn't a good sign.

"You listen to me. You don't want to do this. Your precious Maxwell name isn't as intact as you think. I need the building. My job in the Halsey Group depends on that fucking spa being built."

"Guess what?" Reese said. "You're not getting anything. Gran is like my mom, and she's the best person I know. That building is the first one she bought with Grandpa, and it means a lot to her. You won't take over the upper levels and upset her."

"I'm so tired of this family and your sentimental crap. It's business, and I want it. And none of your cousins or your bitch of a sister or you will stand in the way of what I want."

Tyler stepped right in front of him. "Go away, or I swear to God—"

"Swear to God what, pretty boy?" Malcolm sneered. "You're going to get your hands dirty? Your reputation? What exactly are you worth without it? Nothing. That's right."

"Guys, don't get into trouble on my behalf," Reese said, sounding distressed.

I stepped forward, intending to stop whatever this was before it escalated. Malcolm's only weapon was provoking us, but it was too late. Because one second later, he pushed Tyler back, punching him in the stomach.

The next minutes were a blur. Tyler threw a punch square

in Malcolm's jaw, and then Malcolm hit back with a vengeance, throwing himself at Tyler. They both dropped to the ground, and they didn't stop. They rolled right into the ditch between the gate and the parking lot, which looked to be newly dug, knee deep, and really wide.

Reese shrieked.

"Stop it!" I yelled, jumping in the ditch with them. I pulled Malcolm off Tyler, throwing him far away before extending a hand to my brother. He had a bloody nose and shook his head, refusing my help. I turned to Malcolm, pointing at him.

"Stop right the fuck there, or I start where my brother left off."

"Leave, Malcolm," Reese said, standing straight up. "You're not going to get what you want."

He snorted. "The fuck I won't. I bet if I tried to get back in your good graces, you would have accepted me."

Reese closed her eyes, drawing a deep breath. "You're such a piece of shit."

I wanted to punch that moron, but I had to be mindful of Tyler or he'd jump back into the fight.

The guy in Malcolm's car was holding his phone up. *Fucking hell, is he filming everything?*

"What's going on?" came a familiar voice from the gate. Declan was jogging toward us, exasperated as he took in the scene, from Tyler's bloody lip to Malcolm's red face.

"Leave now, or I'm going to file a complaint," Declan said.

"Tough luck, big boy," Malcolm said with a shit-eating grin. "I'll be the one filing a complaint. And then we'll see how the lawsuit goes."

"You came here to provoke us," Declan said. It always amazed me that he could keep a calm tone even in situations like this, but it was why he was one of the best lawyers in the whole state. "If you call your lawyer now, he'll tell you that what you're doing is not going to help your lawsuit. Know what? I'm going to call him right away, as well as the police. And we'll see what they have to say."

I didn't like the smile Malcolm flashed. "No need. I have what I came for."

I didn't have time to dissect his statement. Reese was close to losing her composure. She was a strong person, but even the strongest of us needed a break from time to time.

Tyler was standing unnaturally still. I instinctively knew something was wrong.

But he didn't say anything. We watched Malcolm get back in the car and pull away.

I went to Tyler immediately, and so did Reese. "Are you okay?" she asked him.

At the same time, Declan asked, "What the fuck were you thinking? We knew he might pull something like that. It was exactly what I warned you all about."

"Oh for fuck's sake, Declan. Just be reckless and stupid like all the rest of us for once." Tyler spoke through gritted teeth.

"Declan," I said harshly, "we don't have time for this right now."

"Really? Why? What do we have better to do?"

"Well, I, for one, need to get to the hospital," Tyler said, and I was shocked at how strained his voice sounded. "Something's wrong with my shoulder. Let's get Sam out here, but I'm sure I need a hospital."

At that precise moment, I realized Tyler must have been in a whole lot of pain. Hockey was a brutal game, and I'd seen my brother fall on the ice plenty of times, but he'd never reacted like this before.

TWENTY-FIVE

Tate

"Well, that was a shit-show," I said later in the evening when Lexi and I got home. Tyler went to the hospital with Reese, Declan, and Blair, but he insisted the party go on. It was impossible to keep the incident from my family, but we still tried our best to make this day worth it for Travis. We managed to keep the party going for another hour, right until Declan texted that Tyler dislocated his shoulder and there were some complications. He was going to need an intensive recovery program.

There was a real risk he was going to be benched for the upcoming season. That put a big damper on the party, and not even Luke or Sam could put a positive spin on it.

Travis took it all in stride. Predictably, he wasn't mad that his party was derailed, but he was pissed that we didn't tell him about Malcolm showing up.

"Yeah, it was," Lexi said.

We had the whole house to ourselves because Paisley was spending the evening with my parents. They were dropping her off tomorrow.

We sat down on the couch, and I pulled Lexi into my lap. She immediately straddled me, her thighs at my sides.

"I'm sorry for the family drama," I said.

"You don't have to apologize. I'm happy you all stick together."

I loved that about her, that she didn't judge, that she understood how much I valued my family. She also seemed to appreciate it. But I couldn't help wondering if it would get to be too much for her at some point.

"What are you thinking about?" she asked.

"Doesn't matter. What's with that smile?"

"I just remembered you told me you loved me today and that you were wishing the party was over. And now it is over."

I smirked. "That's right. I'm going to show you exactly what's going to happen now, and you're going to love it."

"Oh yeah?" she asked in a teasing tone.

"I fucking promise, Lexi. All day long I've been looking forward to this, to being alone with you. I like it when the two of us spend time with Paisley, but I also like it when we're alone. You ground me. You balance me." I kissed down her neck. "You turn me on."

She giggled, shimmying in my lap. "Oh, I really do turn you on, and super fast. Do I get a prize?"

"Yeah, you do. You get everything you want, Lexi, all the time. Anything you want, tell me, and I'll find a way to make it happen, to give you exactly what you deserve."

"And that's what?" she asked, eyes wide.

"Everything." I looked her straight in the eyes. "I want to give you everything I have to give."

She bit her lower lip before leaning in. I kissed her desperately, moving my hands down her thighs and then her ankles. I was hungry for her the whole day, and all that deep need for her slammed into me all at once. I could barely control myself as I pushed my fingers under her dress, enjoying the way her skin turned to goose bumps beneath my touch, right until I reached her ass. I cupped it, hoisting her up in the air as I rose from the couch. She yelped, holding onto me tightly.

I walked through the house with her like that and straight up the staircase to my bedroom. I paused kissing her to lower her to her feet, and then I knew I couldn't take it slow. I yanked off her dress before she was even fully standing on her own. Her skin was tanned from all the time she and Paisley were spending outdoors. I took immense pleasure in taking off her bra and panties, tracing my fingers along the portion of her skin the sun hadn't touched. That was just for me. No one else saw her the way I did.

I could barely stand the touch of my own clothes on my skin. So when she grabbed my T-shirt with hurried, jerking moves, I helped her along, and we got rid of my clothes quickly.

"Sit on the bed, Lexi," I said. "Not on the edge, but farther back on the mattress. Sit on it and spread your legs for me."

I couldn't take my eyes off her. She was so damn gorgeous, all naked and ready for me.

"You're fucking perfect," I told her. She blushed every time I complimented her, but I was going to say the words again and again so she had no doubt. She was the most beautiful woman in the world to me. She was the only woman in the world for me. I'd never want to even *look* at anyone else.

She parted her legs invitingly, touching her breasts, toying with her nipples before moving one hand down to her pussy and circling her clit. Wrapping my hand around my cock, I started pumping up and down in time with her movements.

Her gaze turned feral. She wanted me as much as I wanted her, even though I didn't think that was possible. It was more than hunger. It was a primal need. I doubted there would come a day when I would be completely satisfied, no matter how often I had her.

I stepped closer, taking my time, gripping myself tighter, watching her beautiful body. I kneeled before her in front of the bed, trailing my mouth along her inner thigh, still stroking myself. Her skin was soft and smelled like shower gel. Her scent was still there under the perfume. I couldn't get enough of it.

With my left hand, I gripped her ankle, moving it upward. "You're amazing," I murmured against her skin. "You're mine."

"Yes," she whispered.

"Say it. I want to hear it. Say you're mine."

"I'm yours," she whispered. Her voice was shaking.

I was hovering with my mouth high on her upper thigh, but I wasn't touching her pussy yet. I couldn't hold myself back any longer, though. I pressed the flat of my tongue against her entrance. Satisfaction rocked through me when she curved her body, bringing her thighs together around my ears. I pressed my hand between them. With a groan, she opened them back up.

"Oh, I'm so sorry," she said.

I looked up at her, cocking a brow. "Let's make sure that doesn't happen again." Her eyes widened a bit. "Move farther back on the bed," I said with a wink.

"Okay." She moved backward, putting her feet on the bed.

I immediately grabbed her ankles.

"I'll make sure these stay here," I said before clasping my mouth on her clit, sucking it into my mouth.

Her cries of pleasure filled the room. I'd never get enough of them. Hearing her succumb to me gave me immense satisfaction. I wanted to lure out every drop of pleasure. I wanted her to come like this, spread open for me.

I could feel that she was close. I kept her feet firmly on the bed so she couldn't close them again. Knowing she couldn't move unless I allowed it would intensify every sensation for her. She liked it, and so did I.

Being in control of her ecstasy was intoxicating. I was going to make her come so hard that she'd even forget her own name. I teased and sucked her clit between my lips, hearing her voice become more desperate, her breath quicker. She exploded, rocking her hips into me, back and forth, uttering my name as if in a chant. She was intoxicating, and I needed her. I needed her right now.

She didn't even finish coming by the time I was already pulling her even farther on the bed. I put on a condom before rolling her on top of me. She gasped, eyes wide. She looked between us, grabbing my cock and rubbing the tip against her clit. Pleasure exploded through me. It was so unexpected that it knocked the breath out of my lungs.

"Lexi," I groaned.

She smiled but didn't say anything, and just kept moving back and forth, grazing the tip of my erection before sliding down my cock. I'd been in control before, but I wanted her to take over now. I nearly lost my mind. Every time I was with her, it felt more intense. She rested my hands on her hips. I guided her movement by gripping her hips, moving her faster and faster.

I took one of her nipples in my mouth while she rode me. This right here was perfection. She was perfection. The way she felt around me. The way she gave herself to me, with pure abandon, was unbelievably sexy. She was still sensitive, but I was determined to make this one as good as the one before. I would never tire of seeing her come apart in my arms.

I felt the change in her body. Slowly, her muscles tightened. She squeezed her eyes shut. Her movements became frantic, and she pulsed deliciously around my cock. She cried out my name, and I exploded inside her, pounding and moving until I chased every drop of pleasure for both of us, and we were spent and sated.

We lay down in a dazed state. I liked this moment, just being lazy with her, without a plan, without hurrying anywhere. She was kissing my chest and playing around my nipple with her fingers.

"Someone's happy," she teased me.

"You make me so damn happy, Lexi."

"No one's ever made me feel the way you do," she whispered, and her open confession touched deep inside me.

I decided to open up too. "It's the same for me, Lexi. I've never felt this way about anyone."

Her eyes widened.

"Ever before."

"Really?" Her expression lit up. "Me either."

"I'm serious, baby."

She smiled from ear to ear, rising out of bed and doing a small dance throughout the bedroom. I watched her, laughing wholeheartedly. This woman was something else.

"This is the best day ever. Well, except for Tyler ending up in the hospital." She narrowed her eyes. "Do you think he needs cheering up?"

"I think Tyler's going to need lots of it. Reese is probably already on it."

"I can help. I mean, I don't know Tyler as well as she does, but sometimes that's a good thing."

"Come here, Lexi." I patted the mattress, and she immediately lowered herself onto it, curling against me. The day had been a total shit-show, but I'd never been so gloriously happy. Feeling her body against mine was exactly what I needed. *She* was exactly what I needed.

"Still not tired of fondling me, huh?" she asked between giggles.

"Never."

LAYLA HAGEN

THE NEXT MORNING, I woke up before Lexi and headed downstairs. I went straight to the fridge, taking out the ham, cheese, toast and tomatoes. I made coffee, and put everything on a platter, carrying it up. Lexi was inexplicably happy whenever I brought her breakfast in bed, and I didn't get the chance to do it very often. I wanted to spoil her.

She stirred when I entered the bedroom, opening her eyes slowly. She was gorgeous, even with glazed eyes and her hair sticking out in every direction. Watching her wake up stirred something inside me. I didn't want her to leave my bed or my house. I wanted the privilege of waking up next to her every damn morning.

"Hey," she whispered.

"Morning, gorgeous girl." I put the platter on the nightstand as she pulled the bedsheet up to her nose and then to her eyebrows.

"Lexi, what are you doing?"

"Nothing."

I pulled the sheet back down so I could see her face. Her eyes were still heavy with sleep.

"I feel like a bear. Puffy and swollen. Definitely not gorgeous."

"Trust me, you are." I tilted toward her, rolling a strand of her hair between my fingers. "I'll show you exactly how gorgeous and perfect you are to me. Right after you have breakfast."

I nodded toward the tray on the nightstand. She followed my gaze, and her eyes widened.

"Oh my God. You made me breakfast in bed."

I chuckled. "You seriously didn't see me come in with it a few seconds ago?"

"Umm… I saw you, but the details didn't register." She smiled sheepishly, pushing herself up in a sitting position before setting the tray in her lap.

"Are we sharing it?" she asked.

"Nah, I'm not hungry."

She took a bite, closing her eyes.

"Mmm," she moaned. "This is such a great way to start the day. I love breakfast and coffee."

"And I'm nowhere on the list?"

She opened one eye playfully. "Yes, you are."

"Good. I was getting worried there for a second. What do you want to do today?"

"I don't know. What are you in the mood to do?"

"You." I wiggled my eyebrows. "I should probably talk to Declan, see if we need to do any damage control about yesterday."

"Who is going to tell Beatrice?"

I cleared my throat. "One of my brothers."

Lexi laughed. "Afraid of your own grandmother, huh?"

"Not at all. I choose my battles wisely."

"Aha. Riiiiight. Okay, I'll pretend I believe that. What else do you want to do today besides talking to Declan?"

"Anything you want. I love spending time with you. I mean it. I want to make you happy, Lexi."

"You do just by saying things like that." She sighed. "Wait until I've had coffee to make me swoon, okay?"

"No can do, ma'am. Got to start early." I grinned, taking off the covers and parting her thighs with one hand. I trailed my fingers up the side of her right thigh, enjoying it immensely when she widened her legs even more, opening up for me. I stopped midway between the knee and the apex, leaning in to kiss that spot.

She exhaled a sharp breath, fisting the pillow next to her. I straightened up, flashing her a cheeky smile.

"Oooh, you want to make me swoon *and* turn me on."

"Always. But I know better than to distract you from your food."

She laughed. "You learn fast. I love that about you."

Once she finished breakfast, we showered together. After that, I shaved with the door open, listening to the music Lexi was blasting. From time to time, she sang along, especially during the chorus, making me chuckle. I loved hearing her voice throughout the house and having her here with me.

When I came down the stairs, she was sitting in an armchair and tapping on her iPad. She turned down the volume of the music, bouncing one leg to the rhythm.

"What are you doing?" I asked her.

"Sending my parents a few pictures from the party yesterday."

"Any with the two of us?"

"Uh, no. I just snapped some randomly from the party."

I wiggled my eyebrows, sitting on the armrest. "Want to send them a selfie? How else will they know you're dating a sexy hunk?"

The corners of her mouth twitched. "Are you referring to yourself?"

I cupped her jaw, looking her in the eyes. "You're mine, Lexi. I want them to know it too."

She licked her lips, nodding. "Oh, but I did send them a pic of you, me, and Paisley before we went to the party. But I can send them another one. A word of advice. Put on a parent-approved smile. No smoldering sexy gaze. It's not going to earn you points."

"Duly noted."

I splayed my fingers on her jaw, touching her lower lip before taking my hand away.

She turned on the iPad's camera, keeping it toward both of us. I flashed a professional PR smile. Lexi elbowed me.

"I didn't mean that. A genuine smile."

"So many instructions," I teased but changed to a natural smile.

She snapped a few pics, sending them in a group she had with her parents.

Then she lowered the iPad on the armrest, fidgeting in her spot.

Something was off.

"You seem nervous."

"School is starting in two weeks. We haven't talked about what happens then. Do you want to look for another nanny? I finish one hour earlier than Paisley, so I could pick her up from school and come here with her or do stuff outdoors." She swallowed, averting her gaze before quickly adding, "If that's something you want."

"I have another proposition." I trailed my fingers up her arm, looking her straight in the eyes. "Move in with us."

"Tate, do you mean that?" she whispered.

"Hell yes. I'd love to have you here. Spoil you every evening —properly."

She narrowed her eyes. "You've been very thorough until now too."

"Imagine how much *more* thorough I can be once you're here." I kissed her shoulder, still trailing my fingers up her arms, feeling her tense under my touch.

"I'd love that. I can't wait. It will be so epic. Paisley and I are both going to be low on energy in the afternoon once school starts, but I think we'll still enjoy being out and about by the lake until it gets cold. And if I manage to get some freelance job that I can do remotely while she's finishing homework, even better."

I straightened up, looking at her. "What are you talking about?"

"Umm… I talked to my parents, and there are still a lot of bills due."

I cupped her jaw, looking straight at her. "I can help with that."

"Thanks, but it's not necessary."

"What? How is it not necessary? You just said it is."

"Yes, but I'll manage."

"Lexi—"

"I wouldn't feel comfortable."

"But you're mine."

She chuckled, but I could see her determination falter a fraction.

"I'm still not comfortable."

"We'll talk about this another time." I pressed my thumb on the corner of her mouth, deciding not to press the issue for now. I'd win that battle in time.

She giggled, immediately shifting in her spot and rising on her knees, then she frowned. "Oh crap."

"What's wrong?"

She sat back down, tapping her iPad again and bringing up the notes app.

"I knew I'd opened the iPad for a reason. I need to check the list with stuff I still have to buy for Paisley's birthday. I'm going to show it to her once your parents drop her off. I want everything to be perfect."

The affection she had for my daughter slayed me.

I glanced at the list, and I had to admit half the things didn't make sense to me, but then the item *Shopping with Nora* caught my attention.

"What's that?" I asked, pointing at Nora's name.

"Paisley said she'd love to go shopping with her mom. I said she should check with you first."

"That's not a problem."

"Paisley is excited to see her."

"It's been a long time." I frowned, pacing the room. "Does it bother you that she'll be here?"

"Not at all. Nora is her mom. She'll always be her mother. That's a special bond."

The truth was, Lexi had a much stronger bond with Paisley than Nora did, but she was still her mother. I was relieved that Lexi didn't mind that Nora would be here. I knew Paisley was excited, though I wasn't, because every time she came here, it reminded me of our failed marriage. Of my failure.

An old fear resurfaced. What if I couldn't make things work with Lexi either?

I shook my head, feeling ridiculous. I walked back behind Lexi, bending at the waist to kiss the side of her neck. I loved smelling my shampoo and shower gel on her. Straightening up, I glanced at the list and did a double take. The first time I looked at it, I hadn't realized how long it was, but Lexi was scrolling now.

"Does the list ever end?" I asked.

"Hey! The tenth birthday party is important."

"Do I see the word 'unicorn' there?"

She swatted me away. "Hey, don't judge. Besides, you said I had free rein at organizing it."

"You do." I kissed her neck again, taking the iPad out of her hands.

"What are you doing?" she asked lazily, but she already had goose bumps on her legs. I could practically feel the anticipation coursing through her.

"Carrying on what I started before breakfast."

She pressed her thighs together, and I knew what that meant. She was wet for me. The thought was driving me crazy.

"Please do," she whispered, and I took her upstairs the next second.

———

MY PARENTS DROPPED off Paisley in the afternoon, and from the moment my daughter walked in the house, she barely paid me any attention.

She ran immediately to Lexi. "Grandma and Grandpa gave me some ideas for the party."

"Okay, let's add them to the list," Lexi replied. She sat on the couch where I held her last night. This time, she and Paisley were sitting next to each other with their legs stretched out. Seeing them made me so damn fulfilled. It dawned on me for the first time that we were a family, and the thought used to scare me, but not anymore.

"Hi, pumpkin. Did you have fun at Grandma and Grandpa's?"

"Yes, Daddy. I'll tell you later. Lexi and I have important stuff to do now."

I sat down at their feet, watching them. They both looked up at me in surprise.

"What are you doing?" Lexi asked cautiously.

"I want to help with party planning."

My daughter looked crestfallen, "Daddy, I love you, but you always sort of look through me when I talk about the party."

Jesus! I needed to do better. "I'll focus, I promise."

Lexi pointed a finger at me. "On one condition. You're not allowed to laugh, not even if you hear the word 'unicorn.'"

It was on the tip of my tongue to ask what exactly they meant, but I held up my hands in defense, "No laughing, I promise."

I had a million things to deal with, including talking to Declan, but I'd start tomorrow. I wanted to enjoy today with the two most important women in my life.

TWENTY-SIX

Tate

_____

*a*s Declan predicted, Malcolm didn't attempt to use the incident from the party in the lawsuit. It made Malcolm look worse, so he avoided the situation entirely. Declan was already singing victory, but I didn't want to celebrate early. I was sure Malcolm was going to do something.

The bomb dropped one week later, and it hit differently than expected.

It turned out Malcolm's assistant had indeed recorded the fight—and uploaded the video online. Malcolm had his back to the camera the whole time, so you couldn't see his face. All you could see was Tyler fighting someone.

The hockey team immediately *suspended* him. He wasn't just benched because of the injury. He was fucking suspended. The second he messaged me with the news, I went to his condo. He lived in one of the high-rises downtown, on the twenty-fifth floor.

"What a fucking clusterfuck," Tyler exclaimed. He was pacing his living room, his arm in a sling.

"The good news is Declan says there will be no legal ramifications. Malcolm would have to press charges, which he won't do because then he'd have to admit it was him. And it was obvious the guy you were fighting was the instigator."

Tyler turned to me, running his good hand through his hair.

"It doesn't matter, Tate. I'm suspended. Do you know what that means? Even after my arm recovers, they might not put me back on the ice this season."

He sat on the armrest of his couch, looking out the window.

Damn. I'd never seen Tyler like this.

"Ever since I was a kid, this is all I wanted to do, you know? It's why I begged Mom and Dad to take me to practice and everything. I don't want to let anyone down. The team or our parents."

"Tyler. Everyone's proud of you. You'll get back on the ice. You're one of their best players."

"The team might lose some sponsors because of me, so who knows."

I stepped closer to him, patting his good shoulder. "Focus on your physical therapy. That's all you can do for now."

"I know. Listen, I don't want to be rude, but I'm gonna talk to some of my teammates in ten minutes."

"I'll see myself out. I just wanted to check on you."

"Thanks, brother."

He didn't make even one lousy joke. Things were even worse than I thought.

The second I was out of his building, before even ordering an Uber, I called Declan.

"How is he taking it?" he said instead of hello.

"Even worse than I expected. I think we need to call the gang. Maybe between us, we'll come up with a strategy to help him out."

"Luke, Travis, and Sam are here. I'll call Reese too."

"Thanks. I'm on my way."

I ARRIVED at the office half an hour later. Declan texted me that everyone was up at the bar, so I took the elevator straight to the top floor. Since it was three o'clock in the afternoon, the place was empty except for my family. Reese was here too. They were all sitting at a round table. The bartender, Lance, wasn't around.

"You were fast," I told Reese.

She blushed, fiddling with her thumbs. "I was in the area, sort of. I was heading to Tyler's place, but after Declan called, I came here."

Travis straightened in his chair, looking around the table. "So, the plan is to come up with a strategy to what? Get the team to un-suspend him?"

I frowned. "I think so. I haven't thought this through. I just saw him and knew we had to do something. I usually don't like interfering—"

"Yes, yes, we all know that," Declan said impatiently.

"I was pointing out the irony of *you* being the ones saying *we* have to do something," Sam said with a shit-eating grin.

Luke cocked a brow at me. "Tate, I don't know why you always think you're not interfering. You're the one who suggested from the get-go to take the lawsuit off Gran's hands."

"That was just common sense," I countered.

"Can we focus on Tyler?" Declan said in a no-nonsense tone, silencing everyone at the table. "We need to pool our resources. Who knows the team's management?"

Travis pointed at Declan. "I *really* don't think Tyler would appreciate us talking to his team's management. We need another strategy. I, for one, can entertain him. I have all the time in the world."

Reese looked straight at Travis. "I like that idea."

"That's not going to solve the issue, though," Luke said.

Declan frowned. For him, distractions were not solutions. Travis was usually as practical as Declan, but maybe his perspective was changing now that he'd sold his company and had a lot of free time.

"But it's going to help his morale," Sam added, narrowing his eyes. "Besides, no one said we couldn't multitask. Since we don't know how to actually solve the problem, we can start with the fun part."

Everyone started talking at the same time. It was impossible to follow all the conversations taking place simultaneously.

Reese held a hand up, indicating she wanted to speak. I chuckled, shaking my head. I forgot that things got so loud and crazy when we were together that it was necessary to raise a hand to get to speak.

"I'll coordinate all our efforts," Reese put in. Her shoulders sagged. "I can't believe this is happening. I feel guilty as hell."

I put a hand on her shoulder. She pushed a strand of hair behind her ear in a nervous, jittery movement.

"You don't have to feel guilty about anything, Reese."

"Well, I do. But that's not why I want to spearhead this effort. I'm a master at organizing stuff."

That she was. Her favorite activity as a kid was organizing a *schedule* for games.

"Let me call Kimberly," she continued. "She always has great ideas."

"Does she already know about the video being online?" I asked in surprise. She was back in Paris already.

"Duh. She called me before I got here. Bad news crosses the ocean too."

She took the phone out of her bag, putting it on speakerphone. Kimberly answered after three rings.

"Hey, Reese," she greeted. "Gang all gathered?"

"Yes, and you're on speakerphone. We're coming up with strategies to cheer up Tyler."

"And let me guess. Luke and Sam are on board, Tate hasn't said much yet, Declan is annoyed because that won't solve anything, and Travis is with Declan?"

I chuckled. Yeah, that was pretty close.

"Almost on point, cousin dearest," Travis said. "I'm Team Distract Tyler right now."

"Holy shit, that sale really changed you, huh? I approve. Okay, so what if I bring him to Paris for a week or so? A change of scenery would help."

"He has physical therapy daily," I put in.

"Damn. Okay, so we keep the party in Chicago," Kimberly murmured. "Are Lena and Emmett there too?"

"No," Reese replied. "Should we call them?"

"Hell no," Sam explained. "I have about a million ideas, and none of them should reach our parents' ears."

We all burst out laughing, and for the next half hour, we passed ideas around. We had more than enough to keep Tyler occupied for a year. My ears were ringing even after Kimberly disconnected from the call.

My phone beeped with a message while we were all talking over each other, and I forgot about it. I took it out now, checking my messages.

Lexi: How is Tyler?

Lexi: Tate.

Lexi: Hellooooo. I'm worried.

Tate: Sorry. My siblings and I met up to brainstorm ideas to help Tyler.

Lexi: Wow, you all move fast. I have some ideas too! I'll tell you all about them this evening.

This woman. She kept surprising me at every turn. I'd been with her when I saw the video online, and she was just as concerned as I was. I couldn't believe she cared about my family's troubles so much. Lexi fit in my life so perfectly—as if she'd always been part of it, of me. I couldn't wait to go home and show her *exactly* how much that meant to me. I planned to prove my appreciation with a lot of orgasms.

"Not to be a buzzkill, but what are we doing about Malcolm?" Travis asked, sounding more like his old self.

"Leave Malcolm to Tate and me," Declan said in a calm and collected tone, which could only mean one thing: he was finally doing things my way. We were going in for the kill.

"And me," Reese said. "I'm done playing nice. He doesn't deserve it."

TWENTY-SEVEN

Tate

The next two weeks moved at an insane pace. Declan practically slept at the office. After chatting with all my siblings, plus Reese and Kimberly, they all agreed to my plan: buy the neighboring building. Without access to that building, he couldn't build the spa at all, so then he couldn't sue us for loss of business opportunity anymore.

Since Dean Hanks, the owner of the neighboring building, was involved in the lawsuit too, he wasn't too keen on talking to me and Declan at first.

But he was *very keen* on selling us the building once we told him how much we were willing to pay for it. It was twenty percent above market value. We lost money on it, but it didn't matter.

"Your phone chimed. I think it's a message," Lexi exclaimed on Monday morning. We were both in the bedroom getting ready for the day. It was the first day of school for both her and Paisley. Lexi hadn't moved in yet officially—her lease was expiring at the end of the month—but she spent almost every night here.

I grabbed the phone from the nightstand.

Declan: The judge dismissed the case as soon as I told him the sale went through. I'm going to sleep for a month.

I turned the message to Lexi, who squealed, immediately moving her hips in that funny way she did when she was happy about something.

I gripped her waist, keeping her flat against me. Her breasts pressed against my chest. Feeling her nipples get hard was such a damn turn-on, even at 6:00 a.m.

"You're the only thing keeping me sane these days," I murmured against her skin, mapping her neck with my mouth and her back with my fingers. I meant every word I said. Coming home to Lexi this past week had been the highlight of every single day.

"Hmmm… it *was* an insane week. So, it's over now?"

I pulled back, clearing my throat. "I have to talk to Declan, but we sent Malcolm and the Halsey Group back cowering. That's what they get for messing with the Maxwells. No one hurts my family and gets away with it."

"They certainly don't. I can't believe you bought the neighboring building."

"It was merciless, but I have zero regrets."

She sighed, tugging at my tie. "You're so sexy when you say things like that."

"But we only solved the problem with Gran's building. Tyler's still suspended, and I don't know how to fix it."

"I don't think you can, but I like that you want to. You're this badass tough guy, but then in a few minutes, you're going to be downstairs, making breakfast."

"I have many talents."

"You look sexy, all alpha and tough," she whispered. "I like it."

"I'll give you sexy."

I kissed her against the wall, biting her lower lip before

claiming her mouth and exploring her until she clenched her thighs and rolled her hips against me. I was already semi-hard. If I didn't stop this, I was going to lose my head.

I pulled back, touching her lips with my fingers. Her mouth was a bit swollen. I liked seeing her like this—bearing my mark in one way or another.

"Come on, let's go downstairs before Paisley wakes up," I said.

"Yeah, a word of warning. She's going to talk your ear off about the birthday party. We've been making some changes."

I laughed. "Of course you have."

She loved it even more than Christmas—probably because it was her day. And it seemed that Lexi was enjoying it just as much.

During breakfast, both of them pulled out lists. The party was the only topic of conversation during breakfast.

"Lexi, I think Dad has stopped listening again," Paisley said in a conspiratorial whisper.

I cleared my throat. "Not at all."

Lexi put a hand on her hip, smiling wryly. "Okay, then repeat the last sentence."

I racked my memory but came up blank.

Lexi and Paisley exchanged a glance.

"Can I do it, Lexi?"

"Oh, yes please."

I knew exactly what she wanted to do: employ her technique for making me tell the truth—tickling me. But I deserved it.

I fessed up ten seconds into the tickling session, and then I paid attention for the rest of the morning. Afterward, I drove Lexi to her school first before dropping off Paisley, and then I headed downtown.

I was in a good mood when I arrived at work. I went directly to Declan's office, intending to celebrate with him, but he wasn't there. Remembering he said he was going to sleep for a month, I headed to my own office and started my day by going through the most pressing emails.

At eleven o'clock, my phone buzzed. Paisley's name popped up. This was weird. She was still at school; why would she call me? I answered right away.

"Morning, sweetheart."

"Hey, Daddy." She sounded beat up. My stomach bottomed out.

"What's wrong?"

She sighed. "I spoke to Mom." She sighed, and her voice was uneven. "She said she couldn't come to my birthday."

Anger shot through me. I curled my hand into a fist, forcing myself to draw in a breath. What the fuck? She barely remembered to call her daughter, canceled on their vacation, and now this?

"Baby, when did you talk to your mom?"

"She texted me right before break, and I called her back."

She knew I never wanted her to give Paisley bad news if I wasn't around.

"You'll have a great party anyway. All your friends will be there."

"I know, Daddy."

"I'm sorry, baby, but how about this? I promise this will be the best birthday you ever have."

"You promise?" she asked, and I could feel that smile in her voice.

"Yes. And remember, Lexi will be there," I added, hoping that would make her smile as much as it made me.

"I love her. She makes me feel special, Daddy."

"I know, baby. She does that for me too."

"Can I have as much ice cream as I want?"

I laughed. Of course she'd use this moment to ask me for something she wasn't allowed. When I wanted to comfort her, my girl knew how to use her weapons. I should have been proud of her; she'd make a great lawyer or negotiator if she wanted to.

"We'll talk about this when I pick you up," I said.

"Okay. I have to go. Ms. McDonald says we aren't allowed to use the phone after break ends."

"Bye, Paisley. I love you."

After hanging up, I rose to my feet again. Anger crawled through my veins. What was Nora thinking? I called her immediately. She had the good sense to answer after one ring.

"Before you get annoyed—" she began.

I cut her off. "I'm not annoyed. I'm fucking mad! What do you mean you're not going to come here for your daughter's tenth birthday? And why the hell would you talk to her before talking to me?"

"Well, I knew you were going to get into a state."

"It doesn't matter if I get into a state, Nora. The point of me being next to her when you give her bad news is so I can pick up the pieces. But you wouldn't know that because you're never here!"

"Look, she's not a child anymore."

"She'll be ten," I said through gritted teeth.

"Yes, exactly. She can handle news like this."

"Really? Where did you read that? Because kids don't react according to books, Nora. Paisley is sensitive. She cares, she hurts, she loves, understand? She has emotions and she needs parents that care about her and her wellbeing. And you can't seem to be able to do that, can you? "

She snorted. "Why do you always think the worst of me. I'm doing my best—"

"Come to her birthday," I said, completely ignoring her rant.

"Look, it's impossible. I have a photoshoot with *Vogue* that day."

"I don't care. Reschedule."

"I can't reschedule. I've been waiting for this opportunity for years. I can't pass it up."

"It's your daughter's birthday party. The one you only see once a year, if that. Remember?"

Nora sighed. "Look, I'll make it up to her, okay? I'll come later, and the two of us will have fun, and I will explain it to her. She'll understand."

"No, she won't. She's a kid." What was so hard to understand? "This is important to her."

"*Vogue* is important to me too. Can you be supportive at least once?"

"Not if it means you're disappointing our daughter."

"I heard you're dating her nanny."

I stopped pacing at the abrupt change in topic. "Where did you hear that from?"

"Paisley. Why didn't you tell me?"

"You said you weren't interested in my personal life."

"No, I'm not. I just… well, I assumed that whenever you were serious about someone, you'd tell me."

"It doesn't concern you. And Paisley is happy with it."

"Yes, Paisley can't stop talking about Lexi. I'm glad she's bonding with her. I really hope it lasts."

I scoffed. "What's that supposed to mean?"

"You know how you are, Tate. There's always some drama in your family. I saw the video about Tyler. I'm guessing that's taking up some time. Besides your meetings, obviously. I don't know if that's going to be enough for any woman."

Nora was always able to get a rise out of me, but this time, her words missed the target. I felt completely calm as I answered. "Or maybe I've finally found someone who accepts me for who I am and who likes my life and everyone in it."

As I said the words out loud, I realized Nora and I never had that. Even though we'd been married, our bond—if we'd even had one—had never been as deep as what I had with Lexi. Not even close.

"For your sake, I hope you're right," Nora said. "Now I have to go. I'll make it up to Paisley, I promise. I already switched things around so I can take her on vacation."

That calmed me down, but only a bit. "Good. You'd better not cancel."

"Tate, we both know our marriage was a mistake. We were too young when we decided to get married, and, well, frankly, I don't think we were really in love. I'll admit that I was dazed by the Maxwell name."

"Finally you admit it."

"And when I got pregnant, it was all so unexpected. I was never the maternal type, but I thought perhaps I'd feel different once I was a mom. But I didn't. I just saw my career slipping away. And then after the divorce, I realized it was easier to be away. I know it's selfish." She hesitated before adding, "I think Paisley is getting to a point where she's used to me not being a big part of her life."

"She was very upset on the phone." But even I couldn't deny that lately, Paisley asked less about her mom. She'd even forgotten about their calls these past few weeks.

"I know. And I understand that her birthday is a big thing for her. I've never missed one before. But this is *Vogue*. If I don't do this, it will all be for nothing."

"Goodbye, Nora."

After I finished the phone call, I paced even more than before as I replayed our conversation.

Something clicked in my mind. What I had with Nora didn't fall apart because I hadn't been able to make her happy. We were simply two people who got married when they had nothing in common. Paisley was never going to be Nora's first choice. Even I couldn't make that happen. But it didn't matter. I'd been fixated on the idea that Paisley needed a connection with her mother, but since meeting Lexi, I realized a mother didn't necessarily have to be the person who gave birth. Paisley had me, and now she had Lexi, who was amazing.

IN THE AFTERNOON, I went to pick up Paisley. I was going to take her out for ice cream. Yeah, I was going against my rules, but sometimes you just had to break them.

I parked in a spot next to the school and walked up to the front door. Kids were playing in the courtyard, waiting for their parents to pick them up. I couldn't see Paisley anywhere. Maybe she was still inside. I saw her teacher, Ms. McDonald, at the other end of the courtyard, so I walked in that direction.

"Where is Paisley?" I asked.

She looked around. "She's not here. Maybe she's inside. I'll go look."

"I'll come with you," I said.

The inside of the school was empty, as it usually was at pickup time. We went to the locker area, but Paisley wasn't there.

"Let's check her classroom. Maybe she stayed behind or came to get something," she said.

"Sure." I walked after her, wondering where Paisley was.

"Okay. She's not here either," she informed me after poking her head in the classroom.

My heart rate accelerated. "She's not here, and she's not in the front courtyard. Where could she be?"

"I'm sure she's with the other kids. Maybe they're playing hide-and-seek."

That didn't sound like Paisley, but I didn't say anything as we returned outside. I glanced around the courtyard, taking in every face, but none of them belonged to Paisley.

Ms. McDonald stopped in front of a blonde girl. I recognized Elena, Paisley's friend.

"Elena, do you know where Paisley is?" she asked.

"Yes, Ms. McDonald, she wanted to get tacos. She said tacos always make everything better."

I swear to God, my heart stopped in my chest. "Where did she go?" I asked, trying to control the desperation in my voice.

"She said she was going to the food truck down the street. They sell tacos there."

Hell.

I immediately strode toward the front gate, and Ms. McDonald ran up to me. "I'm sure she couldn't have gotten too far."

I turned to her, narrowing my eyes. "How was she able to leave at all? You have a doorman, and you have cameras. How can any child get away?"

"I assure you it doesn't happen very often. It didn't happen at all last year. You know how unpredictable kids can be."

"That's exactly why you need a better security system in place."

TWENTY-EIGHT

Tate

I went out the front gate, hurrying to the food truck Elena had mentioned. It really was just around the corner. I was going to find Paisley any minute now. I was sure of it. She had to be there, still deciding what she wanted. My girl *had* to be here.

I took a deep breath to steady my nerves.

When I rounded the corner, my whole body went rigid. She wasn't there.

I forced myself to put one foot in front of the other until I reached the food truck.

"Hi. What can I get you?" the vendor asked.

"Nothing. Thank you. I'm wondering if a little girl came here earlier." I tapped the screen of my phone, showing him a picture of Paisley. "She ran off from school."

The guy grimaced. "I'm sorry. She wasn't here."

Fuck. Where is she?

I looked up and down the street. My pulse thumped in my ear. Bile rose at the back of my throat. I called her a couple times. *Come on, baby girl, pick up. Pick up.*

She didn't answer. Then I remembered that she had a tracking app on her phone. I could use it to locate her.

Adrenaline spiked in my veins as I opened the app connected to her phone. It said she didn't have a signal.

Damn it.

Where could she be?

I couldn't think straight. But I immediately knew I needed reinforcements. I called Declan.

"Hey, brother," I said. "Listen, I need your help."

"What's wrong?" he asked in an alarmed tone.

"I'm at Paisley's school, and she ran off."

"What? Why?"

"Long story. I'll tell you later. I need help looking for her."

"I'm on it. I'll leave the office right now. I'll take Tyler too. He's here. And I'll call everyone else, okay?"

"Thanks." I was eternally grateful to my brother, because I didn't even have enough brainpower to think about calling the rest. But I did call Lexi's number. I needed her here with me.

She answered after the second ring. I looked up and down the street as I spoke, not wanting to lose any opportunity to spot Paisley.

"Hey," she said in a soft voice. "I just left school. Where are you?"

"At Paisley's school. She ran off."

"Oh my God. Ran off? Are you sure? That's not like her."

"Well, I don't know. I can't find her," I snapped. "Sorry. I didn't mean... It's not your fault." I was pacing the street, feeling like I'd lost my wits completely. I couldn't think straight. "The family's coming, and they're going to help me search for her. Can you come too?"

"Absolutely. I'm on my way."

The tension between my shoulder blades lessened a bit. Knowing Lexi was going to be here calmed me down.

"Thank you, Lexi. Thanks."

Pocketing the phone, I looked up and down the street again. There was nothing else to do except scour every street around the school.

A sheen of sweat dotted my whole body. *Where is my little girl?*

I walked up the street and then took a sharp right on the street at the back of the school. I was going to walk along the perimeter once. I stopped at a bakery and a butcher shop, but no one had seen Paisley. *Where is she?* I tried calling her phone again, walking street after street. Finally, I returned to the school, in the small hope that someone had seen her or that maybe she'd returned. Why wasn't she answering the phone?

As I approached the front gates, I noticed my family: Mom and Dad, Tyler, Declan, and Luke.

Mom was on the phone talking to my grandmother. "Beatrice, I'll call you as soon as we have news, okay?"

Lexi was here too. She came straight to me, putting her arms around my neck. I kept her soft body against me, drinking in that peace she offered, even though it lasted only a few seconds.

"We'll find her," she promised.

I nodded but didn't say anything. I was drowning in worry.

"Tate, where did you look?" Declan asked. "Point it out on the map."

"I checked the streets surrounding the school in a square and these two adjacent ones."

"Okay. Here's what we're going to do," Declan said. They were all paying attention. "I'll call the police, but in the meantime, everyone is going to take three streets, and we're going to look everywhere, and I mean everywhere. Behind rocks, up in the trees, any place you wouldn't think about checking."

"I didn't look up trees and in the corners," I said.

"Doesn't matter. We'll redo the whole perimeter anyway, just to make sure we're not missing anything."

"She's not answering her phone," I said in a desperate voice. "And the locator app says her phone has no signal."

"That's because she doesn't have it with her. I spoke to Ms. McDonald. They confiscated her phone earlier because she tried to use it during class," Declan explained.

"Great. Fucking great." I felt like lashing out at everyone. The teacher, even my family. And it wasn't fair. This wasn't their fault. It was all Nora's and my fault.

"I'm going to stay with you. Okay, Tate?" Lexi said softly, taking my hand. I nodded, flexing my fingers around hers. I needed her. "Come on, let's go. We're getting a bigger perimeter. But between the two of us, we're going to be fast," she promised.

We scoured street after street. I was growing more desperate with every bench we checked, every three we looked under, and every shop where we asked about Paisley, but no one had seen her. I grew so desperate that I even stopped random strangers, showing them pictures of my daughter. No one saw her.

"Where is she?" I shouted out in frustration. Worry was eating up at me.

"We have one more street," Lexi said, her voice strong. She interlaced our fingers, squeezing my hand.

I was going through the motions, doing everything mechanically. If I thought too much, I was going to lose it.

My phone rang when we were halfway down the street.

"It's the teacher," I said, answering right away. My throat constricted.

"She's here. She came back," Ms. McDonald said.

"Is she okay?" I asked.

"Yes, yes, she's fine. She got lost on the way to the food truck and went in the opposite direction."

Relief washed over me, relaxing my stiff muscles.

"We'll be right there," I replied before hanging up and turning to Lexi. "They found her."

Her eyes watered. I instantly wrapped my arms around her, holding her close. She sobbed into my neck, tugging at my shirt. Her whole body was shaking.

"Oh my God. I was so worried. So worried."

I wrapped my arms around her. My brave, perfect woman. She'd held all this inside her while we were searching, all so she could be strong for me. I kept her in my arms, whispering in her ear.

"It's okay. It's all over. We found her."

"Can we wait for a bit?" she asked through sobs. "I want to calm down."

"Sure." I didn't let go of her, holding her firmly in my arms and giving her all the support she needed. My phenomenal woman. I loved her so fucking much.

A few moments later, she took a step back.

Her eyes widened as she looked at my shoulder. "I'm so sorry. I sobbed all over you."

"That's okay. You're beautiful, even like that," I said, trying to cheer her up.

She half chuckled, half snorted. Then she covered her mouth with her hand and snorted again.

"Okay. Okay. I'm done, I think," she whispered before lowering her hand and drying her eyes. "Come on. Let's go."

I grabbed her hand, kissing the back of it, and then we both went toward the school. Paisley was sitting on the bench near the exit, looking around nervously, clearly realizing something was wrong because we were all here.

"Daddy. I'm so sorry. I went to buy tacos, and I got lost."

I crouched down to her level, caressing her hair. "Elena told us you left because you were upset."

"Just a bit. But I also wanted tacos. They make everything better. I thought for sure I'd be back before you came."

So, she hadn't run away, but still, she could have gotten injured.

"Baby, this isn't right. You can't go off by yourself. We've talked about this."

"I'm really sorry, Daddy."

I knew I had to reinforce that point more, but right now I was too relieved that she was okay to scold her.

Lexi lowered herself on her haunches too.

"Why do you have red eyes, Lexi?"

"I've been crying."

"Why?" Paisley asked, looking struck.

"Because I was afraid we weren't going to find you. I love you."

"I love you too. I'm sorry," Paisley said again.

"Don't worry, sweetheart. It happens," Lexi said.

My daughter went straight into her arms, and Lexi hugged her quietly. We'd found her. She was safe. That was all that mattered.

"You gave us quite the scare, nugget," Declan said.

"I'm so sorry, Uncle Declan."

"No biggie, just don't do it again."

"I won't," she promised.

"Thank you for coming," I told Declan. Then I turned to the rest of my family. Tyler was leaning against a huge oak tree, his eyes fixed on Paisley. Luke was pacing the yard, not saying anything. His shoulders were hunched. He was like me in that regard—it always took him a while to calm down after a scare.

Mom was on the phone with Gran. "Beatrice, she's completely fine. I promise. She took the wrong turn to the food truck."

Dad and Lexi were sitting with Paisley. I went straight to them, lowering myself on my haunches until I was eye level with my daughter.

"Paisley, are you ready to go home?"

"Yes, Daddy. Let's go." She took my hand and then held her other little one out to Lexi.

I just about proposed on the spot. This woman was my rock—my everything. We were a family. There was no doubt in my mind about it.

I rose to my feet. After thanking my family for coming to help, Paisley, Lexi, and I went to the car.

Paisley fell asleep on the drive home. After parking, I carried her in my arms, bringing her up the stairs. Lexi went ahead of me, opening the doors as we entered the house, and headed to my daughter's bedroom, where she threw back the blankets on the bed. Paisley didn't nap during the day, and it was far too early for her to go to bed, but she was obviously exhausted from all the commotion.

I laid her on the mattress, taking off her shoes before drawing the covers up to her chin.

"I'm going to stay with her for a bit," I whispered to Lexi.

She nodded, watching us from the doorway for a few minutes before going downstairs.

I couldn't move from Paisley's side. She was safe. She was with me. I was never going to allow anything like this to happen again. Never. I wanted to protect her at all costs. Nora didn't want to be part of her life, so it was on me to offer Paisley as much stability as possible, and I was going to do a damn fine job.

Lexi and I were going to be there for her. Always.

Doubt slithered in my mind. What if things didn't work out between us? What if one day she walked out of our lives?

I shook my head, focusing on Paisley. She was sleeping peacefully. This day had been an emotional roller coaster for her... and for me too. That's why my thoughts were going in circles. It was the only explanation for why I went from wanting to spontaneously propose to Lexi to contemplating the worst-case scenario.

I rose from the side of the bed, needing to move. I was going to spiral out more if I sat here, so I left the room as quietly as possible and went downstairs to Lexi.

She always balanced me out. She was everything I wanted, and I needed her: her warmth, her calmness, her softness.

I needed all of her.

———

Lexi

I HAD no idea what to do with myself. I was in a state. Adrenaline still coursed through me, and I walked restlessly around the kitchen. Part of me wanted to hurry up the stairs and check if Paisley was indeed in her bed, sleeping soundly. Rationally, I knew she was okay, but I got so scared today that I was still beside myself.

I filled two glasses with ice water for Tate and me for no reason at all, to give myself something to do. When he told me she was missing, everything inside me went numb. I'd never been so afraid about anything in my entire life. I couldn't imagine how he must have felt.

I paced the kitchen, perking up when I heard footsteps coming down.

"She's still asleep," he announced, coming into the kitchen.

"It'll do her good," I said. "How are you feeling? I poured us ice water, but I can get out a bottle of wine or whiskey. I'm sure it's wine time somewhere in the world." I was only half joking.

"That's fine. I don't need any of it." He leaned against the kitchen counter.

"Do you know what happened? Why she left the school? Did she just want tacos?"

"No. Nora told her she couldn't come for her birthday, and she was upset."

"Oh no." My heart sank. "Poor kid. No wonder she was upset. Do you think you can change Nora's mind?"

"No, she has a *Vogue* photoshoot she doesn't want to miss," he said with a sneer.

"Know what? You should sit down. You're tense, and I'm sure a neck massage is going to help you. You're going to forget about today, and we're going to make Paisley's birthday amazing. She won't even realize Nora isn't there."

He was frowning, as if he wasn't really listening to me, just pacing the kitchen. I took in his body language. His shoulders were rigid, his arms and neck stiff. In fact, the way he moved gave away that his whole body was full of tension.

"Earth to Tate. Where are you?"

"What if we break up?" he blurted.

I jerked my head back. "What?"

"You and Paisley, you're so close. She loves you as much as I do."

"I love both of you too," I said, biting the inside of my cheek.

"But what if this between us doesn't work out, say, five years down the road? I don't want to put my daughter through more heartbreak."

I knew he was reacting to everything that happened today with Paisley and Nora ghosting her daughter again. His guard always went up when Paisley was affected. And today, he was in full-on protector mode. It was completely understandable, and I loved him even more for being so consumed by her happiness. I wasn't sure how to make him see that it was all I wanted too. I loved him and Paisley deeply. I'd never felt anything like it in my whole life.

I brought a hand to my stomach, pressing against the knot that popped up there. "Tate. Look, no matter what happens, I care about Paisley, and we can always talk about things with her."

"Or she'll always react like this, and maybe another time I won't find her."

"What are you saying?" I asked in a whisper.

"Nothing. I'm frustrated. I just… I'm wondering if I'm being selfish, choosing my happiness even at the risk of hurting my daughter in the future."

I stared at him, feeling like I couldn't breathe. *He's emotional from today's events. That's all*, I told myself. *That's all.*

But what if it was more?

"So, what, you want to call things off on the off chance it might not work out in the future?" My voice was high-pitched. I pressed my lips together, feeling like I couldn't breathe.

Tate's eyes widened. "Lexi, I don't want to hurt you. Or Paisley. It's just… This is a big fear of mine."

Oh my God, he's not saying no.

"I'm not going to—" I broke off midsentence because my voice was even more high-pitched than before. I couldn't control it. My eyes were burning, and my tear ducts seemed to be connected to the lump in my throat.

"I love you," I whispered, moving closer until he was right in front of me.

He put his hands on my arms, and his touch warmed me. But the concern in his eyes slayed me. If my love wasn't enough…

"I love you too. You know I do. But I can't help fearing that one day, it might fall apart."

"It won't," I said honestly before covering my mouth. My voice was completely undependable. It went from high-pitched to a whisper, and now to high-pitched and loud again. I didn't want to wake Paisley. That was the last thing she needed after how today went.

"Lexi. I love you," he repeated.

"But you don't know if it's enough." My whole body sagged with a bone-deep sadness. "Tate, I'm going to go."

"What? No. Why? Let's talk about this." He moved one hand from my arm to my cheek, but I took a step back, needing distance.

"I can't. Not right now. We've both had a difficult day, and I don't want Paisley to wake up and see us like this."

"Lexi—"

I shook my head, a bit afraid of what he wanted to say. I wasn't ready to hear it. Grabbing my purse from the kitchen counter, I slung it on my shoulder, fiddling with the strap.

"I love you, Tate. You and Paisley. That's all I can tell you."

He opened his mouth, but I shook my head again, hurrying past him.

I needed to get out.

TWENTY-NINE

Tate

*T*he second Lexi was out the door, I regretted every word I said. Fuck, I was a mess, but now I'd *hurt* her. That was unacceptable.

For the next two hours, I paced my living room, torn between staying put or calling someone to stay with Paisley so I could run out the door after Lexi. But I couldn't leave my little girl, not after what happened today. I needed to make things good with Lexi, though. She was so damn important to me, and I wanted her to know that.

I took out my phone, starting to dial Lexi's number when I heard a patter of feet on the staircase.

"Daaaaad?" Paisley asked.

"I'm in the kitchen."

She ran toward me and hugged my waist. I put the phone on the counter. Maybe it was better. There was no way I could make this right over the phone. I hugged my daughter back with all I had.

"Daddy, can I have waffles?"

Today of all days, I couldn't say no to her, so of course I gave in.

"Daddy, is Lexi here?"

No, because your father scared her off. Fuck me.

"No, honey. She went home for a bit." What else could I say? I felt horrible.

"She'll be back, right?"

"Yes, sweetheart." As soon as Paisley was eating, I was going to call and apologize. I'd seriously messed this up.

While preparing the batter, I kept a close eye on her. She brought her coloring book to the island, singing one of her favorite soundtracks.

"How are you feeling?" I asked her a few minutes later, putting a waffle with a smiley face and a party hat on it in front of her. That made her smile. I ruffled her hair, standing right next to her. After today's scare, I didn't want to be farther away than necessary. I couldn't.

"I'm okay. Really. I'm so sorry I scared everyone, Dad."

"Hey, don't worry. It's okay. We all do things we don't mean to when we're upset."

Like me with Lexi. Damn it.

I touched Paisley's shoulder and pulled her into a half hug. I wanted to keep her safe from everything and everyone. But I didn't get to hold her very long because she pushed me away, looking up at me.

"I'm not a baby anymore. I'll be ten soon. I understand stuff."

"What do you mean?"

She shrugged, taking a bite of her waffle. "I spoke to Mom, and she said she might take me to Disneyland for my next vacation. I know Mom's life isn't here anymore, so I won't see her as much. And that's okay. You're here. And so is Lexi." She put her fork down, looking up at me. She seemed nervous.

"What is it, Paisley?"

"Dad, do you think Lexi would want to be my mom?"

Something twisted in my chest. *Shit. I fucked up so badly.* I honestly thought the answer to that was a resounding yes, but I'd hurt Lexi, so now I wasn't sure of anything anymore.

I cupped my daughter's cheek. "I think Lexi loves you very much."

"I love her too, Dad. She's the best mom I could hope for."

And that thing in my chest kept twisting, remembering how upset Lexi was when she left here. At that moment, I wasn't in the right headspace, but I should have kept my mouth shut instead of voicing my fears. It wasn't fair to her.

Paisley focused on eating her waffles, clearly happy in her thoughts about Lexi. My mind was racing at one million miles an hour.

The doorbell rang, startling me.

"Oh, that's Grandma Beatrice," Paisley said.

"How do you know?"

"I spoke to her earlier on the phone. That's why I woke up. She asked if she could come here. She was worried too." My daughter bit her lower lip. "Now she'll see that I'm okay, and she won't worry anymore. And we need to check the list for my birthday party."

"Go on and open the door for her."

She slid down from the chair, leaving the half-eaten waffle on the plate as she darted out of the kitchen.

"You gave us quite the scare, girl," Gran told Paisley seconds after I heard the front door open.

"I know. I'm sorry, Grandma. I promise I won't do it again."

Both of them came into the kitchen.

"Where is your list for the party?" Gran asked.

"It's on my iPad. I'll go get it."

"Perfect. Your dad will keep me company in the mean-time." Something in her voice alerted me that Paisley wasn't the only reason she was here.

The second my daughter was out of the room, Gran

sighed, shaking her head as she pointed at me. "Tate, Tate, Tate, what am I going to do with you?"

I hadn't heard that tone of voice since I was a teenager. "What do you mean?"

"You need to make things right with Lexi," she said without further ado.

I stared at her. "How do you know something is wrong?"

"Because I called to talk to her about Paisley's birthday and the poor girl was out of sorts."

"Fuck."

"Language," she said, giving me the side-eye. "Listen to me, Tate. Lexi cares about you, and you care about her. And I'm going to give you some advice."

I grimaced.

"Don't make that face. Your dad was all full of himself too when he thought he knew how to get your mom back."

I frowned. "When did he have to? He never said anything."

"Of course not. Men don't like to bring up things like that. Your grandfather and I were married for twenty-five years, and we only had one big fight where he almost lost me. And you know what he did after that?"

"No, what?" I asked, now curious and earnest.

"He did everything to make sure I knew exactly how strongly he felt about me. Strong enough that we could go through whatever life had to throw at us together and still come out on the other side loving each other." She paused, and the words sank in. "Is that how you feel about Lexi?"

Lexi meant everything to me. She'd changed my life so much. She'd changed *me*.

"Yes," I said without hesitation.

"Good. Then make it clear to her in no uncertain terms. I don't know what youngsters these days do that counts as big gestures. I'm old as dirt, so my ideas won't be any good. I suggest you come up with something quickly. Make sure it's romantic, because romance never goes out of fashion. And I'll have one of those waffles too."

"Yes, ma'am."

———

Lexi

USUALLY, I was in a good mood when I was working on crafts, but today, that wasn't the case. I was working on the hand-painted decorations I'd promised Paisley for her birthday. I'd started yesterday after leaving Tate's house, and today I jumped on them early in the morning. I only had until eight o'clock; then I was picking up Paisley's birthday dress from Macy's.

I sniffled and then shook my head, mad at myself. I didn't want to be sad. I loved that girl. I loved Tate too. And I really, really hoped he would love me too, that he would believe in us, but clearly, he didn't. And now I was at a loss as to what to do.

My phone rang, and I had to do a double take when I looked at the number. It was Reese.

Oh my God. Did something happen to Tate or Paisley?

I dropped the heart I'd been working on for the past half hour to answer the phone.

"Reese, hi! Is something wrong?"

"No, of course not."

I pressed a palm to my chest to calm my racing heart. "You scared me. Umm… why are you calling?"

"Just wanted to let you know that I dropped by Macy's and picked up Paisley's dress so you can take that off your to-do list for the party."

"Oh, okay. Thanks."

I pouted, taking in a deep breath. I'd been looking forward

to picking up the dress. It gave me something to do since it was a Saturday.

"What are you doing now?" she asked in a chipper voice.

"I'm painting the fairy-themed decorations for the oak tree."

"Want company? I've been told I'm *excellent* with heartbreak."

My heart skipped a beat. *What does she know?* I opened my mouth to ask, then decided against it. I didn't want any details.

"Thanks, but it's not necessary. I'm going to finish the decorations today."

"Hmmm, if you change your mind, call, okay?"

"Sure. Thanks, Reese."

"You're welcome."

After hanging up, I picked up the heart I'd dropped, inspecting it for any damage. It was made of glass, but it seemed intact. Thank goodness. I was painting stars on it, and I'd only managed four so far. I still had ten to go.

———

THE NEXT TWO hours flew by. I finished three pine cones I'd sprayed gold and silver and painted five glass ornaments. My neck was stiff, and my back was hurting from sitting in the wrong position. I needed a break.

Rising to my feet, I grabbed my phone, pacing the living room. I'd put it on airplane mode so I wouldn't be distracted. To my astonishment, I had three missed calls from Tyler.

Holy shit! I stopped in my tracks, feeling like my heart was about to jump through my rib cage. I called him right back. Something bad happened. I was sure of it.

"Finally," he said instead of hello.

"Hey. What happened? Is someone hurt?" I asked, almost breathless.

"No, why would you think that?"

"You called me three times."

"Yeah, that's because I need some advice. I want to take my woman to a super-romantic place to surprise her. Paisley told me you took her to a clearing that she loved, but she can't remember how to get there." His voice sounded a bit off, but I couldn't quite understand why. Maybe the idea of doing something romantic scared him. And even though my heart was heavy, that romantic streak flared up.

"Yes, it's amazing. I think I can grab a snapshot on Google Maps and send it to you. I'm not sure, though, because I don't know if all the trails are on it. I stumbled upon it by mistake."

"If it's not too much trouble, could you show it to me? I have lots of time right now. I have to fill it up somehow."

I was sad for him. It was a good thing that he was in a new relationship because he could at least draw some positive aspects from that and not think all the time about his accident and his career.

"You want us to go there?" I glanced at the crafts table. I still had three glass ornaments to paint. "When?"

"Tonight?"

"You know, it's funny. I was supposed to pick up Paisley's dress tonight, but Reese already did it, so I'm free."

"Cool. Nine o'clock?"

"Hmm… it's gonna be dark, but maybe that's for the better. I think it looks even more romantic at night, but you'll get a chance to check for yourself. I'll text you the address nearest to it."

"Cool. Thanks, Lexi." His voice still seemed off, but I was going to get the bottom of it tonight. I could give him some advice too, if he wanted it. Not that I was an expert in romance, clearly, but if there was anything I could do to lift his mood, I was willing to try it.

I spent the rest of the afternoon finishing up the decorations, trying hard not to think about what would happen when I eventually had to drop them off at the house for the party. Would Tate even want to talk to me? I loved him to the moon and back, but I didn't think I could stand to be on friendly, simple terms when it felt like my heart had a crack right in the middle of it.

At eight o'clock, I left my building and drove my Mini Cooper to the lake, cranking up the A/C because it was hot even at this time of night. When I arrived, Tyler wasn't at our meeting point near the lake. I frowned, picking up my phone. I already had a message from him.

Tyler: Hey, I think I found the clearing.
Lexi: Oh, good. I'll be there in a few minutes.

There was a thick patch of trees separating me from the clearing. I'd never been here in the evening, but it truly was even more romantic than during the day. My bruised heart gave a mighty sigh.

I walked through the trees, drawing in deep breaths and letting the fresh air fill my lungs. I arrived in the clearing a few minutes later, and I swear my heart stopped.

Tyler wasn't there waiting for me at all.

It was Tate.

For a few seconds, I forgot how to breathe. My whole body was stiff. And then I found it in myself to move my legs.

He smiled, coming up to me. His eyes searched me, first my face, then down my body and back up.

"I'm sorry for using subterfuge to get you here."

"I gather Tyler isn't here at all."

"No."

"What's going on?" I whispered. I'd been so focused on him that I didn't see what was next to him. There were a few blankets on the meadow, and on the blankets were flowers, as well as a basket with a bottle of champagne and glasses.

I looked from the blanket to Tate. His eyes were warm. He

stepped closer to me, taking both my hands in his. "I hurt you, Lexi. And I'm so sorry about that."

I was trembling slightly, not sure what to say.

"So you brought me here," I said eventually, because he seemed to be waiting for a reaction.

"Yes." His lips curled into a beautiful smile. "I was advised to make a grand gesture."

For the first time since yesterday, I didn't feel like I had a weight pressing down on my chest anymore. Something else entirely seemed to take hold of me. An immense joy swept through me, electrifying me from the tips of my fingers to my toes.

"By whom? Beatrice?" I whispered.

"Exactly. And then I thought, what to do? I remembered you told me about this place, and I asked Paisley to show it to me."

"Oh my God, that's why Reese picked up Paisley's dress. So I could have the evening free."

His lip curled into a half smile. "That's right."

"And where does Tyler come into this?"

"I needed a good reason to get you here. Something that wouldn't make you suspicious."

He kept my hand against his chest, looking me straight in the eye. "I was wrong, Lexi, in everything I said. What you and I have is stronger than everything. I know we can get through anything life throws at us. I want to be at your side for everything if you'll still have me. I love you with all I have. With all I am."

"Tate, I..." My voice trembled a bit. "I love you and Paisley. And I'd never do anything to hurt her."

"I know. I'm sorry I said all those things. I believe in us. I'm going to spend every day proving it to you. Being the best version of myself, for you and for Paisley. For our life together."

"And how exactly do you plan to do that?"

"I haven't thought that far ahead, I confess."

"We'll find a way," I said.

"Together."

"Yes, together. I love you, Tate. Of course I want you in my life. I want to be next to you for each of those moments. For all of them. And enjoy them with you."

I sensed relief coursing through him. His heartbeat intensified, but his muscles loosened. He tipped my head back, sealing his lips over mine. His mouth was soft and determined at the same time, his kiss deep and full of emotion and need for me.

Joy thrummed through my veins. I could feel it in every inch of my body, mixed with relief. He loved me, and he did want me in his life. He saw us together.

"I love you," he whispered against my cheek. "So damn much."

"I can't believe you brought us here. With champagne." My voice was full of emotion.

He kissed my temple before straightening up and looking me straight in the eyes.

"I wanted tonight to be special, Lexi, so we both remember it."

"I'm sure we will." I kneeled on the blanket, picking up the bottle of champagne.

He effortlessly popped open the cork and poured two glasses. Then he growled, kissing me. I laughed against his mouth, struggling to keep the glass upright so it wouldn't spill all over. But damn, the way this man kissed always made me forget my head and my manners and my decency. He always made everything else blur except *him*.

When we paused to breathe, I said, "You know, I always come here alone. I just came once with Paisley."

"And now with me." He sounded deliciously possessive.

"You look pretty satisfied too." I guess that tickled his Neanderthal bone somewhere. Well, that was fine with me.

We clinked glasses, and I took a sip of the bubbly, letting it course through me. Tate held my other hand, fingers interlaced with mine like he didn't want to let go of me. I flexed my fingers against his, smiling at him.

"I love you, Lexi. I told you once that you made me want. You made me feel. I want more of everything and you. Every damn day, I'm going to love you and prove to you how much you mean to me."

"Tate Maxwell. You brought me to my favorite spot and have my favorite bubbly. What else do you have up your sleeve?"

He winked. "I'm not going to give away all my aces in one evening."

"Hmm… pacing yourself. I like it. Besides, there isn't anything more you could do. This evening is amazing."

This evening was so magical that I knew I'd remember it for the rest of my life. Us here in my favorite spot under the moonlight, listening to the most romantic song with the man I loved. Life couldn't get better than this. It was perfect.

"I'd do anything for you, Lexi. Always."

THIRTY

Lexi

"That was amazing," I said as we stepped inside the house with trash bags. Paisley's birthday party was a total success. It was six o'clock in the evening, and finally, all the guests were gone. We'd been cleaning for the past thirty minutes.

"I loved it. It was the best party ever," Paisley exclaimed, running a hand through her wavy hair. I'd painted pink strands in her braid today, and I'd caught her checking her appearance in every reflective surface possible all day long. She was so cute that I barely resisted hugging her all the time. If I'd learned one thing in all my years of teaching, it was that kids liked to play it cool in front of their friends.

After dropping the bags in the garbage, we went to the living room, where another pile of trash awaited us. Paisley opened all her presents in here, and there was paper everywhere and one unopened gift, a flat rectangular box wrapped in pink paper with a pink ribbon on the couch.

"Hey, where did that come from?" I asked.

"I want to open it," Paisley exclaimed.

"Don't you want to go back in the yard and help your

268

grandparents finish?" We were almost done cleaning the yard of balloons, toys, and discarded paper cups. Lena and Emmett volunteered to help with the cleanup before taking Paisley to their place for a sleepover.

"After I look inside. Pleaaaaase," she said.

Turning my head to her, I noticed that she exchanged a glance with Tate, who had joined us in the living room. A *suspicious* glance.

What's going on?

"Sure, why not?" I said. "Tate?"

"Yeah, I'm on board."

"Come on, Lexi," Paisley said, taking my hand and leading me to the couch.

I sat down, and, to my surprise, so did Tate.

"Lexi, can you help me unwrap it?" she asked.

"Sure. I'll tear off the paper for you."

"Thanks."

I was so busy unwrapping it that I didn't pay attention to the fact that Paisley was sitting unnaturally still. Under the wrapping paper was a beautiful gift box in black velvet that seemed very serious for a ten-year-old's gift.

Opening it, I frowned. Inside was a card, and it was hand-drawn by Paisley. I recognized the stroke of her brush and the way she wrote the letters *For Lexi*. Next to it was a small jewelry box.

I looked up and found Paisley and Tate exchanging yet another glance. "What's going on?" I asked. My palms were a bit sweaty.

"These are for you, Lexi," Tate said in a soft voice.

"I made a card," Paisley added. "Do you want to read it?"

"Sure," I said, a bit bewildered. "But it's your birthday."

"I know. If you want, I can read it to you. I wrote it so I wouldn't forget what I want to say."

"But why would you write me a card and give me a gift? It's not my birthday," I said.

"It's all in the card. I'll explain it."

With a look at Tate, who nodded, Paisley took out the card and opened it. She scrunched her beautiful face in concentration.

"*Dear Lexi,*

Today is a big day because it's my birthday and I am ten years old. I asked Daddy to do this on my birthday because then it's a special day for both of us. We love you, and we hope you want to be with us. I want to ask if you'd like to be my mom. I wrote it down because then it's official."

Her voice wobbled a bit, and she looked over the card at me.

My throat was completely blocked. I had a giant knot in my chest, and I could barely breathe past it, let alone speak. So instead of saying anything, I nodded and opened my arms. Paisley walked right into them, wrapping her arms around me. The card was scratching the back of my neck, but I didn't care. I didn't want to let go.

But only a few short seconds later, Paisley wiggled out of my embrace, taking a step back.

"And Daddy also wants to ask something."

She said a few more words, but I couldn't hear them past the thumping in my ear.

Tate took the small jewelry box out of the big box, and then he dropped to one knee next to Paisley, who was standing still, holding her card with both hands.

"Lexi, I love you," Tate said simply, opening the box. "As Paisley said, we both love you, and we want you with us, forever." He took in a deep breath, and I didn't miss the emotion in his eyes. "Will you marry me? Be my wife, my partner in crime, and my best friend? Will you be my everything, Lexi?"

"Yes," I said in an overly emotional voice, but that was fine because if there was ever a moment to be overly emotional, it was this one. "Yes, I will."

Paisley clapped her hands. "Can I put the ring on?" she asked, and I nodded.

Tate held the box for her while she took out the ring. It wasn't a classic engagement ring, but it was far more beautiful than any I'd seen, with a sapphire sphere set in white gold. She put it on my finger and then clapped her hands again.

"You're going to be my mom. And then we can do mommy things together. We already did some, but now it will be *official*."

"Yes, it will," I said, smiling at her catchy enthusiasm.

"I'm going to tell Grandma and Grandpa the good news and that they can come in," she exclaimed.

Tate kissed her forehead before she darted toward the back door.

He rose to his feet, his eyes trained on me. His gaze seemed even more intense than a few seconds ago. It was still full of emotion and radiating heat, and I was melting under its weight.

He reached out for me, one hand on my cheek, the other on my hip. His lips were hot and determined against mine, moving desperately, like no matter how close he was, it wasn't enough. No matter how much he kissed me, it wasn't enough.

I felt the same. My whole body was alive with excitement; it vibrated through me. Happiness coursed through my veins. A small tremor took hold of me as I skimmed my hands down his muscular arms. He was wearing a T-shirt, and all those delicious muscles were mine to touch. I was smiling when we paused to breathe.

"Did you time everything?" I asked in a shaky tone.

"Yeah, except how much time I had for this kiss," he said as the back door opened and Paisley's and his parents' voices reached us. "Should have told my parents to keep Paisley outside for a while."

"How many helpers did you have, exactly? Your parents, Tyler, Reese, Paisley…"

"Hey. I needed the element of surprise, and I couldn't do it on my own, so I got everyone involved. We each have our set of skills. Reese is an excellent planner, Tyler can distract even the most suspicious of us, and Paisley is quickly learning something from everyone."

"Obviously," I said with a chuckle. I couldn't believe all this. I still couldn't believe the ring on my finger or that this beautiful man wanted to spend his life with me. He'd thought he couldn't open up to love again, but he'd let me in *all the way*.

And Paisley wants me to be her mom.

My eyes stung a bit, and Tate didn't miss it. He touched my cheek with the backs of his fingers, keeping his eyes fixed on me.

"I love you, Lexi. I love you so much. I can't imagine my life without you, babe. You've made me such a happy man today." He gave me another kiss, but this one was short and chaste, because the trio was close enough that we could hear what they were saying clearly.

They entered the living room the next second.

Paisley ran straight to us and hugged us both, looking up at me with a dreamy smile. I'd made this little girl happy, and Tate too. There was no better feeling in the world.

"We hear congratulations are in order," Emmett said, coming up to us. "Well done, son." He clapped a hand on Tate's shoulder before hugging me and kissing each of my cheeks.

Lena hugged me too, and she held on tight for a few seconds. My heart was so happy and full.

"You two make such a lovely pair." Stepping back, Lena looked between Tate and me and then at Paisley. "Paisley, is your backpack ready? If we leave now, we still have time for a movie tonight."

"It's ready," I replied. "We packed it before the party started and put it next to the front door."

"Then I suggest we go. The yard is clean," Lena went on.

Emmett nodded. "That's right. No reason to linger."

My cheeks were a bit red. I mean, I was sure Lena and Emmett just wanted to give us privacy, but I was equally certain that Tate was already harboring sexy thoughts. I could feel it in the stance of his body, the heat radiating off him, the way he put an arm around my shoulders, brushing his fingers up and down my upper arm.

"Okay. What are we going to watch?" Paisley asked.

"Whatever you want, poppet," Lena said. She put a hand at the back of Paisley's neck, steering her toward the front door. Emmett walked out next to them. Tate and I trailed behind, chuckling when Paisley started to negotiate. She wanted to watch two movies.

I had to admit, I wasn't totally listening to the conversation going on. I was too lost in my happiness. But once they left and we were alone, all my senses went into overdrive. Especially when Tate wrapped his arms around my waist, whispering, "We're alone. Finally."

I giggled. "You've been waiting for a while, huh?"

"The whole damn day. I wanted Paisley to be part of the proposal, but now it's just you and me, and I want to tell you a few more things."

"I'm listening." I suspected my man was going to make me swoon again.

"I love you, Lexi, and I can't wait for us to be married, for you to officially be mine. Thank you for teaching me how to feel again, how to want, how to live. You're everything to me."

I'd been right. I *was* swooning.

"And you to me."

"You're mine, Lexi. Do you know what that means?"

"What?" I whispered.

"That I get to spoil you every day. Take care of you. Your problems are my problems too. So, if you changed your mind about me helping with your parents' medical expenses, let me know."

"Hmmm... you had to bring this up while I'm swooning and happy, huh?"

"Yeah," he said with a slight grin. "Thought it might increase the chances of getting a yes."

"I'll take it under consideration," I said in my best stern tone. "And that's all I'm gonna say on the topic today."

His grin turned devilish. "Let's see if I can change your mind."

"I can't wait to tell my parents about this."

The corners of his mouth twitched.

I narrowed my eyes. "What?"

"They already know, babe. I asked them for your hand."

"Oh my God! You did? How? When?"

"That's our secret."

I rose on my toes and touched my lips to his. Desire coursed through me like wildfire. I put my arms around his neck, pressing my body against him. Feeling those hard abs was stirring all my hormones. The effect this man had on me was insane.

My nipples turned hard. They felt almost painful pressing against his chest.

His hands slowly descended to my sides, gripping my hips. He pulled me against him, and I could feel how much he wanted me. He was semi-hard already. With a groan, he took control of the kiss, deepening it, and bunching my dress up until his fingers brushed the bare skin on my outer thigh. The contact turned me on like nothing else. Tendrils of heat flared through me, gathering between my legs. My clit pulsed.

We moved swiftly, and not until I felt a hard surface behind my back did I realize he'd pushed me against the door. His kiss was even more frantic now, as was his touch. His hands were everywhere: on my shoulders and my thighs, under my dress. His tongue stroked mine even faster. I loved being engulfed by him like this.

He led me away from the door, but we didn't get too far. We were too busy devouring each other.

We'd never make it to the bedroom.

He kissed me even more hungrily as we walked through the hallway and into the living room, where he laid me down on the plush carpet. I rolled around because I wanted to be on top of him. He smiled at me lazily while I pushed up his T-shirt, slowly grazing those gorgeous muscles with my fingers. Throwing away his shirt, I mapped the same spots with my tongue and my lips, luring out groan after groan from him. I loved the delicious sounds he made. They turned me on until I was already slick between my legs.

I kissed up his neck and his Adam's apple before straightening again. I moved off him and was immediately even more hungry for him, but I needed to get rid of his pants first, that pesky belt, the boxers, and everything else that was in my way. To my astonishment, he removed a wallet from the back pocket of his pants, taking out a condom while wiggling his eyebrows. Then he started undressing me. His job was way easier.

He tugged at my dress, yanking it up over my head. I wasn't even wearing a bra, since most of my summer dresses had sewn-in cups. I did have panties, though, and I expected him to take them off right away.

Instead, he decided to tease me. Nudging my legs farther apart, he rubbed two fingers along the fabric covering my pussy. The soaked material felt cold against my heated flesh. This time, the pleasure ricocheting through me was downright shocking. I bent at the waist, gasping for air. A tremor shook me when I felt Tate hook his thumbs in the waistband of my panties. He took them off carefully. I had to lean on all fours, lifting one leg and then the other so he could get rid of them.

"Don't you love summer?" I teased, pushing myself up on my knees again. "You can get me naked so fast."

"I fucking love it," he said, kissing up the side of my body and reaching my breasts. He took a nipple in his mouth, and I gasped again. I'd never been as sensitive to his touch. The way he was looking up at me was downright sinful.

He cupped my other breast, flicking his tongue over my nipple, and then he brought one hand between my legs, pressing the heel of his palm straight on my clit. I nearly tumbled down onto him.

"Tate," I gasped.

He moved his hand over my clit in the same rhythm he was circling my nipple with his tongue, and I was so overwhelmed by the sensations that I couldn't even breathe. I wasn't sure where the tension ended and the pleasure began, but I couldn't get enough of it. It vibrated in every cell, through my bones, and spread like wildfire. I didn't even know where it started from: his hand on my clit or his mouth on my breasts. But I came apart so hard that my legs shook and my jaw clenched. I pressed both hands on his shoulders to balance myself.

"I've got you, Lexi. I've got you, babe. Fuck, you're so beautiful when you come. I could watch you come all day long."

I gasped a few times, riding out my orgasm and moving my hips against his hand until I had wrung out every drop of pleasure.

He looked at me with a satisfied grin, and I grinned right back. Then he captured my mouth, kissing me deeply. I loved the lust in his kiss and the way his hands felt against my body, no matter where they touched me. They said the same thing: *You're mine, Lexi. Every inch of you is mine.*

He was sitting on the floor, and I was still on my knees, so I straddled him again, wrapping my hand around his cock and moving it up and down.

He groaned, tipping his head back. "I need you, Lexi," he said in a dangerously calm tone.

I smiled at him, drawing my thumb over the tip of his erection before putting the condom on him and sliding him into my core, moving slowly, taking him in inch by inch. I was still sated from before, and my inner muscles were clenched tight. I was feeling everything even more intensely; I never thought it was possible, but apparently it was. My legs shook with every inch I took in. Little tremors spread through me with every move, like aftershocks from the orgasm.

We locked gazes, and I hoped he'd look at me like this for the rest of our lives. The passion, the love, the possessive streak in that gaze was everything to me. When I took him all the way to the hilt, he grabbed my hands, lacing our fingers, and I moved my hips back and forth, slowly at first but then harder and faster.

I was still so spent from before that I didn't have much strength, not as much as I wanted. Leaning forward, I propped my hand on his chest, taking in a deep breath, just feeling him inside me, hard and hot and so damn delicious.

He groaned again and gripped my hips, and I knew he wanted to take over. The next thing I knew, he'd rolled us over so we were lying down on one side.

"I love this angle," I whispered before he sealed his mouth over mine. I was so overwhelmed by Tate: his hands on me, his cock inside me, his mouth on mine coaxing my tongue. He brushed my clit on every thrust, pushing his pelvis against me. I felt him thicken and widen inside me, and I knew he was close. I didn't think I had it in me to come again, but oh wow, was I wrong.

Whereas I could feel the first orgasm building up, this one took me by surprise, rocking my world.

I came hard while I felt Tate explode too, and our thrusts became even more frantic, more desperate. We both chased our pleasure until we were completely out of breath and could barely move. My body was exhausted but so full of happiness.

Neither of us could move, but I liked the way we were lying down on the floor, limbs intertwined, heads resting on the carpet.

He grinned. "I love this smile. I promise to put this happy, sated expression on your face every single day."

I felt my smile widen. "That's a promise right there, mister, and I'll make sure you keep it."

"You have my word."

Epilogue

LEXI

Two weeks later

"Are you having fun?" I asked Paisley, holding the phone between my ear and my shoulder as I slipped on shoes. Paisley was spending a weekend with Nora. They were at Disneyland. Tate was watching me closely. He'd just spoken to Paisley, but I wanted to hear her voice too.

"Yes. Lots. Did you get the fabric samples? Pleaaaase don't choose them without me."

I chuckled. Paisley was obsessed with wedding details. I'd moved in with them officially, with all my things, and even though Tate and I hadn't even set a date, she already wanted us to choose the fabric for her dress. She was going to be our flower girl, of course.

"I promise I won't. I won't even open the box. I'll wait for you."

"Thanks. I'm going to hang up now. We're going to eat pizza."

"Have fun," I replied before the line disconnected.

Handing the phone back to Tate, I added, "She sounds happy."

Fortunately, Nora was more than pleased with the news that Tate was remarrying, giving her the space to be less involved in her daughter's life. Paisley understood her mother more than any of us and took it all in stride. She knew her real family was her dad and me, and she could always count on us.

He nodded, glancing at me with a scorching-hot look.

Oh Lord.

I pointed at him. "Hey, don't make smoldering eyes at me."

He could convince me of anything when he looked at me like that... even of helping me with my parents' bills. One week ago, they got yet another huge bill that caused all three of us to hyperventilate. Tate immediately offered his assistance, and he did an excellent job of convincing me. Before meeting him, I'd never in a million years agree to this, but I trusted Tate with all I had. He was my soul mate.

He stepped closer to me, catching my wrist and kissing the back of my hand.

"Why not? Afraid you can't resist me?"

I scoffed. "Please. I'm very good at ignoring these sexy vibes you're giving off."

"We can test that theory anytime. Like right now." His voice was dangerously seductive and delicious. He reached for my waist, but I scooted back before he could touch me.

I was lying, of course.

I was shit at ignoring the super-sexy vibes. Ever since Paisley left yesterday, the looks he'd been giving me grew progressively more shameless. I was so on edge that one innocent touch might make my panties go up in flames.

"Nope. We can't be late," I admonished. "Tyler is waiting, remember?"

"I can't believe you're even more involved in Operation Cheer Up Tyler than I am."

"Hey, I have skills. It would be a shame not to use them."

"True." With a groan, Tate stepped back, opening the front door. "Let's go before I lose my head completely."

Pride surged inside me. I *loved* having that effect on him, and I planned to use it thoroughly once we were back, but now we were on a mission.

We drove Tyler to meet the coordinator of a volunteering program that his team's management wanted him to participate in. Tyler was still benched due to his injury and suspended because of the fight, but he was still hopeful to make a comeback this season. After all, they hadn't *fired* him. All because of Malcolm.

At least he got his due. The Halsey Group kicked him out. He also filed for bankruptcy, because it turned out he'd invested his personal money in the business too.

As Reese put it, this was *not* Tyler's year. Tate was right, though. Every Maxwell had their strengths, and they came in handy now that Tyler needed them. Declan was fiercely watching out for Tyler, doing it in the typical way he showed he cared about everyone: by employing tough love. But Declan's relentlessness was what won the lawsuit and kept Beatrice's building safe.

Luke kept telling Tyler he could always employ him as a poster boy for his company.

Travis was throwing party after party to celebrate the sale of his company, and Tyler was the guest of honor at every one of them. According to Tate, he threw them more for Tyler's benefit.

Sam, who'd requested a short leave from his Doctors Without Borders placement, was barhopping with him whenever he had free time, much to Declan's chagrin, who insisted Tyler should keep a low profile. Reese was coordinating everyone's efforts, and Kimberly *tried* to appease Declan. She wasn't very successful, though. Everyone agreed that Tyler's reputation was important, but so was his happiness, which took precedence. So far, the odds were 7 to 1, and I doubted they'd change anytime soon.

Tyler was waiting for us in front of the building. Tate stopped the car right in front of him.

"I don't need babysitting," he said the second he was in the car, "but I do appreciate the company. In fact, I think I'll be sick more often. Every Maxwell seems to find a reason to bring me food or booze, or just spend time with me," he said in a lighthearted tone.

I liked how they stuck together. They were there for each other to celebrate the good times, but also to get through the bad times, and I knew that even though Tyler was putting on a brave face, this wasn't easy for him.

The goal was simple. We had to spend time with him so he wouldn't be so painfully aware of how much free time he had without daily training and games and meeting with sponsors. So far, it wasn't going too bad, but it was only three weeks into the new season.

"How is Blair?" I asked as the car lurched forward.

I caught his grimace in the rearview mirror and instantly realized something had to be wrong. Tate and I exchanged a glance, and I half turned, looking straight at Tyler in the back.

"Blair decided I'm not famous enough for her anymore."

"What?" Tate sputtered.

"Yeah. When it became obvious that I would sit out for the whole season and some of my sponsors stepped back, she realized life with me would be boring, I guess. Hey, her loss, because I'm pretty damn amazing," he said with a lazy smile.

I looked him straight in the eyes. He said all that with humor, but I knew it stung even someone like Tyler, who was perpetually in a good mood and laid-back and happy.

He avoided eye contact, confirming my fears. *Oh, heavens.* I was going to text Reese after dropping him off, because it was obvious we had to double our efforts. I was so mad at Blair. Who did something like that?

"So, what exactly will you do in this volunteer program?"

"Coach school kids in hockey. I'm actually looking forward to it, because I'm bored as fuck even with all the visits. No offense."

"None taken," Tate said.

"Hockey is all I know how to do, so my goal is to get back in shape and get back to doing it as soon as possible. I don't even really care about the sponsors. I just want to get back in the game, on the ice, and play."

We arrived at the address he gave us twenty minutes later. A beautiful brunette was waiting in front of a building.

"Tyler Maxwell?" she said. "Hey, I'm Kendra. I spoke to you team's PR person."

Wow, she was pretty. I automatically glanced at Tyler and could barely hold back a laugh, because the guy looked like he'd just swallowed his tongue. Tate was also looking at him, frowning slightly.

"How do you do, Kendra?" Tyler said. "Nice to meet you. I heard you've got a magic way of pairing volunteers with volunteer programs."

She smiled wholeheartedly, shrugging. "Well, some like to oversell my abilities, but I'm good at what I do. You'll be happy. As long as you follow my instructions to a T," she added with a wink.

Tate burst out laughing, patting Tyler's good shoulder. "This one's barely good at following orders. I'm not sure if he can stick to instructions."

Tyler wiggled his eyebrows. "Oh, he's right."

"Let's see if there's anything I can do about that," Kendra said with sass in her voice.

A twinkle appeared in Tyler's eyes that I hadn't seen in weeks.

Well, well. This was going to be interesting.

"Challenge accepted," Tyler exclaimed.

Kendra chuckled. "Game on, Tyler Maxwell."

Tate laughed, shaking his head. "He's all yours, Kendra."

"I'll take good care of him. I promise."

Once Tate and I were back in the car, we were both silent, looking at Tyler and Kendra walking inside the building.

"Was it just me, or did Tyler look like he likes Kendra a *lot*?" I asked.

"No, not just you. That was the exact impression I got."

"Well, this is a good thing, right? He needs a distraction."

"Yeah, but not with Kendra. Declan will have a field day if he finds out about it. With all the trouble he's in with team management, I think it would be a bad idea."

"Think that's going to hold him back?" I asked.

Tate grinned. "Absolutely not."

Also by Layla Hagen

Very Irresistible Bachelors Series

You're The One

Just One Kiss

One Perfect Touch

One Beautiful Promise

My One and Only

The Gallagher's

Say You're Mine

When You're Mine

Because You're Mine

The Connor Family

Anything For You

Wild With You

Meant For You

Only With You

Fighting For You

Always With You

The Bennett Family

Your Irresistible Love

Your Captivating Love

Your Forever Love

Your Inescapable Love

Your Tempting Love

Your Alluring Love

Your Fierce Love

Your One True Love

Your Endless Love

Your Christmas Love

The Lost Series

Lost in Us

Found in Us

Caught in Us

Withering Hope – soon to be made into a Passionflix movie

Printed in Great Britain
by Amazon

45361962R00165